Vision Of Supreme Horror

And then, suddenly, Randolph Carter felt a greater terror than that which any of the Forms could give—a terror from which he could not flee because it was connected with himself. In a chaos of scenes whose infinite multiplicity and monstrous diversity brought him close to the brink of madness, were a limitless confusion of beings which he knew were himself . . . forms both human and non-human.

He reeled in the clutch of supreme horror. He was no longer a being distinguished from other beings. He had reached the nameless summit of agony and dread. . . .

"The Kadath stories take place in a parallel world that men of this Earth visit in dreams . . . Lovecraft's dream world of Kadath was never concretely visualized. He never, in fact, committed himself as to this world's location and was even uncertain as to whether it exists now or in the remote past. That, however, does not interfere with our enjoyment."

—L. Sprague de Camp

Also by H. P. Lovecraft
Published by Ballantine Books:

AT THE MOUNTAINS OF MADNESS
and Other Tales of Terror

THE TOMB
and Other Tales

THE LURKING FEAR

THE CASE OF CHARLES DEXTER WARD

THE DOOM THAT CAME TO SARNATH

THE DREAM-QUEST
OF UNKNOWN KADATH

H. P. Lovecraft

A Del Rey Book

BALLANTINE BOOKS • NEW YORK

A Del Rey Book
Published by Ballantine Books

ISBN 0-345-30233-8

Manufactured in the United States of America

First U.S. Printing: May 1970
Sixth U.S. Printing: March 1982

First Canadian Printing: May 1970
Second Canadian Printing: July 1971

Cover art by Michael Whelan

Contents

THE DREAM-QUEST OF UNKNOWN KADATH   1

CELEPHAIS   142

THE SILVER KEY   151

THROUGH THE GATES OF THE SILVER KEY   168

THE WHITE SHIP   220

THE STRANGE HIGH HOUSE IN THE MIST   229

THE
DREAM-QUEST
OF UNKOWN
KADATH

The Dream Quest
of Unknown Kadath

THREE TIMES Randolph Carter dreamed of the marvellous city, and three times was he snatched away while still he paused on the high terrace above it. All golden and lovely it blazed in the sunset, with walls, temples, colonnades and arched bridges of veined marble, silver-basined fountains of prismatic spray in broad squares and perfumed gardens, and wide streets marching between delicate trees and blossom-laden urns and ivory statues in gleaming rows; while on steep northward slopes climbed tiers of red roofs and old peaked gables harbouring little lanes of grassy cobbles. It was a fever of the gods, a fanfare of supernal trumpets and a clash of immortal cymbals. Mystery hung about it as clouds about a fabulous unvisited mountain; and as Carter stood breathless and expectant on that balustraded parapet there swept up to him the poignancy and suspense of almost-vanished memory, the pain of lost things and the maddening need to place again what once had been an awesome and momentous place.

He knew that for him its meaning must once have been supreme; though in what cycle or incarnation he had known it, or whether in dream or in waking, he could not tell. Vaguely it called up glimpses of a far forgotten first youth, when wonder and pleasure lay in all the mystery of days, and dawn and dusk alike strode forth prophetic to the eager sound of lutes and song, unclosing fiery gates toward further and surprising marvels. But each night as he stood on that high marble terrace with the curious urns and carven rail and looked off over that hushed sunset city of beauty and unearthly immanence he felt the bondage of dream's tyrannous gods; for in no wise could he leave that lofty spot, or descend the wide marmoreal flights flung endlessly down to where those streets of elder witchery lay outspread and beckoning.

When for the third time he awakened with those flights still undescended and those hushed sunset streets still untraversed, he prayed long and earnestly to the hidden gods of dream that brood capricious above the clouds on unknown Kadath, in the cold waste where no man treads. But the gods made no answer and shewed no relenting, nor did they give any favouring sign when he prayed to them in dream, and invoked them sacrificially through the bearded priests of Nasht and Kaman-Thah, whose cavern-temple with its pillar of flame lies not far from the gates of the waking world. It seemed, however, that his prayers must have been adversely heard, for after even the first of them he ceased wholly to behold the marvellous city; as if his three glimpses from afar had been mere accidents or over-sights, and against some hidden plan or wish of the gods.

At length, sick with longing for those glittering sunset streets and cryptical hill lanes among ancient tiled roofs, nor able sleeping or waking to drive them from his mind, Carter resolved to go with bold entreaty whither no man had gone before, and dare the icy deserts through the dark to where unknown Kadath, veiled in cloud and crowned with unimagined stars, holds secret and nocturnal the onyx castle of the Great Ones.

In light slumber he descended the seventy steps to the cavern of flame and talked of this design to the bearded priests Nasht and Kaman-Thah. And the priests shook their pshent-bearing heads and vowed it would be the death of his soul. They pointed out that the Great Ones had shown already their wish, and that it is not agreeable to them to be harassed by insistent pleas. They reminded him, too, that not only had no man ever been to Kadath, but no man had ever suspected in what part of space it may lie; whether it be in the dreamlands around our own world, or in those surrounding some unguessed companion of Fomalhaut or Aldebaran. If in our dreamland, it might conceivably be reached, but only three human souls since time began had ever crossed and recrossed the black impious gulfs to other dreamlands, and of that three, two had come back quite mad. There were, in such voyages, incalculable local dangers; as well as that shocking final peril which gibbers unmentionably outside the ordered universe, where no dreams reach; that last amorphous blight of nethermost confusion which blasphemes and bubbles at the centre of all infinity—the boundless daemon sultan Azathoth, whose name no lips dare speak aloud, and who gnaws hungrily in inconceivable, unlighted chambers beyond time amidst the muffled, maddening beating of vile drums and the thin, monotonous whine of accursed flutes; to which detestable pounding and piping dance slowly, awkwardly, and absurdly the gigantic Ultimate gods, the blind, voiceless, tenebrous, mindless Other gods whose soul and messenger is the crawling chaos Nyarlathotep.

Of these things was Carter warned by the priests Nasht and Kaman-Thah in the cavern of flame, but still he resolved to find the gods on unknown Kadath in the cold waste, wherever that might be, and to win from them the sight and remembrance and shelter of the marvellous sunset city. He knew that his journey would be strange and long, and that the Great Ones would be against it; but being old in the land of dream he counted on many useful memories and devices to aid him. So asking a formal blessing of the priests and thinking shrewdly on his course, he boldly descended the seven hundred steps to the Gate of Deeper Slumber and set out through the Enchanted Wood.

In the tunnels of that twisted wood, whose low prodigious oaks twine groping boughs and shine dim with the phosphorescence of strange fungi, dwell the furtive and secretive Zoogs; who know many obscure secrets of the dream world and a few of the waking world, since the wood at two places touches the lands of men, though it would be disastrous to say where. Certain unexplained rumours, events, and vanishments occur among men where the Zoogs have access, and it is well that they cannot travel far outside the world of dream. But over the nearer parts of the dream world they pass freely, flitting small and brown and unseen and bearing back piquant tales to beguile the hours around their hearths in the forest they love. Most of them live in burrows, but some inhabit the trunks of the great trees; and although they live mostly on fungi it is muttered that they have also a slight taste for meat, either physical or spiritual, for certainly many dreamers have entered that wood who have not come out. Carter, however, had no fear; for he was an old dreamer and had learnt their fluttering language and made many a treaty with them; having found through their help the splendid city of Celephais in Ooth-Nargai beyond the Tanarian Hills, where reigns half the year the great King Kuranes, a man he had known by another name in life. Kuranes was the one soul who had been to the star-gulfs and returned free from madness.

Threading now the low phosphorescent aisles between those gigantic trunks, Carter made fluttering sounds in the manner of the Zoogs, and listened now and then for responses. He remembered one particular village of the creatures was in the centre of the wood, where a circle of great mossy stones in what was once a clearing tells of older and more terrible dwellers long forgotten, and toward this spot he hastened. He traced his way by the grotesque fungi, which always seem better nourished as one approaches the dread circle where elder beings danced and sacrificed. Finally the great light of those thicker fungi revealed a sinister green and grey vastness pushing up through the roof of the forest and out of sight. This was the nearest of the great ring of stones, and Carter knew he was close to the Zoog village. Renewing his fluttering sound, he waited patiently; and was at last rewarded by an impression of many eyes watching him. It was the Zoogs, for one sees their weird eyes long before one can discern their small, slippery brown outlines.

Out they swarmed, from hidden burrow and honeycombed tree, till the whole dim-litten region was alive with them. Some of the wilder ones brushed Carter unpleasantly, and one even nipped loathesomely at his ear; but these lawless spirits were soon restrained by their elders. The Council of Sages, recognizing the visitor, offered a gourd of fermented sap from a haunted tree unlike the others, which had grown from a seed dropt down by someone on the moon; and as Carter drank it ceremoniously a very strange colloquy began. The Zoogs did not, unfortunately, know where the peak of Kadath lies, nor could they even say whether the cold waste is in our dream world or in another. Rumours of the Great Ones came equally from all points; and one might only say that they were likelier to be seen on high mountain peaks than in valleys, since on such peaks they dance reminiscently when the moon is above and the clouds beneath.

Then one very ancient Zoog recalled a thing unheard-of by the others; and said that in Ulthar, beyond the River Skai, there still lingered the last copy of those inconceivably old Pnakotic Manuscripts made by waking men in forgotten boreal kingdoms and borne into the land of dreams when the hairy cannibal Gnophkehs overcame many-templed Olathoe and slew all the heroes of the land of Lomar. Those manuscripts he said, told much of the gods, and besides, in Ulthar there were men who had seen the signs of the gods, and even one old priest who had scaled a great mountain to behold them dancing by moonlight. He had failed, though his companion had succeeded and perished namelessly.

So Randolph Carter thanked the Zoogs, who fluttered amicably and gave him another gourd of moon-tree wine to take with him, and set out through the phosphorescent wood for the other side, where the rushing Skai flows down from the slopes of Lerion, and Hatheg and Nir and Ulthar dot the plain. Behind him, furtive and unseen, crept several of the curious Zoogs; for they wished to learn what might befall him, and bear back the legend to their people. The vast oaks grew thicker as he pushed on beyond the village, and he looked sharply for a certain spot where they would thin somewhat, standing quite dead or dying among the unnaturally dense fungi and the rotting mould and mushy logs of their fallen brothers. There he would turn sharply aside, for at that spot a mighty slab of stone rests on the forest floor; and those who have dared approach it say that it bears an iron ring three feet wide. Remembering the archaic circle of great mossy rocks, and what it was possibly set up for, the Zoogs do not pause near that expansive slab with its huge ring; for they realise that all which is forgotten need not necessarily be dead, and they would not like to see the slab rise slowly and deliberately.

Carter detoured at the proper place, and heard behind him the frightened fluttering of some of the more timid Zoogs. He had known they would follow him, so he was not disturbed; for one grows accustomed to the anomalies of these prying creatures. It was twilight when he came to the edge of the wood, and the strengthening glow told him it was the twilight of morning. Over fertile plains rolling down to the Skai he saw the smoke of cottage chimneys, and on every hand were the hedges and ploughed fields and thatched roofs of a peaceful land. Once he stopped at a farmhouse well for a cup of water, and all the dogs barked affrightedly at the inconspicuous Zoogs that crept through the grass behind. At another house, where people were stirring; he asked questions about the gods, and whether they danced often upon Lerion; but the farmer and his wife would only make the Elder Sign and tell him the way to Nir and Ulthar.

At noon he walked through the one broad high street of Nir, which he had once visited and which marked his farthest former travels in this direction; and soon afterward he came to the great stone bridge across the Skai, into whose central piece the masons had sealed a living human sacrifice when they built it thirteen-hundred years before. Once on the other side, the frequent presence of cats (who all arched their backs at the trailing Zoogs) revealed the near neighborhood of Ulthar; for in Ulthar, according to an ancient and significant law, no man may kill a cat. Very pleasant were the suburbs of Ulthar, with their little green cottages and neatly fenced farms; and still pleasanter was the quaint town itself, with its old peaked roofs and overhanging upper stories and numberless chimney-pots and narrow hill streets where one can see old cobbles whenever the graceful cats afford space enough. Carter, the cats being somewhat dispersed by the half-seen Zoogs, picked his way directly to the modest Temple of the Elder Ones where the priests and old records were said to be; and once within that venerable circular tower of ivied stone—which crown Ulthar's highest hill—he sought out the patriarch Atal, who had been up the forbidden peak Hatheg-Kla in the stony desert and had come down again alive.

Atal, seated on an ivory dais in a festooned shrine at the top of the temple, was fully three centuries old; but still very keen of mind and memory. From him Carter learned many things about the gods, but mainly that they are indeed only Earth's gods, ruling feebly our own dreamland and having no power or habitation elsewhere. They might, Atal said, heed a man's prayer if in good humour; but one must not think of climbing to their onyx stronghold atop Kadath in the cold waste. It was lucky that no man knew where Kadath towers, for the fruits of ascending it would be very grave. Atal's companion Barzai the Wise had been drawn screaming into the sky for climbing merely the known peak of Hatheg-Kla. With unknown Kadath, if ever found, matters would be much worse; for although Earth's gods may sometimes be surpassed by a wise mortal, they are protected by the Other Gods from Outside, whom it is better not to discuss. At least twice in the world's history the Other Gods set their seal upon Earth's primal granite; once in antediluvian times, as guessed from a drawing in those parts of the Pnakotic Manuscripts too ancient to be read, and once on Hatheg-Kla when Barzai the Wise tried to see Earth's gods dancing by moonlight. So, Atal said, it would be much better to let all gods alone except in tactful prayers.

Carter, though disappointed by Atal's discouraging advice and by the meagre help to be found in the Pnakotic Manuscripts and the Seven Cryptical Books of Hsan, did not wholly despair. First he questioned the old priest about that marvellous sunset city seen from the railed terrace, thinking that perhaps he might find it without the gods' aid; but Atal could tell him nothing. Probably, Atal said, the place belonged to his especial dream world and not to the general land of vision that many know; and conceivably it might be on another planet. In that case Earth's gods could not guide him if they would. But this was not likely, since the stopping of the dreams shewed pretty clearly that it was something the Great Ones wished to hide from him.

Then Carter did a wicked thing, offering his guileless host so many draughts of the moon-vine which the Zoogs had given him that the old man became irresponsibly talkative. Robbed of his reserve, poor Atal babbled freely of forbidden things; telling of a great image reported by travellers as carved on the solid rock of the mountain Ngranek, on the isle of Oriab in the Southern Sea, and hinting that it may be a likeness which Earth's gods once wrought of their own features in the days when they danced by moonlight on that mountain. And he hiccoughed likewise that the features of that image are very strange, so that one might easily recognize them, and that they are sure signs of the authentic race of the gods.

Now the use of all this in finding the gods became at once apparent to Carter. It is known that in disguise the younger among the Great Ones often espouse the daughters of men, so that around the borders of the cold waste wherein stands Kadath the peasants must all bear their blood. This being so, the way to find that waste must be to see the stone face on Ngranek and mark the features; then, having noted them with care, to search for such features among living men. Where they are plainest and thickest, there must the gods dwell nearest; and whatever stony waste lies back of the villages in that place must be that wherein stands Kadath.

Much of the Great Ones might be learnt in such regions, and those with their blood might inherit little memories very useful to a seeker. They might not know their parentage, for the gods so dislike to be known among men that none can be found who has seen their faces wittingly; a thing which Carter realized even as he sought to scale Kadath. But they would have queer lofty thoughts misunderstood by their fellows, and would sing of far places and gardens so unlike any known even in the dreamland that common folk would call them fools; and from all this one could perhaps learn old secrets of Kadath, or gain hints of the marvellous sunset city which the gods held secret. And more, one might in certain cases seize some well-loved child of a god as hostage; or even capture some young god himself, disguised and dwelling amongst men with a comely peasant maiden as his bride.

Atal, however, did not know how to find Ngranek on its isle of Oriab; and recommended that Carter follow the singing Skai under its bridges down to the Southern Sea; where no burgess of Ulthar has ever been, but whence the merchants come in boats or with long caravans of mules and two-wheeled carts. There is a great city there, Dylath-Leen, but in Ulthar its reputation is bad because of the black three-banked galleys that sail to it with rubies from no clearly named shore. The traders that come from those galleys to deal with the jewellers are human, or nearly so, but the rowers are never beheld; and it is not thought wholesome in Ulthar that merchants should trade with black ships from unknown places whose rowers cannot be exhibited.

By the time he had given this information Atal was very drowsy, and Carter laid him gently on a couch of inlaid ebony and gathered his long beard decorously on his chest. As he turned to go, he observed that no suppressed fluttering followed him, and wondered why the Zoogs had become so lax in their curious pursuit. Then he noticed all the sleek complacent cats of Ulthar licking their chops with unusual gusto, and recalled the spitting and caterwauling he had faintly heard, in lower parts of the temple while absorbed in the old priest's conversation. He recalled, too, the evilly hungry way in which an especially impudent young Zoog had regarded a small black kitten in the cobbled street outside. And because he loved nothing on earth more than small black kittens, he stooped and petted the sleek cats of Ulthar as they licked their chops, and did not mourn because those inquisitive Zoogs would escort him no farther.

It was sunset now, so Carter stopped at an ancient inn on a steep little street overlooking the lower town. And as he went out on the balcony of his room and gazed down at the sea of red tiled roofs and cobbled ways and the pleasant fields beyond, all mellow and magical in the slanted light, he swore that Ulthar would be a very likely place to dwell in always, were not the memory of a greater sunset city ever goading one onward toward unknown perils. Then twilight fell, and the pink walls of the plastered gables turned violet and mystic, and little yellow lights floated up one by one from old lattice windows. And sweet bells pealed in the temple tower above, and the first star winked softly above the meadows across the Skai. With the night came song, and Carter nodded as the lutanists praised ancient days from beyond the filigreed balconies and tesselated courts of simple Ulthar. And there might have been sweetness even in the voices of Ulthar's many cats, but that they were mostly heavy and silent from strange feasting. Some of them stole off to those cryptical realms which are known only to cats and which villagers say are on the moon's dark side, whither the cats leap from tall housetops, but one small black kitten crept upstairs and sprang in Carter's lap to purr and play, and curled up near his feet when he lay down at last on the little couch whose pillows were stuffed with fragrant, drowsy herbs.

In the morning Carter joined a caravan of merchants bound for Dylath-Leen with the spun wool of Ulthar and the cabbages of Ulthar's busy farms. And for six days they rode with tinkling bells on the smooth road beside the Skai; stopping some nights at the inns of little quaint fishing towns, and on other nights camping under the stars while snatches of boatmen's songs came from the placid river. The country was very beautiful, with green hedges and groves and picturesque peaked cottages and octagonal windmills.

On the seventh day a blur of smoke rose on the horizon ahead, and then the tall black towers of Dylath-Leen, which is built mostly of basalt. Dylath-Leen with its thin angular towers looks in the distance like a bit of the Giant's Causeway, and its streets are dark and uninviting. There are many dismal sea-taverns near the myriad wharves, and all the town is thronged with the strange seamen of every land on earth and of a few which are said to be not on earth. Carter questioned the oddly robed men of that city about the peak of Ngranek on the isle of Oriab, and found that they knew of it well. Ships came from Baharna on that island, one being due to return thither in only a month, and Ngranek is but two days' zebra-ride from that port. But few had seen the stone face of the god, because it is on a very difficult side of Ngranek, which overlooks only sheer crags and a valley of sinister lava. Once the gods were angered with men on that side, and spoke of the matter to the Other Gods.

It was hard to get this information from the traders and sailors in Dylath-Leen's sea taverns, because they mostly preferred to whisper of the black galleys. One of them was due in a week with rubies from its unknown shore, and the townsfolk dreaded to see it dock. The mouths of the men who came from it to trade were too wide, and the way their turbans were humped up in two points above their foreheads was in especially bad taste. And their shoes were the shortest and queerest ever seen in the Six Kingdoms. But worst of all was the matter of the unseen rowers. Those three banks of oars moved too briskly and accurately and vigorously to be comfortable, and it was not right for a ship to stay in port for weeks while the merchants traded, yet to give no glimpse of its crew. It was not fair to the tavern-keepers of Dylath-Leen, or to the grocers and butchers, either; for not a scrap of provisions was ever sent aboard. The merchants took only gold and stout black slaves from Parg across the river. That was all they ever took, those unpleasantly featured merchants and their unseen rowers; never anything from the butchers and grocers, but only gold and the fat black men of Parg whom they bought by the pound. And the odours from those galleys which the south wind blew in from the wharves are not to be described. Only by constantly smoking strong thagweed could even the hardiest denizen of the old sea-taverns bear them. Dylath-Leen would never have tolerated the black galleys had such rubies been obtainable elsewhere, but no mine in all earth's dreamland was known to produce their like.

Of these things Dylath-Leen's cosmopolitan folk chiefly gossiped whilst Carter waited patiently for the ship from Baharna, which might bear him to the isle whereon carven Ngranek towers lofty and barren. Meanwhile he did not fail to seek through the haunts of far travellers for any tales they might have concerning Kadath in the cold waste or a marvellous city of marble walls and silver fountains seen below terraces in the sunset. Of these things, however, he learned nothing; though he once thought that a certain old slant-eyed merchant looked queerly intelligent when the cold waste was spoken of. This man was reputed to trade with the horrible stone villages on the icy desert plateau of Leng, which no healthy folk visit and whose evil fires are seen at night from afar. He was even rumoured to have dealt with that highpriest not to be described, which wears a yellow silken mask over its face and dwells all alone in a prehistoric stone monastery. That such a person might well have had nibbling traffick with such beings as may conceivably dwell in the cold waste was not to be doubted, but Carter soon found that it was no use questioning him.

Then the black galley slipped into the harbour past the basalt wale and the tall lighthouse, silent and alien, and with a strange stench that the south wind drove into the town. Uneasiness rustled through the taverns along that waterfront, and after a while the dark wide-mouthed merchants with humped turbans and short feet clumped stealthily ashore to seek the bazaars of the jewellers. Carter observed them closely, and disliked them more the longer he looked at them. Then he saw them drive the stout black men of Parg up the gang-plank grunting and sweating into that singular galley, and wondered in what lands—or if in any lands at all—those fat pathetic creatures might be destined to serve.

And on the third evening of that galley's stay one of the uncomfortable merchants spoke to him, smirking sinfully and hinting of what he had heard in the taverns of Carter's quest. He appeared to have knowledge too secret for public telling; and although the sound of his voice was unbearably hateful, Carter felt that the lore of so far a traveller must not be overlooked. He bade him therefore be his guest in locked chambers above, and drew out the last of the Zoog's moon-wine to loosen his tongue. The strange merchant drank heavily, but smirked unchanged by the draught. Then he drew forth a curious bottle with wine of his own, and Carter saw that the bottle was a single hollowed ruby, gro-tesquely carved in patterns too fabulous to be compre-hended. He offered his wine to his host, and though Carter took only the least sip, he felt the dizziness of space and the fever of unimagined jungles. All the while the guest had been smiling more and more broad-ly, and as Carter slipped into blankness the last thing he saw was that dark odious face convulsed with evil laugh-ter and something quite unspeakable where one of the two frontal puffs of that orange turban had become disarranged with the shakings of that epileptic mirth.

Carter next had consciousness amidst horrible odours beneath a tent-like awning on the deck of a ship, with the marvellous coasts of the Southern Sea flying by in unnatural swiftness. He was not chained, but three of the dark sardonic merchants stood grinning nearby, and the sight of those humps in their turbans made him almost as faint as did the stench that filtered up through the sinister hatches. He saw slip past him the glorious lands and cities of which a fellow-dreamer of earth—a lighthouse-keeper in ancient Kingsport—had often discoursed in the old days, and recognized the templed terraces of Zak, abode of forgotten dreams; the spires of infamous Thalarion, that daemon-city of a thousand wonders where the eidolon Lathi reigns; the charnel gardens of Zura, land of pleasures unattained, and the twin headlands of crystal, meeting above in a resplendent arch, which guard the harbour of Sona-Nyl, blessed land of fancy.

Past all these gorgeous lands the malodourous ship flew unwholesomely, urged by the abnormal strokes of those unseen rowers below. And before the day was done Carter saw that the steersman could have no other goal than the Basalt Pillars of the West, beyond which simple folk say splendid Cathuria lies, but which wise dreamers well know are the gates of a monstrous cataract wherein the oceans of earth's dreamland drop wholly to abysmal nothingness and shoot through the empty spaces toward other worlds and other stars and the awful voids outside the ordered universe where the daemon-sultan Azathoth gnaws hungrily in chaos amid pounding and piping and the hellish dancing of the Other Gods, blind, voiceless, tenebrous, and mindless, with their soul and messenger Nyarlathotep.

Meanwhile the three sardonic merchants would give no word of their intent, though Carter well knew that they must be leagued with those who wished to hold him from his quest. It is understood in the land of dream that the Other Gods have many agents moving among men; and all these agents, whether wholly human or slightly less than human, are eager to work the will of those blind and mindless things in return for the favour of their hideous soul and messenger, the crawling chaos Nyarlathotep. So Carter inferred that the merchants of the humped turbans, hearing of his daring search for the Great Ones in their castle of Kadath, had decided to take him away and deliver him to Nyarlathotep for whatever nameless bounty might be offered for such a prize. What might be the land of those merchants, in our known universe or in the eldritch spaces outside, Carter could not guess; nor could he imagine at what hellish trysting-place they would meet the crawling chaos to give him up and claim their reward. He knew, however, that no beings as nearly human as these would dare approach the ultimate nighted throne of the daemon Azathoth in the formless central void.

At the set of sun the merchants licked their excessively wide lips and glared hungrily and one of them went below and returned from some hidden and offensive cabin with a pot and basket of plates. Then they squatted close together beneath the awning and ate the smoking meat that was passed around. But when they gave Carter a portion, he found something very terrible in the size and shape of it; so that he turned even paler than before and cast that portion into the sea when no eye was on him. And again he thought of those unseen rowers beneath, and of the suspicious nourishment from which their far too mechanical strength was derived.

It was dark when the galley passed betwixt the Basalt Pillars of the West and the sound of the ultimate cataract swelled portentous from ahead. And the spray of that cataract rose to obscure the stars, and the deck grew damp, and the vessel reeled in the surging current of the brink. Then with a queer whistle and plunge the leap was taken, and Carter felt the terrors of nightmare as earth fell away and the great boat shot silent and comet-like into planetary space. Never before had he known what shapeless black things lurk and caper and flounder all through the aether, leering and grinning at such voyagers as may pass, and sometimes feeling about with slimy paws when some moving object excites their curiosity. These are the nameless larvae of the Other Gods, and like them are blind and without mind, and possessed of singular hungers and thirsts.

But that offensive galley did not aim as far as Carter had feared, for he soon saw that the helmsman was steering a course directly for the moon. The moon was a crescent shining larger and larger as they approached it, and shewing its singular craters and peaks uncomfortably. The ship made for the edge, and it soon became clear that its destination was that secret and mysterious side which is always turned away from earth, and which no fully human person, save perhaps the dreamer Snireth-Ko, has ever beheld. The close aspect of the moon as the galley drew near proved very disturbing to Carter, and he did not like the size and shape of the ruins which crumbled here and there. The dead temples on the mountains were so placed that they could have glorified no suitable or wholesome gods, and in the symmetries of the broken columns there seemed to be some dark and inner meaning which did not invite solution. And what the structure and proportions of the olden worshippers could have been, Carter steadily refused to conjecture.

When the ship rounded the edge, and sailed over those lands unseen by man, there appeared in the queer landscape certain signs of life, and Carter saw many low, broad, round cottages in fields of grotesque whitish fungi. He noticed that these cottages had no windows, and thought that their shape suggested the huts of Esquimaux. Then he glimpsed the oily waves of a sluggish sea, and knew that the voyage was once more to be by water—or at least through some liquid. The galley struck the surface with a peculiar sound, and the odd elastic way the waves received it was very perplexing to Carter. They now slid along at great speed, once passing and hailing another galley of kindred form, but generally seeing nothing but that curious sea and a sky that was black and star-strewn even though the sun shone scorchingly in it.

There presently rose ahead the jagged hills of a leprous-looking coast, and Carter saw the thick unpleasant grey towers of a city. The way they leaned and bent, the manner in which they were clustered, and the fact that they had no windows at all, was very disturbing to the prisoner; and he bitterly mourned the folly which had made him sip the curious wine of that merchant with the humped turban. As the coast drew nearer, and the hideous stench of that city grew stronger, he saw upon the jagged hills many forests, some of whose trees he recognized as akin to that solitary moon-tree in the enchanted wood of earth, from whose sap the small brown Zoogs ferment their curious wine.

Carter could now distinguish moving figures on the noisome wharves ahead, and the better he saw them the worse he began to fear and detest them. For they were not men at all, or even approximately men, but great greyish-white slippery things which could expand and contract at will, and whose principal shape—though it often changed—was that of a sort of toad without any eyes, but with a curious vibrating mass of short pink tentacles on the end of its blunt, vague snout. These objects were waddling busily about the wharves, moving bales and crates and boxes with preternatural strength, and now and then hopping on or off some anchored galley with long oars in their forepaws. And now and then one would appear driving a herd of clumping slaves, which indeed were approximate human beings with wide mouths like those merchants who traded in Dylath-Leen; only these herds, being without turbans or shoes or clothing, did not seem so very human after all. Some of the slaves—the fatter ones, whom a sort of overseer would pinch experimentally— were unloaded from ships and nailed in crates which workers pushed into the low warehouses or loaded on great lumbering vans.

Once a van was hitched and driven off, and the fabulous thing which drew it was such that Carter gasped, even after having seen the other monstrosities of that hateful place. Now and then a small herd of slaves dressed and turbaned like the dark merchants would be driven aboard a galley, followed by a great crew of the slippery toad-things as officers, navigators, and rowers. And Carter saw that the almost-human creatures were reserved for the more ignominious kinds of servitude which required no strength, such as steering and cooking, fetching and carrying, and bargaining with men on the earth or other planets where they traded. These creatures must have been convenient on earth, for they were truly not unlike men when dressed and carefully shod and turbaned, and could haggle in the shops of men without embarrassment or curious explanations. But most of them, unless lean or ill-favoured, were unclothed and packed in crates and drawn off in lumbering lorries by fabulous things. Occasionally other beings were unloaded and crated; some very like these semi-humans, some not so similar, and some not similar at all. And he wondered if any of the poor stout black men of Parg were left to be unloaded and crated and shipped inland in those obnoxious drays.

When the galley landed at a greasy-looking quay of spongy rock a nightmare horde of toad-things wiggled out of the hatches, and two of them seized Carter and dragged him ashore. The smell and aspect of that city are beyond telling, and Carter held only scattered images of the tiled streets and black doorways and endless precipices of grey vertical walls without windows. At length he was dragged within a low doorway and made to climb infinite steps in pitch blackness. It was, apparently, all one to the toad-things whether it were light or dark. The odour of the place was intolerable, and when Carter was locked into a chamber and left alone he scarcely had strength to crawl around and ascertain its form and dimensions. It was circular, and about twenty feet across.

From then on time ceased to exist. At intervals food was pushed in, but Carter would not touch it. What his fate would be, he did not know; but he felt that he was held for the coming of that frightful soul and messenger of infinity's Other Gods, the crawling chaos Nyarlathotep. Finally, after an unguessed span of hours or days, the great stone door swung wide again, and Carter was shoved down the stairs and out into the red-litten streets of that fearsome city. It was night on the moon, and all through the town were stationed slaves bearing torches.

In a detestable square a sort of procession was formed; ten of the toad-things and twenty-four almost human torch-bearers, eleven on either side, and one each before and behind. Carter was placed in the middle of the line; five toad-things ahead and five behind, and one almost-human torch-bearer on either side of him. Certain of the toad-things produced disgustingly carven flutes of ivory and made loathsome sounds. To that hellish piping the column advanced out of the tiled streets and into nighted plains of obscene fungi, soon commencing to climb one of the lower and more gradual hills that lay behind the city. That on some frightful slope or blasphemous plateau the crawling chaos waited, Carter could not doubt; and he wished that the suspense might soon be over. The whining of those impious flutes was shocking, and he would have given worlds for some even half-normal sound; but these toad-things had no voices, and the slaves did not talk.

Then through that star-specked darkness there did come a normal sound. It rolled from the higher hills, and from all the jagged peaks around it was caught up and echoed in a swelling pandaemoniac chorus. It was the midnight yell of the cat, and Carter knew at last that the old village folk were right when they made low guesses about the cryptical realms which are known only to cats, and to which the elders among cats repair by stealth nocturnally, springing from high housetops. Verily, it is to the moon's dark side that they go to leap and gambol on the hills and converse with ancient shadows, and here amidst that column of foetid things

Carter heard their homely, friendly cry, and thought of the steep roofs and warm hearths and little lighted windows of home.

Now much of the speech of cats was known to Randolph Carter, and in this far terrible place he uttered the cry that was suitable. But that he need not have done, for even as his lips opened he heard the chorus wax and draw nearer, and saw swift shadows against the stars as small graceful shapes leaped from hill to hill in gathering legions. The call of the clan had been given, and before the foul procession had time even to be frightened a cloud of smothering fur and a phalanx of murderous claws were tidally and tempestuously upon it. The flutes stopped, and there were shrieks in the night. Dying almost-humans screamed, and cats spit and yowled and roared, but the toad-things made never a sound as their stinking green ichor oozed fatally upon that porous earth with the obscene fungi.

It was a stupendous sight while the torches lasted, and Carter had never before seen so many cats. Black, grey, and white; yellow, tiger, and mixed; common, Persian, and Manx, Thibetan, Angora, and Egyptian; all were there in the fury of battle, and there hovered over them some trace of that profound and inviolate sanctity which made their goddess great in the temples of Bubastis. They would leap seven strong at the throat of an almost-human or the pink tentacled snout of a toad-thing and drag it down savagely to the fungous plain, where myriads of their fellows would surge over it and into it with the frenzied claws and teeth of a divine battle-fury. Carter had seized a torch from a stricken slave, but was soon overborne by the surging waves of his loyal defenders. Then he lay in the utter blackness hearing the clangour of war and the shouts of the victors, and feeling the soft paws of his friends as they rushed to and fro over him in the fray.

At last awe and exhaustion closed his eyes, and when he opened them again it was upon a strange scene. The great shining disc of the earth, thirteen times greater than that of the moon as we see it, had risen with floods of weird light over the lunar landscape; and across all those leagues of wild plateau and ragged crest there squatted one endless sea of cats in orderly array. Circle on circle they reached, and two or three leaders out of the ranks were licking his face and purring to him consolingly. Of the dead slaves and toad-things there were not many signs, but Carter thought he saw one bone a little way off in the open space between him and the warriors.

Carter now spoke with the leaders in the soft language of cats, and learned that his ancient friendship with the species was well known and often spoken of in the places where cats congregate. He had not been unmarked in Ulthar when he passed through, and the sleek old cats had remembered how he patted them after they had attended to the hungry Zoogs who looked evilly at a small black kitten. And they recalled, too, how he had welcomed the very little kitten who came to see him at the inn, and how he had given it a saucer of rich cream in the morning before he left. The grandfather of that very little kitten was the leader of the army now assembled, for he had seen the evil procession from a far hill and recognized the prisoner as a sworn friend of his kind on earth and in the land of dream.

A yowl now came from the farther peak, and the old

leader paused abruptly in his conversation. It was one of the army's outposts, stationed on the highest of the mountains to watch the one foe which Earth's cats fear; the very large and peculiar cats from Saturn, who for some reason have not been oblivious of the charm of our moon's dark side. They are leagued by treaty with the evil toad-things, and are notoriously hostile to our earthly cats; so that at this juncture a meeting would have been a somewhat grave matter.

After a brief consultation of generals, the cats rose and assumed a closer formation, crowding protectingly around Carter and preparing to take the great leap through space back to the housetops of our earth and its dreamland. The old field-marshal advised Carter to let himself be borne along smoothly and passively in the massed ranks of furry leapers, and told him how to spring when the rest sprang and land gracefully when the rest landed. He also offered to deposit him in any spot he desired, and Carter decided on the city of Dylath-Leen whence the black galley had set out; for he wished to sail thence for Oriab and the carven crest Ngranek, and also to warn the people of the city to have no more traffick with black galleys, if indeed that traffick could be tactfully and judiciously broken off. Then, upon a signal, the cats all leaped gracefully with their friend packed securely in their midst; while in a black cave on an unhallowed summit of the moon-mountains still vainly waited the crawling chaos Nyarlathotep.

The leap of the cats through space was very swift; and being surrounded by his companions Carter did not see this time the great black shapelessnesses that lurk and caper and flounder in the abyss. Before he fully realised what had happened he was back in his familiar room at the inn at Dylath-Leen, and the stealthy, friendly cats were pouring out of the window in streams. The old leader from Ulthar was the last to leave, and as Carter shook his paw he said he would be able to get home by cockcrow. When dawn came, Carter went downstairs and learned that a week had elapsed since his capture and leaving. There was still nearly a fortnight to wait for the ship bound toward Oriab, and during that time he said what he could against the black galleys and their infamous ways. Most of the townsfolk believed him; yet so fond were the jewellers of great rubies that none would wholly promise to cease trafficking with the wide-mouthed merchants. If aught of evil ever befalls Dylath-Leen through such traffick, it will not be his fault.

In about a week the desiderate ship put in by the black wale and tall lighthouse, and Carter was glad to see that she was a barque of wholesome men, with painted sides and yellow lateen sails and a grey captain in silken robes. Her cargo was the fragrant resin of Oriab's inner groves, and the delicate pottery baked by the artists of Baharna, and the strange little figures carved from Ngranek's ancient lava. For this they were paid in the wool of Ulthar and the iridescent textiles of Hatheg and the ivory that the black men carve across the river in Parg. Carter made arrangements with the captain to go to Baharna and was told that the voyage would take ten days. And during his week of waiting he talked much with that captain of Ngranek, and was told that very few had seen the carven face thereon; but that most travellers are content to learn its legends from old people and lava-gatherers and image-makers in

Baharna and afterward say in their far homes that they have indeed beheld it. The captain was not even sure that any person now living had beheld that carven face, for the wrong side of Ngranek is very difficult and barren and sinister, and there are rumours of caves near the peak wherein dwell the night-gaunts. But the captain did not wish to say just what a night-gaunt might be like, since such cattle are known to haunt most persistently the dreams of those who think too often of them. Then Carter asked that captain about unknown Kadath in the cold waste, and the marvellous sunset city, but of these the good man could truly tell nothing.

Carter sailed out of Dylath-Leen one early morning when the tide turned, and saw the first rays of sunrise on the thin angular towers of that dismal basalt town. And for two days they sailed eastward in sight of green coasts, and saw often the pleasant fishing towns that climbed up steeply with their red roofs and chimney-pots from old dreaming wharves and beaches where nets lay drying. But on the third day they turned sharply south where the roll of water was stronger, and soon passed from sight of any land. On the fifth day the sailors were nervous, but the captain apologized for their fears, saying that the ship was about to pass over the weedy walls and broken columns of a sunken city too old for memory, and that when the water was clear one could see so many moving shadows in that deep place that simple folk disliked it. He admitted, more-over, that many ships had been lost in that part of the sea; having been hailed when quite close to it, but never seen again.

That night the moon was very bright, and one could see a great way down in the water. There was so little wind that the ship could not move much, and the ocean was very calm. Looking over the rail Carter saw many fathoms deep the dome of the great temple, and in front of it an avenue of unnatural sphinxes leading to what was once a public square. Dolphins sported merrily in and out of the ruins, and porpoises revelled clumsily here and there, sometimes coming to the surface and leaping clear out of the sea. As the ship drifted on a little the floor of the ocean rose in hills, and one could clearly mark the lines of ancient climbing streets and the washed-down walls of myriad little houses.

Then the suburbs appeared, and finally a great lone building on a hill, of simpler architecture than the other structures, and in much better repair. It was dark and low and covered four sides of a square, with a tower at each corner, a paved court in the centre, and small curious round windows all over it. Probably it was of basalt, though weeds draped the greater part; and such was its lonely and impressive place on that far hill that it may have been a temple or a monastery. Some phosphorescent fish inside it gave the small round windows an aspect of shining, and Carter did not blame the sailors much for their fears. Then by the watery moonlight he noticed an odd high monolith in the middle of that central court, and saw that something was tied to it. And when after getting a telescope from the captain's cabin he saw that that bound thing was a sailor in the silk robes of Oriab, head downward and without any eyes, he was glad that a rising breeze soon took the ship ahead to more healthy parts of the sea.

The next day they spoke with a ship with violet sails bound for Zar, in the land of forgotten dreams, with bulbs of strange coloured lilies for cargo. And on the evening of the eleventh day they came in sight of the isle of Oriab with Ngranek rising jagged and snow-crowned in the distance. Oriab is a very great isle, and its port of Baharna a mighty city. The wharves of Baharna are of porphyry, and the city rises in great stone terraces behind them, having streets of steps that are frequently arched over by buildings and the bridges between buildings. There is a great canal which goes under the whole city in a tunnel with granite gates and leads to the inland lake of Yath, on whose farther shore are the vast clay-brick ruins of a primal city whose name is not remembered. As the ship drew into the harbour at evening the twin beacons Thon and Thal gleamed a welcome, and in all the million windows of Baharna's terraces mellow lights peeped out quietly and gradually as the stars peep out overhead in the dusk, till that steep and climbing seaport became a glittering constellation hung between the stars of heaven and the reflections of those stars in the still harbour.

The captain, after landing, made Carter a guest in his own small house on the shores of Yath where the rear of the town slopes down to it; and his wife and servants brought strange toothsome foods for the traveller's delight. And in the days after that Carter asked for rumours and legends of Ngranek in all the taverns and public places where lava-gatherers and image-makers meet, but could find no one who had been up the higher slopes or seen the carven face. Ngranek was a hard mountain with only an accursed valley behind it, and besides, one could never depend on the certainty that night-gaunts are altogether fabulous.

When the captain sailed back to Dylath-Leen Carter took quarters in an ancient tavern opening on an alley of steps in the original part of the town, which is built of brick and resembles the ruins of Yath's farther shore. Here he laid his plans for the ascent of Ngranek, and correlated all that he had learned from the lava-gatherers about the roads thither. The keeper of the tavern was a very old man, and had heard so many legends that he was a great help. He even took Carter to an upper room in that ancient house and shewed him a crude picture which a traveller had scratched on the clay wall in the old days when men were bolder and less reluctant to visit Ngranek's higher slopes. The old tavern-keeper's great-grandfather had heard from his great-grandfather that the traveller who scratched that picture had climbed Ngranek and seen the carven face, here drawing it for others to behold; but Carter had very great doubts, since the large rough features on the wall were hasty and careless, and wholly overshadowed by a crowd of little companion shapes in the worst possible taste, with horns and wings and claws and curling tails.

At last, having gained all the information he was likely to gain in the taverns and public places of Baharna, Carter hired a zebra and set out one morning on the road by Yath's shore for those inland parts wherein towers stony Ngranek. On his right were rolling hills and pleasant orchards and neat little stone farmhouses, and he was much reminded of those fertile fields that flank the Skai. By evening he was near the nameless ancient ruins on Yath's farther shore, and though old lava-gatherers had warned him not to camp there at night, he tethered his zebra to a curious pillar before a crumbling wall and laid his blanket in a sheltered corner beneath some carvings whose meaning none could decipher. Around him he wrapped another blanket, for the nights are cold in Oriab; and when upon awaking once he thought he felt the wings of some insect brushing his face he covered his head altogether and slept in peace till roused by the magah birds in distant resin groves.

The sun had just come up over the great slope whereon leagues of primal brick foundations and worn walls and occasional cracked pillars and pedestals stretched down desolate to the shore of Yath, and Carter looked about for his tethered zebra. Great was his dismay to see that docile beast stretched prostrate beside the curious pillar to which it had been tied, and still greater was he vexed on finding that the steed was quite dead, with its blood all sucked away through a singular wound in its throat. His pack had been disturbed, and several shiny knickknacks taken away, and all round on the dusty soil were great webbed footprints for which he could not in any way account. The legends and warnings of lava-gatherers occurred to him, and he thought of what had brushed his face in the night. Then he shouldered his pack and strode on toward Ngranek, though not without a shiver when he saw close to him as the highway passed through the ruins a great gaping arch low in the wall of an old temple, with steps leading down into darkness farther than he could peer.

His course now lay uphill through wilder and partly wooded country, and he saw only the huts of charcoal-burners and the camp of those who gathered resin from the groves. The whole air was fragrant with balsam, and all the magah birds sang blithely as they flashed their seven colours in the sun. Near sunset he came on a new camp of lava-gatherers returning with laden sacks from Ngranek's lower slopes; and here he also camped, listening to the songs and tales of the men, and overhearing what they whispered about a companion they had lost. He had climbed high to reach a mass of fine lava above him, and at nightfall did not return to his fellows. When they looked for him the next day they found only his turban, nor was there any sign on the crags below that he had fallen. They did not search any more, because the old man among them said it would be of no use. No one ever found what the night-gaunts took, though those beasts themselves were so uncertain as to be almost fabulous. Carter asked them if night-gaunts sucked blood and liked shiny things and left webbed footprints, but they all shook their heads negatively and seemed frightened at his making such an inquiry. When he saw how taciturn they had become he asked them no more, but went to sleep in his blanket.

The next day he rose with the lava-gatherers and exchanged farewells as they rode west and he rode east on a zebra he bought of them. Their older men gave him blessings and warnings, and told him he had better not climb too high on Ngranek, but while he thanked them heartily he was in no wise dissuaded. For still did he feel that he must find the gods on unknown Kadath; and win from them a way to that haunting and marvellous city in the sunset. By noon, after a long uphill ride, he came upon some abandoned brick villages of the hill-people who had once dwelt thus close to Ngranek and carved images from its smooth lava. Here they had dwelt till the days of the old tavernkeeper's grandfather, but about that time they felt that their presence was disliked. Their homes had crept even up the mountain's slope, and the higher they built the more people they would miss when the sun rose. At last they decided it would be better to leave altogether, since things were sometimes glimpsed in the darkness which no one could interpret favourably; so in the end all of them went down to the sea and dwelt in Baharna, inhabiting a very old quarter and teaching their sons the old art of image-making which to this day they carry on. It was from these children of the exiled hill-people that Carter had heard the best tales about Ngranek when searching through Baharna's ancient taverns.

All this time the great gaunt side of Ngranek was looming up higher and higher as Carter approached it. There were sparse trees on the lower slopes and feeble shrubs above them, and then the bare hideous rock rose spectral into the sky, to mix with frost and ice and eternal snow. Carter could see the rifts and ruggedness of that sombre stone, and did not welcome the prospect of climbing it. In places there were solid streams of lava, and scoriac heaps that littered slopes and ledges. Ninety aeons ago, before even the gods had danced upon its pointed peak, that mountain had spoken with fire and roared with the voices of the inner thunders. Now it towered all silent and sinister, bearing on the hidden side that secret titan image whereof rumour told. And there were caves in that mountain, which might be empty and alone with elder darkness, or might—if legend spoke truly—hold horrors of a form not to be surmised.

The ground sloped upward to the foot of Ngranek, thinly covered with scrub oaks and ash trees, and strewn with bits of rock, lava, and ancient cinder. There were the charred embers of many camps, where the lava-gatherers were wont to stop, and several rude altars which they had built either to propitiate the Great Ones or to ward off what they dreamed of in Ngranek's high passes and labyrinthine caves. At evening Carter reached the farthermost pile of embers and camped for the night, tethering his zebra to a sapling and wrapping himself well in his blankets before going to sleep. And all through the night a voonith howled distantly from the shore of some hidden pool, but Carter felt no fear of that amphibious terror, since he had been told with certainty that not one of them dares even approach the slope of Ngranek.

In the clear sunshine of morning Carter began the long ascent, taking his zebra as far as that useful beast could go, but tying it to a stunted ash tree when the floor of the thin wood became too steep. Thereafter he scrambled up alone; first through the forest with its ruins of old villages in overgrown clearings, and then over the tough grass where anaemic shrubs grew here and there. He regretted coming clear of the trees, since the slope was very precipitous and the whole thing rather dizzying. At length he began to discern all the countryside spread out beneath him whenever he looked about; the deserted huts of the image-makers, the groves of resin trees and the camps of those who gathered from them, the woods where prismatic magahs nest and sing, and even a hint very far away of the shores of Yath and of those forbidding ancient ruins whose name is forgotten. He found it best not to look around, and kept on climbing and climbing till the shrubs became very sparse and there was often nothing but the tough grass to cling to.

Then the soil became meagre, with great patches of

bare rock cropping out, and now and then the nest of a condor in a crevice. Finally there was nothing at all but the bare rock, and had it not been very rough and weathered, he could scarcely have ascended farther. Knobs, ledges, and pinnacles, however, helped greatly; and it was cheering to see occasionally the sign of some lava-gatherer scratched clumsily in the friable stone, and know that wholesome human creatures had been there before him. After a certain height the presence of man was further shewn by handholds and footholds hewn where they were needed, and by little quarries and excavations where some choice vein or stream of lava had been found. In one place a narrow ledge had been chopped artificially to an especially rich deposit far to the right of the main line of ascent. Once or twice Carter dared to look around, and was almost stunned by the spread of landscape below. All the island betwixt him and the coast lay open to his sight, with Baharna's stone terraces and the smoke of its chimneys mystical in the distance. And beyond that the illimitable Southern Sea with all its curious secrets.

Thus far there had been much winding around the mountain, so that the farther and carven side was still hidden. Carter now saw a ledge running upward and to the left which seemed to head the way he wished, and this course he took in the hope that it might prove continuous. After ten minutes he saw it was indeed no cul-de-sac, but that it led steeply on in an arc which would, unless suddenly interrupted or deflected, bring him after a few hours' climbing to that unknown southern slope overlooking the desolate crags and the accursed valley of lava. As new country came into view below him he saw that it was bleaker and wilder than those seaward lands he had traversed. The mountain's side, too, was somewhat different; being here pierced by curious cracks and caves not found on the straighter route he had left. Some of these were above him and some beneath him, all opening on sheerly perpendicular cliffs and wholly unreachable by the feet of man. The air was very cold now, but so hard was the climbing that he did not mind it. Only the increasing rarity bothered him, and he thought that perhaps it was this which had turned the heads of other travellers and excited those absurd tales of night-gaunts whereby they explained the loss of such climbers as fell from these perilous paths. He was not much impressed by traveller's tales, but had a good curved scimitar in case of any trouble. All lesser thoughts were lost in the wish to see that carven face which might set him on the track of the gods atop unknown Kadath.

At last, in the fearsome iciness of upper space, he came round fully to the hidden side of Ngranek and saw in infinite gulfs below him the lesser crags and sterile abysses of lava which marked the olden wrath of the Great Ones. There was unfolded, too, a vast expanse of country to the south; but it was a desert land without fair fields or cottage chimneys, and seemed to have no ending. No trace of the sea was visible on this side, for Oriab is a great island. Black caverns and odd crevices were still numerous on the sheer vertical cliffs, but none of them was accessible to a climber. There now loomed aloft a great beetling mass which hampered the upward view, and Carter was for a moment shaken with doubt lest it prove impassable. Poised in windy insecurity miles above earth, with only space and death on one side and only slippery walls of rock on the other, he knew for a moment the fear that makes men shun Ngranek's hidden side. He could not turn round, yet the sun was already low. If there were no way aloft, the night would find him crouching there still, and the dawn would not find him at all.

But there was a way, and he saw it in due season. Only a very expert dreamer could have used those imperceptible footholds, yet to Carter they were sufficient. Surmounting now the outward-hanging rock, he found the slope above much easier than that below, since a great glacier's melting had left a generous space with loam and ledges. To the left a precipice dropped straight from unknown heights to unknown depths, with a cave's dark mouth just out of reach above him. Elsewhere, however, the mountain slanted back strongly, and even gave him space to lean and rest.

He felt from the chill that he must be near the snow line, and looked up to see what glittering pinnacles might be shining in that late ruddy sunlight. Surely enough, there was the snow uncounted thousands of feet above, and below it a great beetling crag like that he had just climbed; hanging there forever in bold outline. And when he saw that crag he gasped and cried out aloud, and clutched at the jagged rock in awe; for the titan bulge had not stayed as earth's dawn had shaped it, but gleamed red and stupendous in the sunset with the carved and polished features of a god.

Stern and terrible shone that face that the sunset lit with fire. How vast it was no mind can ever measure, but Carter knew at once that man could never have fashioned it. It was a god chiselled by the hands of the gods, and it looked down haughty and majestic upon the seeker. Rumour had said it was strange and not to be mistaken, and Carter saw that it was indeed so; for those long narrow eyes and long-lobed ears, and that thin nose and pointed chin, all spoke of a race that is not of men but of gods.

He clung overawed in that lofty and perilous eyrie, even though it was this which he had expected and come to find; for there is in a god's face more of marvel than prediction can tell, and when that face is vaster than a great temple and seen looking downward at sunset in the scyptic silences of that upper world from whose dark lava it was divinely hewn of old, the marvel is so strong that none may escape it.

Here, too, was the added marvel of recognition; for although he had planned to search all dreamland over for those whose likeness to this face might mark them as the god's children, he now knew that he need not do so. Certainly, the great face carven on that mountain was of no strange sort, but the kin of such as he had seen often in the taverns of the seaport Celephais which lies in Ooth-Nargai beyond the Tanarian Hills and is ruled over by that King Kuranes whom Carter once knew in waking life. Every year sailors with such a face came in dark ships from the north to trade their onyx for the carved jade and spun gold and little red singing birds of Celephais, and it was clear that these could be no others than the half-gods he sought. Where they dwelt, there must the cold waste lie close, and within it unknown Kadath and its onyx castle for the Great Ones. So to Celephais he must go, far distant from the isle of Oriab, and in such parts as would take him back to Dylath-Leen and up the Skai to the bridge by Nir, and again into the enchanted wood of the Zoogs, whence the way would bend northward through the garden lands by Oukranos to the gilded spires of Thran, where he might find a galleon bound over the Cerenarian sea.

But dusk was now thick, and the great carven face looked down even sterner in shadow. Perched on that ledge night found the seeker; and in the blackness he might neither go down nor go up, but only stand and cling and shiver in that narrow place till the day came, praying to keep awake lest sleep loose his hold and send him down the dizzy miles of air to the crags and sharp rocks of the accursed valley. The stars came out, but save for them there was only black nothingness in his eyes; nothingness leagued with death, against whose beckoning he might do no more than cling to the rocks and lean back away from an unseen brink. The last thing of earth that he saw in the gloaming was a condor soaring close to the westward precipice beside him, and darting screaming away when it came near the cave whose mouth yawned just out of reach.

Suddenly, without a warning sound in the dark, Carter felt his curved scimitar drawn stealthily out of his belt by some unseen hand. Then he heard it clatter down over the rocks below. And between him and the Milky Way he thought he saw a very terrible outline of something noxiously thin and horned and tailed and bat-winged. Other things, too, had begun to blot out patches of stars west of him, as if a flock of vague entities were flapping thickly and silently out of that inaccessible cave in the face of the precipice. Then a sort of cold rubbery arm seized his neck and something else seized his feet, and he was lifted inconsiderately up and swung about in space. Another minute and the stars were gone, and Carter knew that the night-gaunts had got him.

They bore him breathless into that cliffside cavern and through monstrous labyrinths beyond. When he struggled, as at first he did by instinct, they tickled him with deliberation. They made no sound at all themselves, and even their membranous wings were silent. They were frightfully cold and damp and slippery, and their paws kneaded one detestably. Soon they were plunging hideously downward through inconceivable abysses in a whirling, giddying, sickening rush of dank, tomb-like air; and Carter felt they were shooting into the ultimate vortex of shrieking and daemonic madness. He screamed again and again, but whenever he did so the black paws tickled him with greater subtlety. Then he saw a sort of grey phosphorescence about, and guessed they were coming even to that inner world of subterrene horror of which dim legends tell, and which is litten only by the pale death-fire wherewith reeks the ghoulish air and the primal mists of the pits at earth's core.

At last far below him he saw faint lines of grey and ominous pinnacles which he knew must be the fabled Peaks of Throk. Awful and sinister they stand in the haunted disc of sunless and eternal depths; higher than man may reckon, and guarding terrible valleys where the Dholes crawl and burrow nastily. But Carter preferred to look at them than at his captors, which were indeed shocking and uncouth black things with smooth, oily, whale-like surfaces, unpleasant horns that curved inward toward each other, bat wings whose beating made no sound, ugly prehensile paws, and barbed tails that lashed needlessly and disquietingly. And worst of all, they never spoke or laughed, and never smiled because they had no faces at all to smile with, but only a suggestive blankness where a face ought to be. All they ever did was clutch and fly and tickle; that was the way of night-gaunts.

As the band flew lower the Peaks of Throk rose grey and towering on all sides, and one saw clearly that nothing lived on that austere and impressive granite of the endless twilight. At still lower levels the death-fires in the air gave out, and one met only the primal blackness of the void save aloft where the thin peaks stood out goblin-like. Soon the peaks were very far away, and nothing about but great rushing winds with the dankness of nethermost grottoes in them. Then in the end the night-gaunts landed on a floor of unseen things which felt like layers of bones, and left Carter all alone in that black valley. To bring him thither was the duty of the night-gaunts that guard Ngranek; and this done, they flapped away silently. When Carter tried to trace their flight he found he could not, since even the Peaks of Throk had faded out of sight. There was nothing anywhere but blackness and horror and silence and bones.

Now Carter knew from a certain source that he was in the vale of Pnoth, where crawl and burrow the enormous Dholes; but he did not know what to expect, because no one has ever seen a Dhole or even guessed what such a thing may be like. Dholes are known only by dim rumour, from the rustling they make amongst mountains of bones and the slimy touch they have when they wriggle past one. They cannot be seen because they creep only in the dark. Carter did not wish to meet a Dhole, so listened intently for any sound in the unknown depths of bones about him. Even in this fearsome place he had a plan and an objective, for whispers of Pnoth were not unknown to one with whom he had talked much in the old days. In brief, it seemed fairly likely that this was the spot into which all the ghouls of the waking world cast the refuse of their feastings; and that if he but had good luck he might stumble upon that mighty crag taller even than Throk's peaks which marks the edge of their domain. Showers of bones would tell him where to look, and once found he could call to a ghoul to let down a ladder; for strange to say, he had a very singular link with these terrible creatures.

A man he had known in Boston—a painter of strange pictures with a secret studio in an ancient and unhallowed alley near a graveyard—had actually made friends with the ghouls and had taught him to understand the simpler part of their disgusting meeping and glibbering. This man had vanished at last, and Carter was not sure but that he might find him now, and use for the first time in dreamland that far-away English of his dim waking life. In any case, he felt he could persuade a ghoul to guide him out of Pnoth; and it would be better to meet a ghoul, which one can see, than a Dhole, which one cannot see.

So Carter walked in the dark, and ran when he thought he heard something among the bones underfoot. Once he bumped into a stony slope, and knew it must be the base of one of Throk's peaks. Then at last he heard a monstrous rattling and clatter which reached far up in the air, and became sure he had come nigh the crag of the ghouls. He was not sure he could be heard from this valley miles below, but realised that the inner world has strange laws. As he pondered he was struck by a flying bone so heavy that it must have been a skull, and therefore realising his nearness to the fateful crag he sent up as best he might that meeping cry which is the call of the ghoul.

Sound travels slowly, so that was some time before he heard an answering glibber. But it came at last, and before long he was told that a rope ladder would be lowered. The wait for this was very tense, since there was no telling what might not have been stirred up among those bones by his shouting. Indeed, it was not long before he actually did hear a vague rustling afar off. As this thoughtfully approached, he became more and more uncomfortable; for he did not wish to move away from the spot where the ladder would come. Finally the tension grew almost unbearable, and he was about to flee in panic when the thud of something on the newly heaped bones nearby drew his notice from the other sound. It was the ladder, and after a minute of groping he had it taut in his hands. But the other sound did not cease, and followed him even as he climbed. He had gone fully five feet from the ground when the rattling beneath waxed emphatic, and was a good ten feet up when something swayed the ladder from below. At a height which must have been fifteen or twenty feet he felt his whole side brushed by a great slippery length which grew alternately convex and concave with wriggling; and hereafter he climbed desperately to escape the unendurable nuzzling of that loathsome and overfed Dhole whose form no man might see.

For hours he climbed with aching and blistered hands, seeing again the grey death-fire and Throk's uncomfortable pinnacles. At last he discerned above him the projecting edge of the great crag of the ghouls, whose vertical side he could not glimpse; and hours later he saw a curious face peering over it as a gargoyle peers over a parapet of Notre Dame. This almost made him lose his hold through faintness, but a moment later he was himself again; for his vanished friend Richard Pickman had once introduced him to a ghoul, and he knew well their canine faces and slumping forms and unmentionable idiosyncrasies. So he had himself well under control when that hideous thing pulled him out of the dizzy emptiness over the edge of the crag, and did not scream at the partly consumed refuse heaped at one side or at the squatting circles of ghouls who gnawed and watched curiously.

He was now on a dim-litten plain whose sole topographical features were great boulders and the entrances of burrows. The ghouls were in general respectful, even if one did attempt to pinch him while several others eyed his leanness speculatively. Through patient glibbering he made inquiries regarding his vanished friend, and found he had become a ghoul of some prominence in abysses nearer the waking world. A greenish elderly ghoul offered to conduct him to Pickman's present habitation, so despite a natural loathing he followed the creature into a capacious burrow and crawled after him for hours in the blackness of rank mould. They emerged on a dim plain strewn with singular relics of earth—old gravestones, broken urns, and grotesque fragments of monuments—and Carter realised with some emotion that he was probably nearer the waking world than at any other time since he had gone down the seven hundred steps from the cavern of flame to the Gate of Deeper Slumber.

There, on a tombstone of 1768 stolen from the

Granary Burying Ground in Boston, sat a ghoul which was once the artist Richard Upton Pickman. It was naked and rubbery, and had acquired so much of the ghoulish physiognomy that its human origin was already obscure. But it still remembered a little English, and was able to converse with Carter in grunts and monosyllables, helped out now and then by the glibbering of ghouls. When it learned that Carter wished to get to the enchanted wood and from there to the city Celephais in Ooth-Nargai beyond the Tanarian Hills, it seemed rather doubtful; for these ghouls of the waking world do no business in the graveyards of upper dreamland (leaving that to the red-footed wamps that are spawned in dead cities), and many things intervene betwixt their gulf and the enchanted wood, including the terrible kingdom of the Gugs.

The Gugs, hairy and gigantic, once reared stone circles in that wood and made strange sacrifices to the Other Gods and the crawling chaos Nyarlathotep, until one night an abomination of theirs reached the ears of earth's gods and they were banished to caverns below. Only a great trap door of stone with an iron ring connects the abyss of the earth-ghouls with the enchanted wood, and this the Gugs are afraid to open because of a curse. That a mortal dreamer could traverse their cavern realm and leave by that door is inconceivable; for mortal dreamers were their former food, and they have legends of the toothsomeness of such dreamers even though banishment has restricted their diet to the ghasts, those repulsive beings which die in the light, and which live in the vaults of Zin and leap on long hind legs like kangaroos.

So the ghoul that was Pickman advised Carter either

to leave the abyss at Sarkomand, that deserted city in the valley below Leng where black nitrous stairways guarded by winged diarote lions lead down from dreamland to the lower gulfs, or to return through a churchyard to the waking world and begin the quest anew down the seventy steps of light slumber to the cavern of flame and the seven hundred steps to the Gate of Deeper Slumber and the enchanted wood. This, however, did not suit the seeker; for he knew nothing of the way from Leng to Ooth-Nargai, and was likewise reluctant to awake lest he forget all he had so far gained in this dream. It were disastrous to his quest to forget the august and celestial faces of those seamen from the north who traded onyx in Celephais, and who, being the sons of gods, must point the way to the cold waste and Kadath where the Great Ones dwell.

After much persuasion the ghoul consented to guide his guest inside the great wall of the Gugs' kingdom. There was one chance that Carter might be able to steal through that twilight realm of circular stone towers at an hour when the giants would be all gorged and snoring indoors, and reach the central tower with the sign of Koth upon it, which has the stairs leading up to that stone trap door in the enchanted wood. Pickman even consented to lend three ghouls to help with a tombstone lever in raising the stone door; for of ghouls the Gugs are somewhat afraid, and they often flee from their own colossal graveyards when they see them feasting there.

He also advised Carter to disguise as a ghoul himself; shaving the beard he had allowed to grow (for ghouls have none), wallowing naked in the mould to get the correct surface, and loping in the usual slumping way, with his clothing carried in a bundle as if it were a choice morsel from a tomb. They would reach the city of Gugs—which is conterminous with the whole kingdom—through the proper burrows, emerging in a cemetery not far from the stair-containing Tower of Koth. They must beware, however, of a large cave near the cemetery; for this is the mouth of the vaults of Zin, and the vindictive ghasts are always on watch there murderously for those denizens of the upper abyss who hunt and prey on them. The ghasts try to come out when the Gugs sleep and they attack ghouls as readily as Gugs, for they cannot discriminate. They are very primitive, and eat one another. The Gugs have a sentry at a narrow place in the vaults of Zin, but he is often drowsy and is sometimes surprised by a party of ghasts. Though ghasts cannot live in real light, they can endure the grey twilight of the abyss for hours.

So at length Carter crawled through endless burrows with three helpful ghouls bearing the slate gravestone of Col. Nepemiah Derby, obit 1719, from the Charter Street Burying Ground in Salem. When they came again into open twilight they were in a forest of vast lichened monoliths reaching nearly as high as the eye could see and forming the modest gravestones of the Gugs. On the right of the hole out of which they wriggled, and seen through aisles of monoliths, was a stupendous vista of cyclopean round towers mounting up illimitable into the grey air of inner earth. This was the great city of the Gugs, whose doorways are thirty feet high. Ghouls come here often, for a buried Gug will feed a community for almost a year, and even with the added peril it is better to burrow for Gugs than to bother with the graves of men. Carter now understood the occasional titan bones he had felt beneath him in the vale of Pnoth.

Straight ahead, and just outside the cemetery, rose a sheer perpendicular cliff at whose base an immense and forbidding cavern yawned. This the ghouls told Carter to avoid as much as possible, since it was the entrance to the unhallowed vaults of Zin where Gugs hunt ghasts in the darkness. And truly, that warning was soon well justified; for the moment a ghoul began to creep toward the towers to see if the hour of the Gugs' resting had been rightly timed, there glowed in the gloom of that great cavern's mouth first one pair of yellowish-red eyes and then another, implying that the Gugs were one sentry less, and that ghasts have indeed an excellent sharpness of smell. So the ghoul returned to the burrow and motioned his companions to be silent. It was best to leave the ghasts to their own devices, and there was a possibility that they might soon withdraw, since they must naturally be rather tired after coping with a Gug sentry in the black vaults. After a moment something about the size of a small horse hopped out into the grey twilight, and Carter turned sick at the aspect of that scabrous and unwholesome beast, whose face is so curiously human despite the absence of a nose, a forehead, and other important particulars.

Presently three other ghasts hopped out to join their fellow, and a ghoul glibbered softly at Carter that their absence of battle-scars was a bad sign. It proved that they had not fought the Gug sentry at all, but had merely slipped past him as he slept, so that their strength and savagery were still unimpaired and would remain so till they had found and disposed of a victim. It was very unpleasant to see those filthy and disproportioned animals which soon numbered about fifteen, grubbing about and making their kangaroo leaps in the grey twilight where titan towers and monoliths arose, but it was still more unpleasant when they spoke among themselves in the coughing gutturals of ghasts. And yet, horrible as they were, they were not so horrible as what presently came out of the cave after them with disconcerting suddenness.

It was a paw, fully two feet and a half across, and equipped with formidable talons. After it came another paw, and after that a great black-furred arm to which both of the paws were attached by short forearms. Then two pink eyes shone, and the head of the awakened Gug sentry, large as a barrel, wabbled into view. The eyes jutted two inches from each side, shaded by bony protuberances overgrown with coarse hairs. But the head was chiefly terrible because of the mouth. That mouth had great yellow fangs and ran from the top to the bottom of the head, opening vertically instead of horizontally.

But before that unfortunate Gug could emerge from the cave and rise to his full twenty feet, the vindictive ghasts were upon him. Carter feared for a moment that he would give an alarm and arouse all his kin, till a ghoul softly glibbered that Gugs have no voice but talk by means of facial expression. The battle which then ensued was truly a frightful one. From all sides the venomous ghasts rushed feverishly at the creeping Gug, nipping and tearing with their muzzles, and mauling murderously with their hard pointed hooves. All the time they coughed excitedly, screaming when the great vertical mouth of the Gug would occasionally bite into one of their number, so that the noise of the combat would surely have aroused the sleeping city had not the weakening of the sentry begun to transfer the action farther and farther within the cavern. As it was, the tumult soon receded altogether from sight in the blackness, with only occasional evil echoes to mark its continuance.

Then the most alert of the ghouls gave the signal for all to advance, and Carter followed the loping three out of the forest of monoliths and into the dark noisome streets of that awful city whose rounded towers of cyclopean stone soared up beyond the sight. Silently they shambled over that rough rock pavement, hearing with disgust the abominable muffled snortings from great black doorways which marked the slumber of the Gugs. Apprehensive of the ending of the rest hour, the ghouls set a somewhat rapid pace; but even so the journey was no brief one, for distances in that town of giants are on a great scale. At last, however, they came to a somewhat open space before a tower even vaster than the rest; above whose colossal doorway was fixed a monstrous symbol in bas-relief which made one shudder without knowing its meaning. This was the central tower with the sign of Koth, and those huge stone steps just visible through the dusk within were the beginning of the great flight leading to upper dreamland and the enchanted wood.

There now began a climb of interminable length in utter blackness: made almost impossible by the monstrous size of the steps, which were fashioned for Gugs, and were therefore nearly a yard high. Of their number Carter could form no just estimate, for he soon became so worn out that the tireless and elastic ghouls were forced to aid him. All through the endless climb there lurked the peril of detection and pursuit; for though no Gug dares lift the stone door to the forest because of the Great One's curse, there are no such restraints concerning the tower and the steps, and escaped ghasts are often chased, even to the very top. So sharp are the ears of Gugs, that the bare feet and hands of the climbers might readily be heard when the city awoke; and it would of course take but little time for the striding giants, accustomed from their ghast-hunts in the vaults of Zin to seeing without light, to overtake their smaller and slower quarry on those cyclopean steps. It was very depressing to reflect that the silent pursuing Gugs would not be heard at all, but would come very suddenly and shockingly in the dark upon the climbers. Nor could the traditional fear of Gugs for ghouls be depended upon in that peculiar place where the advantages lay so heavily with the Gugs. There was also some peril from the furtive and venomous ghasts, which frequently hopped up onto the tower during the sleep hour of the Gugs. If the Gugs slept long, and the ghasts returned soon from their deed in the cavern, the scent of the climbers might easily be picked up by those loathsome and ill-disposed things; in which case it would almost be better to be eaten by a Gug.

Then, after aeons of climbing, there came a cough from the darkness above; and matters assumed a very grave and unexpected turn. It was clear that a ghast, or perhaps even more, had strayed into that tower before the coming of Carter and his guides; and it was equally clear that this peril was very close. After a breathless second the leading ghoul pushed Carter to the wall and arranged his kinfolk in the best possible way, with the old slate tombstone raised for a crushing blow whenever the enemy might come in sight. Ghouls can see in the dark, so the party was not as badly off as Carter would have been alone. In another moment the clatter of hooves revealed the downward hopping of at least one beast, and the slab-bearing ghouls poised their weapon for a desperate blow. Presently two yellowish-red eyes flashed into view, and the panting of the ghast became audible above its clattering. As it hopped down to the step above the ghouls, they wielded the ancient gravestone with prodigious force, so that there was only a wheeze and a choking before the victim collapsed in a noxious heap. There seemed to be only this one animal, and after a moment of listening the ghouls tapped Carter as a signal to proceed again. As before, they were obliged to aid him; and he was glad to leave that place of carnage where the ghast's uncouth remains sprawled invisible in the blackness.

At last the ghouls brought their companion to a halt; and feeling above him, Carter realised that the great stone trap door was reached at last. To open so vast a thing completely was not to be thought of, but the ghouls hoped to get it up just enough to slip the gravestone under as a prop, and permit Carter to escape through the crack. They themselves planned to descend again and return through the city of the Gugs, since their elusiveness was great, and they did not know the way overland to spectral Sarkomand with its lion-guarded gate to the abyss.

Mighty was the straining of those three ghouls at the stone of the door above them, and Carter helped push with as much strength as he had. They judged the edge next the top of the staircase to be the right one, and to this they bent all the force of their disreputably nour-

ished muscles. After a few moments a crack of light
appeared; and Carter, to whom that task had been
entrusted, slipped the end of the old gravestone in the
aperture. There now ensued a mighty heaving; but
progress was very slow, and they had of course to return
to their first position every time they failed to turn the
slab and prop the portal open.

Suddenly their desperation was magnified a thousand
fold by a sound on the steps below them. It was only
the thumping and rattling of the slain ghast's hooved
body as it rolled down to lower levels; but of all the
possible causes of that body's dislodgment and rolling,
none was in the least reassuring. Therefore, knowing
the ways of Gugs, the ghouls set to with something of a
frenzy; and in a surprisingly short time had the door so
high that they were able to hold it still whilst Carter
turned the slab and left a generous opening. They now
helped Carter through, letting him climb up to their
rubbery shoulders and later guiding his feet as he
clutched at the blessed soil of the upper dreamland
outside. Another second and they were through themselves, knocking away the gravestone and closing the
great trap door while a panting became audible
beneath. Because of the Great One's curse no Gug
might ever emerge from that portal, so with a deep
relief and sense of repose Carter lay quietly on the thick
grotesque fungi of the enchanted wood while his guides
squatted near in the manner that ghouls rest.

Weird as was that enchanted wood through which he
had fared so long ago, it was verily a haven and a
delight after those gulfs he had now left behind. There
was no living denizen about, for Zoogs shun the mysterious door in fear, and Carter at once consulted with his

ghouls about their future course. To return through the tower they no longer dared, and the waking world did not appeal to them when they learned that they must pass the priests Nasht and Kaman-Thah in the cavern of flame. So at length they decided to return through Sarkomand and its gate of the abyss, though of how to get there they knew nothing. Carter recalled that it lies in the valley below Leng, and recalled likewise that he had seen in Dylath-Leen a sinister, slant-eyed old merchant reputed to trade on Leng, therefore he advised the ghouls to seek out Dylath-Leen, crossing the fields to Nir and the Skai and following the river to its mouth. This they at once resolved to do, and lost no time in loping off, since the thickening of the dusk promised a full night ahead for travel. And Carter shook the paws of those repulsive beasts, thanking them for their help and sending his gratitude to the beast which once was Pickman; but could not help sighing with pleasure when they left. For a ghoul is a ghoul, and at best an unpleasant companion for man. After that Carter sought a forest pool and cleansed himself of the mud of nether earth, thereupon reassuming the clothes he had so carefully carried.

It was now night in that redoubtable wood of monstrous trees, but because of the phosphorescence one might travel as well as by day; wherefore Carter set out upon the well-known route toward Celephais, in Ooth-Nargai beyond the Tanarian Hills. And as he went he thought of the zebra he had left tethered to an ash-tree on Ngranek in far-away Oriab so many aeons ago, and wondered if any lava-gatherers had fed and released it. And he wondered, too, if he would ever return to Baharna and pay for the zebra that was slain by night in those ancient ruins by Yath's shore, and if the old tavernkeeper would remember him. Such were the thoughts that came to him in the air of the regained upper dreamland.

But presently his progress was halted by a sound from a very large hollow tree. He had avoided the great circle of stones, since he did not care to speak with Zoogs just now; but it appeared from the singular fluttering in that huge tree that important councils were in session elsewhere. Upon drawing nearer he made out the accents of a tense and heated discussion; and before long became conscious of matters which he viewed with the greatest concern. For a war on the cats was under debate in that sovereign assembly of Zoogs. It all came from the loss of the party which had sneaked after Carter to Ulthar, and which the cats had justly punished for unsuitable intentions. The matter had long rankled; and now, or at least within a month, the marshalled Zoogs were about to strike the whole feline tribe in a series of surprise attacks, taking individual cats or groups of cats unawares, and giving not even the myriad cats of Ulthar a proper chance to drill and mobilise. This was the plan of the Zoogs, and Carter saw that he must foil it before leaving upon his mighty quest.

Very quietly therefore did Randolph Carter steal to the edge of the wood and send the cry of the cat over the starlit fields. And a great grimalkin in a nearby cottage took up the burden and relayed it across leagues of rolling meadow to warriors large and small, black, grey, tiger, white, yellow, and mixed; and it echoed through Nir and beyond the Skai even into Ulthar, and Ulthar's numerous cats called in chorus and fell into a line of march. It was fortunate that the moon was not up, so that all the cats were on earth. Swiftly and silently leaping, they sprang from every hearth and housetop and poured in a great furry sea across the plains to the edge of the wood. Carter was there to greet them, and the sight of shapely, wholesome cats was indeed good for his eyes after the things he had seen and walked with in the abyss. He was glad to see his venerable friend and one-time rescuer at the head of Ulthar's detachment, a collar of rank around his sleek neck, and whiskers bristling at a martial angle. Better still, as a sub-lieutenant in that army was a brisk young fellow who proved to be none other than the very little kitten at the inn to whom Carter had given a saucer of rich cream on that long-vanished morning in Ulthar. He was a strapping and promising cat now, and purred as he shook hands with his friend. His grandfather said he was doing very well in the army, and that he might well expect a captaincy after one more campaign.

Carter now outlined the peril of the cat tribe, and was rewarded by deep-throated purrs of gratitude from all sides. Consulting with the generals, he prepared a plan of instant action which involved marching at once upon the Zoog council and other known strongholds of Zoogs; forestalling their surprise attacks and forcing them to terms before the mobilization of their army of invasion. Thereupon without a moment's loss that great ocean of cats flooded the enchanted wood and surged around the council tree and the great stone circle. Flutterings rose to panic pitch as the enemy saw the newcomers and there was very little resistance among the furtive and curious brown Zoogs. They saw that they were beaten in advance, and turned from thoughts of vengeance to thoughts of present self-preservation.

Half the cats now seated themselves in a circular formation with the captured Zoogs in the centre, leaving open a lane down which were marched the additional captives rounded up by the other cats in other parts of the wood. Terms were discussed at length, Carter acting as interpreter, and it was decided that the Zoogs might remain a free tribe on condition of rendering to the cats a large tribute of grouse, quail, and pheasants from the less fabulous parts of the forest. Twelve young Zoogs of noble families were taken as hostages to be kept in the Temple of Cats at Ulthar, and the victors made it plain that any disappearances of cats on the borders of the Zoog domain would be followed by consequences highly disastrous to Zoogs. These matters disposed of, the assembled cats broke ranks and permitted the Zoogs to slink off one by one to their respective homes, which they hastened to do with many a sullen backward glance.

The old cat general now offered Carter an escort through the forest to whatever border he wished to reach, deeming it likely that the Zoogs would harbour dire resentment against him for the frustration of their warlike enterprise. This offer he welcomed with gratitude; not only for the safety it afforded, but because he liked the graceful companionship of cats. So in the midst of a pleasant and playful regiment, relaxed after the successful performance of its duty, Randolph Carter walked with dignity through that enchanted and phosphorescent wood of titan trees, talking of his quest with the old general and his grandson whilst others of the band indulged in fantastic gambols or chased fallen leaves that the wind drove among the fungi of that primeval floor. And the old cat said that he had heard much of unknown Kadath in the cold waste, but did not know where it was. As for the marvellous sunset city, he had not even heard of that, but would gladly relay to Carter anything he might later learn.

He gave the seeker some passwords of great value among the cats of dreamland, and commended him especially to the old chief of the cats in Celephais, whither he was bound. That old cat, already slightly known to Carter, was a dignified maltese; and would prove highly influential in any transaction. It was dawn when they came to the proper edge of the wood, and Carter bade his friends a reluctant farewell. The young sub-lieutenant he had met as a small kitten would have followed him had not the old general fobidden it, but that austere patriarch insisted that the path of duty lay with the tribe and the army. So Carter set out alone over the golden fields that stretched mysterious beside a willow-fringed river, and the cats went back into the wood.

Well did the traveller know those garden lands that lie betwixt the wood of the Cerenerian Sea, and blithely did he follow the singing river Oukranos that marked his course. The sun rose higher over gentle slopes of grove and lawn, and heightened the colours of the thousand flowers that starred each knoll and dingle. A blessed haze lies upon all this region, wherein is held a little more of the sunlight than other places hold, and a little more of the summer's humming music of birds and bees; so that men walk through it as through a faery place, and feel greater joy and wonder than they ever afterward remember.

By noon Carter reached the jasper terraces of Kiran which slope down to the river's edge and bear that temple of loveliness wherein the King of Ilek-Vad comes from his far realm on the twilight sea once a year in a golden palanquin to pray to the god of Oukranos, who sang to him in youth when he dwelt in a cottage by its banks. All of jasper is that temple, and covering an acre of ground with its walls and courts, its seven pinnacled towers, and its inner shrine where the river enters through hidden channels and the god sings softly in the night. Many times the moon hears strange music as it shines on those courts and terraces and pinnacles, but whether that music be the song of the god or the chant of the cryptical priests, none but the King of Ilek-Vad may say; for only he had entered the temple or seen the priests. Now, in the drowsiness of day, that carven and delicate fane was silent, and Carter heard only the murmur of the great stream and the hum of the birds and bees as he walked onward under the enchanted sun.

All that afternoon the pilgrim wandered on through perfumed meadows and in the lee of gentle riverward hills bearing peaceful thatched cottages and the shrines of amiable gods carven from jasper or chrysoberyl. Sometimes he walked close to the bank of Oukranos and whistled to the sprightly and iridescent fish of that crystal stream, and at other times he paused amidst the whispering rushes and gazed at the great dark wood on the farther side, whose trees came down clear to the water's edge. In former dreams he had seen quaint lumbering buopoths come shyly out of that wood to drink, but now he could not glimpse any. Once in a while he paused to watch a carnivorous fish catch a fishing bird, which it lured to the water by showing its tempting scales in the sun, and grasped by the beak with its enormous mouth as the winged hunter sought to dart down upon it.

Toward evening he mounted a low grassy rise and saw before him flaming in the sunset the thousand gilded spires of Thran. Lofty beyond belief are the alabaster walls of that incredible city, sloping inward toward the top and wrought in one solid piece by what means no man knows, for they are more ancient than memory. Yet lofty as they are with their hundred gates and two hundred turrets, the clustered towers within, all white beneath their golden spires, are loftier still; so that men on the plain around see them soaring into the sky, sometimes shining clear, somtimes caught at the top in tangles of cloud and mist, and sometimes clouded lower down with their utmost pinnacles blazing free above the vapours. And where Thran's gates open on the river are great wharves of marble, with ornate galleons of fragrant cedar and calamander riding gently at anchor, and strange bearded sailors sitting on casks and bales with the hieroglyphs of far places. Landward beyond the walls lies the farm country, where small white cottages dream between little hills, and narrow roads with many stone bridges wind gracefully among streams and gardens.

Down through this verdant land Carter walked at evening, and saw twilight float up from the river to the marvellous golden spires of Thran. And just at the hour of dusk he came to the southern gate, and was stopped by a red-robed sentry till he had told three dreams beyond belief, and proved himself a dreamer worthy to walk up Thran's steep mysterious streets and linger in the bazaars where the wares of the ornate galleons were sold. Then into that incredible city he walked; through a wall so thick that the gate was a tunnel, and thereafter amidst curved and undulant ways winding deep and narrow between the heavenward towers. Lights shone through grated and balconied windows, and the sound of lutes and pipes stole timid from inner courts where marble fountains bubbled. Carter knew his way, and edged down through darker streets to the river, where at an old sea tavern he found the captains and seamen he had known in myriad other dreams. There he bought his passage to Celephaïs on a great green galleon, and there he stopped for the night after speaking gravely to the venerable cat of that inn, who blinked dozing before an enormous hearth and dreamed of old wars and forgotten gods.

In the morning Carter boarded the galleon bound for Celephaïs, and sat in the prow as the ropes were cast off and the long sail down to the Cerenerian Sea begun. For many leagues the banks were much as they were above Thran, with now and then a curious temple rising on the farther hills toward the right, and a drowsy village on the shore, with steep red roofs and nets spread in the sun. Mindful of his search, Carter questioned all the mariners closely about those whom they had met in the taverns of Celephaïs, asking the names and ways of the strange men with long, narrow eyes, long-lobed ears, thin noses, and pointed chins who came in dark ships from the north and traded onyx for the carved jade and spun gold and little red singing birds of Celephaïs. Of these men the sailors knew not much, save that they talked but seldom and spread a kind of awe about them.

Their land, very far away, was called Inquanok, and not many people cared to go thither because it was cold twilight land, and said to be close to unpleasant Leng; although high impassable mountains towered on the side where Leng was thought to lie, so that none might say whether this evil plateau with its horrible stone villages and unmentionable monastery were really there, or whether the rumour were only a fear that timid people felt in the night when those formidable barrier peaks loomed black against a rising moon. Certainly, men reached Leng from very different oceans. Of other boundaries of Inquanok those sailors had no notion, nor had they heard of the cold waste and unknown Kadath save from vague unplaced report. And of the marvellous sunset city which Carter sought they knew nothing at all. So the traveller asked no more of far things, but bided his time till he might talk with those strange men from cold and twilight Inquanok who are the seed of such gods as carved their features on Ngranek.

Late in the day the galleon reached those bends of the river which traverse the perfumed jungles of Kled. Here Carter wished he might disembark, for in those tropic tangles sleep wondrous palaces of ivory, lone and unbroken, where once dwelt fabulous monarchs of a land whose name is forgotten. Spells of the Elder Ones keep those places unharmed and undecayed, for it is written that there may one day be need of them again; and elephant caravans have glimpsed them from afar by moonlight, though none dares approach them closely because of the guardians to which their wholeness is due. But the ship swept on, and dusk hushed the hum of the day, and the first stars above blinked answers to the early fireflies on the banks as that jungle fell far behind, leaving only its fragrance as a memory that it had

been. And all through the night that galleon floated on
past mysteries unseen and unsuspected. Once a lookout
reported fires on the hills to the east, but the sleepy
captain said they had better not be looked at too much,
since it was highly uncertain just who or what had lit
them.

In the morning the river had broadened out greatly,
and Carter saw by the houses along the banks that they
were close to the vast trading city of Hlanith on the
Cerenerian Sea. Here the walls are of rugged granite,
and the houses peakedly fantastic with beamed and
plastered gables. The men of Hlanith are more like
those of the waking world than any others in dreamland; so that the city is not sought except for barter, but
is prized for the solid work of its artisans. The wharves
of Hlanith are of oak, and there the galleon made fast
while the captain traded in the taverns. Carter also went
ashore, and looked curiously upon the rutted streets
where wooden ox carts lumbered and feverish merchants cried their wares vacuously in the bazaars. The
sea taverns were all close to the wharves on cobbled
lanes salt with the spray of high tides, and seemed
exceedingly ancient with their low black-beamed ceilings and casements of greenish bull's-eye panes. Ancient
sailors in those taverns talked much of distant ports, and
told many stories of the curious men from twilight
Inquanok, but had little to add to what the seamen of
the galleon had told. Then at last, after much unloading
and loading, the ship set sail once more over the sunset
sea, and the high walls and gables of Hlanith grew less
as the last golden light of day lent them a wonder and
beauty beyond any that men had given them.

Two nights and two days the galleon sailed over the

Cerenerian Sea, sighting no land and speaking but one other vessel. Then near sunset of the second day there loomed up ahead the snowy peak of Aran with its gingko-trees swaying on the lower slope, and Carter knew that they were come to the land of Ooth-Nargai and the marvellous city of Celephais. Swiftly there came into sight the glittering minarets of that fabulous town, and the untarnished marble walls with their bronze statues, and the great stone bridge where Naraxa joins the sea. Then rose the gentle hills behind the town, with their groves and gardens of asphodels and the small shrines and cottages upon them; and far in the background the purple ridge of the Tanarians, potent and mystical, behind which lay forbidden ways into the waking world and toward other regions of dream.

The harbour was full of painted galleys, some of which were from the marble cloud-city of Serannian, that lies in ethereal space beyond where the sea meets the sky, and some of which were from more substantial parts of dreamland. Among these the steersman thread-ed his way up to the spice-fragrant wharves, where the galleon made fast in the dusk as the city's million lights began to twinkle out over the water. Ever new seemed this deathless city of vision, for here time has no power to tarnish or destroy. As it has always been is still the turquoise of Nath-Horthath, and the eighty orchid-wreathed priests are the same who builded it ten thou-sand years ago. Shining still is the bronze of the great gates, nor are the onyx pavements ever worn or broken. And the great bronze statues on the walls look down on merchants and camel drivers older than fable, yet with-out one grey hair in their forked beards.

Carter did not once seek out the temple or the palace

or the citadel, but stayed by the seaward wall among traders and sailors. And when it was too late for rumours and legends he sought out an ancient tavern he knew well, and rested with dreams of the gods on unknown Kadath whom he sought. The next day he searched all along the quays for some of the strange mariners of Inquanok, but was told that none were now in port, their galley not being due from the north for full two weeks. He found, however, one Thorabonian sailor who had been to Inquanok and had worked in the onyx quarries of that twilight place; and this sailor said there was certainly a descent to the north of the peopled region, which everybody seemed to fear and shun. The Thorabonian opined that this desert led around the utmost rim of impassable peaks into Leng's horrible plateau, and that this was why men feared it; though he admitted there were other vague tales of evil presences and nameless sentinels. Whether or not this could be the fabled waste wherein unknown Kadath stands he did not know; but it seemed unlikely that those presences and sentinels, if indeed they existed, were stationed for nought.

On the following day Carter walked up the Street of the Pillars to the turquoise temple and talked with the High Priest. Though Nath-Horthath is chiefly worshipped in Celephais, all the Great Ones are mentioned in diurnal prayers; and the priest was reasonably versed in their moods. Like Atal in distant Ulthar, he strongly advised against any attempts to see them; declaring that they are testy and capricious, and subject to strange protection from the mindless Other Gods from Outside, whose soul and messenger is the crawling chaos Nyarlathotep. Their jealous hiding of the marvellous sunset city shewed clearly that they did not wish Carter to reach it, and it was doubtful how they would regard a guest whose object was to see them and plead before them. No man had ever found Kadath in the past, and it might be just as well if none ever found it in the future. Such rumours as were told about that onyx castle of the Great Ones were not by any means reassuring.

Having thanked the orchid-crowned High Priest, Carter left the temple and sought out the bazaar of the sheep-butchers, where the old chief of Celephais' cats dwelt sleek and contented. That grey and dignified being was sunning himself on the onyx pavement, and extended a languid paw as his caller approached. But when Carter repeated the passwords and introductions furnished him by the old cat general of Ulthar, the furry patriarch became very cordial and communicative; and told much of the secret lore known to cats on the seaward slopes of Ooth-Nargai. Best of all, he repeated several things told him furtively by the timid waterfront cats of Celephais about the men of Inquanok, on whose dark ships no cat will go.

It seems that these men have an aura not of earth about them, though that is not the reason why no cat will sail on their ships. The reason for this is that Inquanok holds shadows which no cat can endure, so that in all that cold twilight realm there is never a cheering purr or a homely mew. Whether it be because of things wafted over the impassable peaks from hypothetical Leng, or because of things filtering down from the chilly desert to the north, none may say; but it remains a fact that in that far land there broods a hint of outer space which cats do not like, and to which they are more sensitive than men. Therefore they will not go on the dark ships that seek the basalt quays of In-quanok.

The old chief of the cats also told him where to find his friend King Kuranes, who in Carter's latter dreams had reigned alternately in the rose-crystal Palace of the Seventy Delights at Celephais and in the turreted cloud-castle of sky-floating Serannian. It seemed that he could no more find content in those places, but had formed a mighty longing for the English cliffs and downlands of his boyhood; where in little dreaming villages England's old songs hover at evening behind lattice windows, and where grey church towers peep lovely through the verdure of distant valleys. He could not go back to these things in the waking world because his body was dead; but he had done the next best thing and dreamed a small tract of such countryside in the region east of the city where meadows roll gracefully up from the sea-cliffs to the foot of the Tanarian Hills. There he dwelt in a grey Gothic manor-house of stone looking on the sea, and tried to think it was ancient Tre-vor Towers, where he was born and where thirteen gen-erations of his forefathers had first seen the light. And on the coast nearby he had built a little Cornish fishing village with steep cobbled ways, settling therein such people as had the most English faces, and seeking ever to teach them the dear remembered accents of old Corn-wall fishers. And in a valley not far off he had reared a great Norman Abbey whose tower he could see from his window, placing around it in the churchyard grey stones with the names of his ancestors carved thereon, and with a moss somewhat like Old England's moss. For though Kuranes was a monarch in the land of dream, with all imagined pomps and marvels, splendours and beauties, ecstasies and delights, novelties and excitements at his command, he would gladly have resigned for ever the whole of his power and luxury and freedom for one blessed day as a simple boy in that pure and quiet England, that ancient, beloved England which had moulded his being and of which he must always be immutably a part.

So when Carter bade that old grey chief of the cats adieu, he did not seek the terraced palace of rose crystal but walked out the eastern gate and across the daisied fields toward a peaked gable which he glimpsed through the oaks of a park sloping up to the sea-cliffs. And in time he came to a great hedge and a gate with a little brick lodge, and when he rang the bell there hobbled to admit him no robed and annointed lackey of the palace, but a small stubby old man in a smock who spoke as best he could in the quaint tones of far Cornwall. And Carter walked up the shady path between trees as near as possible to England's trees, and clumbed the terraces among gardens set out as in Queen Anne's time. At the door, flanked by stone cats in the old way, he was met by a whiskered butler in suitable livery; and was presently taken to the library where Kuranes, Lord of Ooth-Nargai and the Sky around Serannian, sat pensive in a chair by the window looking on his little seacoast village and wishing that his old nurse would come in and scold him because he was not ready for that hateful lawn-party at the vicar's, with the carriage waiting and his mother nearly out of patience.

Kuranes, clad in a dressing gown of the sort favoured by London tailors in his youth, rose eagerly to meet his guest; for the sight of an Anglo-Saxon from the waking world was very dear to him, even if it was a Saxon from Boston, Massachusetts, instead of from Cornwall. And for long they talked of old times, having much to say because both were old dreamers and well versed in the wonders of incredible places. Kuranes, indeed, had been out beyond the stars in the ultimate void, and was said to be the only one who had ever returned sane from such a voyage.

At length Carter brought up the subject of his quest, and asked of his host those questions he had asked of so many others. Kuranes did not know where Kadath was, or the marvellous sunset city; but he did know that the Great Ones were very dangerous creatures to seek out, and that the Other Gods had strange ways of protecting them from impertinent curiosity. He had learned much of the Other Gods in distant parts of space, especially in that region where form does not exist, and coloured gases study the innermost secrets. The violet gas S'ngac had told him terrible things of the crawling chaos Nyarlathotep, and had warned him never to approach the central void where the daemon sultan Azathoth gnaws hungrily in the dark. Altogether, it was not well to meddle with the Elder Ones; and if they persistently denied all access to the marvellous sunset city, it were better not to seek that city.

Kuranes furthermore doubted whether his guest would profit aught by coming to the city even were he to gain it. He himself had dreamed and yearned long years for lovely Celephaïs and the land of Ooth-Nargai, and for the freedom and colour and high experience of life devoid of its chains, and conventions, and stupidities. But now that he was come into that city and that land, and was the king thereof, he found the freedom and the vividness all too soon worn out, and monotonous for want of linkage with anything firm in his feelings and memories. He was a king in Ooth-Nargai, but found no meaning therein, and drooped always for the old familiar things of England that had shaped his youth. All his kingdom would he give for the sound of Cornish church bells over the downs, and all the thousand minarets of Celephaïs for the steep homely roofs of the village near his home. So he told his guest that the unknown sunset city might not hold quite that content he sought, and that perhaps it had better remain a glorious and half-remembered dream. For he had visited Carter often in the old waking days, and knew well the lovely New England slopes that had given him birth.

At the last, he was very certain, the seeker would long only for the early remembered scenes; the glow of Beacon Hill at evening, the tall steeples and winding hill streets of quaint Kingsport, the hoary gambrel roofs of ancient and witch-haunted Arkham, and the blessed meads and valleys where stone walls rambled and white farmhouse gables peeped out from bowers of verdure. These things he told Randolph Carter, but still the seeker held to his purpose. And in the end they parted each with his own conviction, and Carter went back through the bronze gate into Celephaïs and down the Street of Pillars to the old sea wall, where he talked more with the mariners of far ports and waited for the dark ship from cold and twilight Inquanok, whose strange-faced sailors and onyx-traders had in them the blood of the Great Ones.

One starlit evening when the Pharos shone splendid over the harbour the longed-for ship put in, and strange-faced sailors and traders appeared one by one and group by group in the ancient taverns along the sea wall. It was very exciting to see again those living faces so like the godlike features of Ngranek, but Carter did not hasten to speak with the silent seamen. He did not know how much of pride and secrecy and dim supernal memory might fill those children of the Great Ones, and was sure it would not be wise to tell them of his quest or ask too closely of that cold desert stretching north of their twilight land. They talked little with the other folk in those ancient sea taverns; but would gather in groups in remote corners and sing among themselves the haunting airs of unknown places, or chant long tales to one another in accents alien to the rest of dreamland. And so rare and moving were those airs and tales that one might guess their wonders from the faces of those who listened, even though the words came to common ears only as strange cadence and obscure melody.

For a week the strange seamen lingered in the taverns and traded in the bazaars of Celephais, and before they sailed Carter had taken passage on their dark ship, telling them that he was an old onyx miner and wishful to work in their quarries. That ship was very lovely and cunningly wrought, being of teakwood with ebony fittings and traceries of gold, and the cabin in which the traveller lodged had hangings of silk and velvet. One morning at the turn of the tide the sails were raised and the anchor lifted, and as Carter stood on the high stern he saw the sunrise-blazing walls and bronze statues and golden minarets of ageless Celephais sink into the distance, and the snowy peak of Mount Aran grow smaller and smaller. By noon there was nothing in sight save the gentle blue of the Cerenerian Sea, with one painted galley afar off bound for that realm of Serannian where the sea meets the sky.

And the night came with gorgeous stars, and the dark ship steered for Charles' Wain and the Little Bear as they swung slowly round the pole. And the sailors sang strange songs of unknown places, and they stole off one by one to the forecastle while the wistful watchers murmured old chants and leaned over the rail to glimpse the luminous fish playing in bowers beneath the sea. Carter went to sleep at midnight, and rose in the glow of a young morning, marking that the sun seemed farther south than was its wont. And all through that second day he made progress in knowing the men of the ship, getting them little by little to talk of their cold twilight land, of their exquisite onyx city, and of their fear of the high and impassable peaks beyond which Leng was said to be. They told him how sorry they were that no cats would stay in the land of Inquanok, and how they thought the hidden nearness of Leng was to blame for it. Only of the stony desert to the north they would not talk. There was something disquieting about that desert, and it was thought expedient not to admit its existence.

On later days they talked of the quarries in which Carter said he was going to work. There were many of them, for all the city of Inquanok was builded of onyx, whilst great polished blocks of it were traded in Rinar, Ogrothan, and Celephais and at home with the merchants of Thraa, Ilarnek, and Kadatheron, for the beautiful wares of those fabulous ports. And far to the north, almost in the cold desert whose existence the men of Inquanok did not care to admit, there was an unused quarry greater than all the rest; from which had been hewn in forgotten times such prodigious lumps and blocks that the sight of their chiselled vacancies struck terror to all who beheld. Who had mined those incredible blocks, and whither they had been transported, no man might say; but it was thought best not to trouble that quarry, around which such inhuman memories might conceivably cling. So it was left all alone in the twilight, with only the raven and the rumoured Shantak-bird to brood on its immensities. When Carter heard of this quarry he was moved to deep thought, for he knew from old tales that the Great Ones' castle atop unknown Kadath is of onyx.

Each day the sun wheeled lower and lower in the sky, and the mists overhead grew thicker and thicker. And in two weeks there was not any sunlight at all, but only a weird grey twilight shining through a dome of eternal cloud by day, and a cold starless phosphorescence from the under side of that cloud by night. On the twentieth day a great jagged rock in the sea was sighted from afar, the first land glimpsed since Aran's snowy peak had dwindled behind the ship. Carter asked the captain the name of that rock, but was told that it had no name and had never been sought by any vessel because of the sounds that came from it at night. And when, after dark, a dull and ceaseless howling arose from that jagged granite place, the traveller was glad that no stop had been made, and that the rock had no name. The seamen prayed and chanted till the noise was out of earshot, and Carter dreamed terrible dreams within dreams in the small hours.

Two mornings after that there loomed far ahead and to the east a line of great grey peaks whose tops were lost in the changeless clouds of that twilight world. And at the sight of them the sailors sang glad songs, and some knelt down on the deck to pray; so that Carter knew they were come to the land of Inquanok and would soon be moored to the basalt quays of the great town bearing that land's name. Toward noon a dark coastline appeared, and before three o'clock there stood out against the north the bulbous domes and fantastic spires of the onyx city. Rare and curious did that archaic city rise above its walls and quays, all of delicate black with scrolls, flutings, and arabesques of inlaid gold. Tall and many-windowed were the houses, and carved on every side with flowers and patterns whose dark symmetries dazzled the eye with a beauty more poignant than light. Some ended in swelling domes that tapered to a point, others in terraced pyramids whereon rose clustered minarets displaying every phase of strangeness and imagination. The walls were low, and pierced by frequent gates, each under a great arch rising high above the general level and capped by the head of a god chiselled with that same skill displayed in the monstrous face on distant Ngranek. On a hill in the centre rose a sixteen-angled tower greater than all the rest and bearing a high pinnacled belfry resting on a flattened dome. This, the seamen said, was the Temple of the Elder Ones, and was ruled by an old High-Priest sad with inner secrets.

At intervals the clang of a strange bell shivered over the onyx city, answered each time by a peal of mystic music made up of horns, viols, and chanting voices. And from a row of tripods on a galley round the high dome of the temple there burst flares of flame at certain moments; for the priests and people of that city were wise in the primal mysteries, and faithful in keeping the rhythms of the Great Ones as set forth in scrolls older than the Pnakotic Manuscripts. As the ship rode past the great basalt breakwater into the harbour the lesser noises of the city grew manifest, and Carter saw the slaves, sailors, and merchants on the docks. The sailors and merchants were of the strange-faced race of the gods, but the slaves were squat, slant-eyed folk said by rumour to have drifted somehow across or around the impassable peaks from the valleys beyond Leng. The wharves reached wide outside the city wall and bore upon them all manner of merchandise from the galleys anchored there, while at one end were great piles of onyx both carved and uncarved awaiting shipment to the far markets of Rinar, Ograthan and Celephais.

It was not yet evening when the dark ship anchored beside a jutting quay of stone, and all the sailors and traders filed ashore and through the arched gate into the city. The streets of that city were paved with onyx and some of them were wide and straight whilst others were crooked and narrow. The houses near the water were lower than the rest, and bore above their curiously arched doorways certain signs of gold said to be in honour of the respective small gods that favoured each. The captain of the ship took Carter to an old sea tavern where flocked the mariners of quaint countries, and promised that he would next day shew him the wonders of the twilight city, and lead him to the taverns of the onyx-miners by the northern wall. And evening fell, and little bronze lamps were lighted, and the sailors in that tavern sang songs of remote places. But when from its high tower the great bell shivered over the city, and the peal of the horns and viols and voices rose cryptical in answer thereto, all ceased their songs or tales and bowed silent till the last echo died away. For there is a wonder and a strangeness on the twilight city of Inquanok, and men fear to be lax in its rites lest a doom and a vengeance lurk unsuspectedly close.

Far in the shadows of that tavern Carter saw a squat form he did not like, for it was unmistakably that of the old slant-eyed merchant he had seen so long before in the taverns of Dylath-Leen, who was reputed to trade with the horrible stone villages of Leng which no healthy folk visit and whose evil fires are seen at night from afar, and even to have dealt with that high-priest not to be described, which wears a yellow silken mask over its face and dwells all alone in a prehistoric stone monastery. This man had seemed to shew a queer gleam of knowing when Carter asked the traders of Dylath-Leen about the cold waste and Kadath; and somehow his presence in dark and haunted Inquanok, so close to the wonders of the north, was not a reassuring thing. He slipped wholly out of sight before Carter could speak to him, and sailors later said that he had come with a yak caravan from some point not well determined, bearing the colossal and rich-flavoured eggs of the rumoured Shantak-bird to trade for the dextrous jade goblets that merchants brought from Ilarnek.

On the following morning the ship-captain led Carter through the onyx streets of Inquanok, dark under their twilight sky. The inlaid doors and figured housefronts, carven balconies and crystal-paned oriels all gleamed with a sombre and polished loveliness; and now and then a plaza would open out with black pillars, colonades, and the statues of curious beings both human and fabulous. Some of the vistas down long and unbending streets, or through side alleys and over bulbous domes, spires, and arabesqued roofs, were weird and beautiful beyond words; and nothing was more splendid than the massive heights of the great central Temple of the Elder Ones with its sixteen carven sides, its flattened dome, and its lofty pinnacled belfry, overtopping all else, and majestic whatever its foreground. And always to the east, far beyond the city walls and the leagues of pasture land, rose the gaunt grey sides of those topless and impassable peaks across which hideous Leng was said to lie.

The captain took Carter to the mighty temple, which is set with its walled garden in a great round plaza whence the streets go as spokes from a wheel's hub. The seven arched gates of that garden, each having over it a carven face like those on the city's gates, are always open, and the people roam reverently at will down the tiled paths and through the little lanes lined with grotesque termini and the shrines of modest gods. And there are fountains, pools, and basins there to reflect the frequent blaze of the tripods on the high balcony, all of onyx and having in them small luminous fish taken by divers from the lower bowers of ocean. When the deep clang from the temple belfry shivers over the garden and the city, and the answer of the horns and viols and voices peals out from the seven lodges by the garden gates, there issue from the seven doors of the temple long columns of masked and hooded priests in black, bearing at arm's length before them great golden bowls from which a curious steam rises. And all the seven columns strut peculiarly in single file, legs thrown far forward without bending the knees, down the walks that lead to the seven lodges, wherein they disappear and do not appear again. It is said that subterrene paths connect the lodges with the temple, and that the long files of priests return through them; nor is it unwhispered that deep flights of onyx steps go down to mysteries that are never told. But only a few are those who hint that the priests in the masked and hooded columns are not human beings.

Carter did not enter the temple, because none but the Veiled King is permitted to do that. But before he left the garden the hour of the bell came, and he heard the shivering clang deafeningly above him, and the wailing of the horns and viols and voices loud from the lodges by the gates. And down the seven great walks stalked the long files of bowl-bearing priests in their singular way, giving to the traveller a fear which human priests do not often give. When the last of them had vanished he left that garden, noting as he did so a spot on the pavement over which the bowls had passed. Even the ship-captain did not like that spot, and hurried him on toward the hill whereon the Veiled King's palace rises many-domed and marvellous.

The ways to the onyx palace are steep and narrow, all but the broad curving one where the king and his companions ride on yaks or in yak-drawn chariots. Carter and his guide climbed up an alley that was all steps, between inlaid walls bearing strange signs in gold, and under balconies and oriels whence sometimes floated soft strains of music or breaths of exotic fragrance. Always ahead loomed those titan walls, mighty buttresses, and clustered and bulbous domes for which the Veiled King's palace is famous; and at length they passed under a great black arch and emerged in the gardens of the monarch's pleasure. There Carter paused in faintness at so much beauty; for the onyx terraces and colonnaded walks, the gay porterres and delicate flowering trees espaliered to golden lattices, the brazen urns and tripods with cunning bas-reliefs, the pedestalled and almost breathing statues of veined black marble, the basalt-bottomed lagoon's tiled fountains with luminous fish, the tiny temples of iridescent singing birds atop carven columns, the marvellous scrollwork of the great bronze gates, and the blossoming vines trained along every inch of the polished walls all joined to form a sight whose loveliness was beyond reality, and half-fabulous even in the land of dream. There it shimmered like a vision under that grey twilight sky, with the domed and fretted magnificence of the palace ahead, and the fantastic silhouette of the distant impassable peaks on the right. And ever the small birds and the fountains sang, while the perfume of rare blossoms spread like a veil over that incredible garden. No other human presence was there, and Carter was glad it was so. Then they turned and descended again the onyx alley of steps, for the palace itself no visitor may enter; and it is not well to look too long and steadily at the great central dome, since it is said to house the archaic father of all the rumoured Shantak-birds, and to send out queer dreams to the curious.

After that the captain took Carter to the north quarter of the town, near the Gate of the Caravans, where are the taverns of the yak-merchants and the onyx-miners. And there, in a low-ceiled inn of quarrymen, they said farewell; for business called the captain whilst Carter was eager to talk with miners about the north. There were many men in that inn, and the traveller was not long in speaking to some of them; saying that he was an old miner of onyx, and anxious to know somewhat of Inquanok's quarries. But all that he learned was not much more than he knew before, for the miners were timid and evasive about the cold desert to the north and the quarry that no man visits. They had fears of fabled emmissaries from around the mountains where Leng is said to lie, and of evil presences and nameless sentinels far north among the scattered rocks. And they whispered also that the rumoured Shantak-birds are no wholesome things; it being indeed for the best that no man has ever truly seen one (for that fabled father of Shantaks in the king's dome is fed in the dark).

The next day, saying that he wished to look over all the various mines for himself and to visit the scattered farms and quaint onyx villages of Inquanok, Carter hired a yak and stuffed great leathern saddle-bags for a journey. Beyond the Gate of the Caravans the road lay straight betwixt tilled fields, with many odd farmhouses crowned by low domes. At some of these houses the seeker stopped to ask questions; once finding a host so austere and reticent, and so full of an unplaced majesty like to that in the huge features on Ngranek, that he felt certain he had come at last upon one of the Great Ones themselves, or upon one with full nine-tenths of their blood, dwelling amongst men. And to that austere and reticent cotter he was careful to speak very well of the gods, and to praise all the blessings they had ever accorded him.

That night Carter camped in a roadside meadow beneath a great lygath-tree to which he tied his yak, and in the morning resumed his northward pilgrimage. At about ten o'clock he reached the small-domed village of

Urg, where traders rest and miners tell their tales, and paused in its taverns till noon. It is here that the great caravan road turns west toward Selarn, but Carter kept on north by the quarry road. All the afternoon he followed that rising road, which was somewhat narrower than the great highway, and which now led through a region with more rocks than tilled fields. And by evening the low hills on his left had risen into sizable black cliffs, so that he knew he was close to the mining country. All the while the great gaunt sides of the impassable mountains towered afar off at his right, and the farther he went, the worse tales he heard of them from the scattered farmers and traders and drivers of lumbering onyx-carts along the way.

On the second night he camped in the shadow of a large black crag, tethering his yak to a stake driven in the ground. He observed the greater phosphorescence of the clouds at this northerly point, and more than once thought he saw dark shapes outlined against them. And on the third morning he came in sight of the first onyx quarry, and greeted the men who there laboured with picks and chisels. Before evening he had passed eleven quarries; the land being here given over altogether to onyx cliffs and boulders, with no vegetation at all, but only great rocky fragments scattered about a floor of black earth, with the grey impassable peaks always rising gaunt and sinister on his right. The third night he spent in a camp of quarry men whose flickering fires cast weird reflections on the polished cliffs to the west. And they sang many songs and told many tales, shewing such strange knowledge of the olden days and the habits of gods that Carter could see they held many latent memories of their sires the Great Ones. They asked him whither he went, and cautioned him not to go too far to the north; but he replied that he was seeking new cliffs of onyx, and would take no more risks than were common among prospectors. In the morning he bade them adieu and rode on into the darkening north, where they had warned him he would find the feared and unvisited quarry whence hands older than men's hands had wrenched prodigious blocks. But he did not like it when, turning back to wave a last farewell, he thought he saw approaching the camp that squat and evasive old merchant with slanting eyes, whose conjectured traffick with Leng was the gossip of distant Dylath-Leen.

After two more quarries the inhabited part of Inquanok seemed to end, and the road narrowed to a steeply rising yak-path among forbidding black cliffs. Always on the right towered the gaunt and distant peaks, and as Carter climbed farther and farther into this untraversed realm he found it grew darker and colder. Soon he preceived that there were no prints of feet or hooves on the black path beneath, and realised that he was indeed come into strange and deserted ways of elder time. Once in a while a raven would croak far overhead, and now and then a flapping behind some vast rock would make him think uncomfortably of the rumoured Shantak-bird. But in the main he was alone with his shaggy steed, and it troubled him to observe that this excellent yak became more and more reluctant to advance, and more and more disposed to snort affrightedly at any small noise along the route.

The path now contracted between sable and glistening walls, and began to display an even greater steepness than before. It was a bad footing, and the yak often slipped on the stony fragments strewn thickly about. In two hours Carter saw ahead a definite crest, beyond which was nothing but dull grey sky, and blessed the prospect of a level or downward course. To reach this crest, however, was no easy task; for the way had grown nearly perpendicular, and was perilous with loose black gravel and small stones. Eventually Carter dismounted and led his dubious yak; pulling very hard when the animal balked or stumbled, and keeping his own footing as best he might. Then suddenly he came to the top and saw beyond, and gasped at what he saw.

The path indeed led straight ahead and slightly down, with the same lines of high natural walls as before; but on the left hand there opened out a monstrous space, vast acres in extent, where some archaic power had riven and rent the native cliffs of onyx in the form of a giant's quarry. Far back into the solid precipice ran that cyclopean gouge, and deep down within earth's bowels its lower delvings yawned. It was no quarry of man, and the concave sides were scarred with great squares, yards wide, which told of the size of the blocks once hewn by nameless hands and chisels. High over its jagged rim huge ravens flapped and croaked, and vague whirrings in the unseen depths told of bats or urhags or less mentionable presences haunting the endless blackness. There Carter stood in the narrow way amidst the twilight with the rocky path sloping down before him; tall onyx cliffs on his right that led on as far as he could see and tall cliffs on the left chopped off just ahead to make that terrible and unearthly quarry.

All at once the yak uttered a cry and burst from his control, leaping past him and darting on in a panic till it vanished down the narrow slope toward the north. Stones kicked by its flying hooves fell over the brink of the quarry and lost themselves in the dark without any sound of striking bottom; but Carter ignored the perils of that scanty path as he raced breathlessly after the flying steed. Soon the left-hand cliffs resumed their course, making the way once more a narrow lane; and still the traveller leaped on after the yak whose great wide prints told of its desperate flight.

Once he thought he heard the hoofbeats of the frightened beast, and doubled his speed from this encouragement. He was covering miles, and little by little the way was broadening in front till he knew he must soon emerge on the cold and dreaded desert to the north. The gaunt grey flanks of the distant impassable peaks were again visible above the right hand crags, and ahead were the rocks and boulders of an open space which was clearly a foretaste of the dark and limitless plain. And once more those hoofbeats sounded in his ears, plainer than before, but this time giving terror instead of encouragement because he realised that they were not the frightened hoofbeats of his fleeing yak. The beats were ruthless and purposeful, and they were behind him.

Carter's pursuit of the yak became now a flight from an unseen thing, for though he dared not glance over his shoulder he felt that the presence behind him could be nothing wholesome or mentionable. His yak must have heard or felt it first, and he did not like to ask himself whether it had followed him from the haunts of men or had floundered up out of that black quarry pit. Meanwhile the cliffs had been left behind, so that the oncoming night fell over a great waste of sand and spectral rocks wherein all paths were lost. He could not see the hoofprints of his yak, but always from behind him there came that detestable clopping; mingled now and then with what he fancied were titanic flappings and whirrings. That he was losing ground seemed unhappily clear to him, and he knew he was hopelessly lost in this broken and blasted desert of meaningless rocks and untravelled sands. Only those remote and impassable peaks on the right gave him any sense of direction, and even they were less clear as the grey twilight wand and the sickly phosphorescence of the clouds took its place.

Then dim and misty in the darkling north before him he glimpsed a terrible thing. He had thought it for some moments a range of black mountains, but now he saw it was something more. The phosphorescence of the brooding clouds shewed it plainly, and even silhouetted parts of it as vapours glowed behind. How distant it was he could not tell, but it must have been very far. It was thousands of feet high, stretching in a great concave arc from the grey impassable peaks to the unimagined westward spaces, and had once indeed been a ridge of mighty onyx hills. But now these hills were hills no more, for some hand greater than man's had touched them. Silent they squatted there atop the world like wolves or ghouls, crowned with clouds and mists and guarding the secrets of the north for ever. All in a great half circle they squatted, those dog-like mountains carven into monstrous watching statues, and their right hands were raised in menace against mankind.

It was only the flickering light of the clouds that made their pitred double heads seem to move, but as Carter stumbled on he saw arise from their shadowy caps great forms whose motions were no delusion. Winged and whirring, those forms grew larger each moment, and the traveller knew his stumbling was at an end. They were not any birds or bats known elsewhere on earth or in dreamland, for they were larger than elephants and had heads like a horse's. Carter knew that they must be the Shantak-birds of ill rumour, and wondered no more what evil guardians and nameless sentinels made men avoid the boreal rock desert. And as he stopped in final resignation he dared at last to look behind him, where indeed was trotting the squat slant-eyed trader of evil legend, grinning astride a lean yak and leading on a noxious horde of leering Shantaks to whose wings still clung the rime and nitre of the nether pits.

Trapped though he was by fabulous and hippo-cephalic winged nightmares that pressed around in great unholy circles. Randolph Carter did not lose consciousness. Lofty and horrible those titan gargoyles towered above him, while the slant-eyed merchant leaped down from his yak and stood grinning before the captive. Then the man motioned Carter to mount one of the repugnant Shantaks, helping him up as his judgment struggled with his loathing. It was hard work ascending, for the Shantak-bird has scales instead of feathers, and those scales are very slippery. Once he was seated, the slant-eyed man hopped up behind him, leaving the lean yak to be led away northward toward the ring of carven mountains by one of the incredible bird colossi.

There now followed a hideous whirl through frigid space, endlessly up and eastward toward the gaunt grey flanks of those impassable mountains beyond which Leng was said to be. Far above the clouds they flew, till at last there lay beneath them those fabled summits which the folk of Inquanok have never seen, and which lie always in high vortices of gleaming mist. Carter beheld them very plainly as they passed below, and saw upon their topmost peaks strange caves which made him think of those on Ngranek; but he did not question his captor about these things when he noticed that both the man and the horse-headed Shantak appeared oddly fearful of them, hurrying past nervously and shewing great tension until they were left far in the rear.

The Shantak now flew lower, revealing beneath the canopy of cloud a grey barren plain whereon at great distances shone little feeble fires. As they descended there appeared at intervals lone huts of granite and bleak stone villages whose tiny windows glowed with pallid light. And there came from those huts and villages a shrill droning of pipes and a nauseous rattle of crotala which proved at once that Inquanok's people are right in their geographic rumours. For travellers have heard such sounds before, and know that they float only from that cold desert plateau which healthy folk never visit; that haunted place of evil and mystery which is Leng.

Around the feeble fires dark forms were dancing, and Carter was curious as to what manner of beings they might be; for no healthy folk have ever been to Leng, and the place is known only by its fires and stone huts as seen from afar. Very slowly and awkwardly did those forms leap, and with an insane twisting and bending not good to behold; so that Carter did not wonder at the monstrous evil imputed to them by vague legend, or the fear in which all dreamland holds their abhorrent frozen plateau. As the Shantak flew lower, the repulsivness of the dancers became tinged with a certain hellish familiarity; and the prisoner kept straining his eyes and racking his memory for clues to where he had seen such creatures before.

They leaped as though they had hooves instead of feet, and seemed to wear a sort of wig or headpiece with small horns. Of other clothing they had none, but most of them were quite furry. Behind they had dwarfish tails, and when they glanced upward he saw the excessive width of their mouths. Then he knew what they were, and that they did not wear any wigs or headpieces after all. For the cryptic folk of Leng were of one race with the uncomfortable merchants of the black galleys that traded rubies at Dylath-Leen; those not quite human merchants who are the slaves of the monstrous moon-things! They were indeed the same dark folk who had shanghaied Carter on their noisome galley so long ago, and whose kith he had seen driven in herds about the unclean wharves of that accursed lunar city, with the leaner ones toiling and the fatter ones taken away in crates for other needs of their polypous and amorphous masters. Now he saw where such ambiguous creatures came from, and shuddered at the thought that Leng must be known to these formless abominations from the moon.

But the Shantak flew on past the fires and the stone huts and the less than human dancers, and soared over sterile hills of grey granite and dim wastes of rock and ice and snow. Day came, and the phosphorescence of low clouds gave place to the misty twilight of that northern world, and still the vile bird winged meaningly through the cold and silence. At times the slant-eyed man talked with his steed in a hateful and guttural language, and the Shantak would answer with tittering tones that rasped like the scratching of ground glass. All this while the land was getting higher, and finally they came to a wind-swept table-land which seemed the very roof of a blasted and tenantless world. There, all alone in the hush and the dusk and the cold, rose the uncouth stones of a squat windowless building, around which a circle of crude monoliths stood. In all this arrangement there was nothing human, and Carter surmised from old tales that he was indeed come to that most dreadful and legendary of all places, the remote and prehistoric monastery wherein dwells uncompanioned the High-Priest not to be described, which wears a yellow silken mask over its face and prays to the Other Gods and their crawling chaos Nyarlathotep.

The loathsome bird now settled to the ground, and the slant-eyed man hopped down and helped his captive alight. Of the purpose of his seizure Carter now felt very sure; for clearly the slant-eyed merchant was an agent of the darker powers, eager to drag before his masters a mortal whose presumption had aimed at the finding of unknown Kadath and the saying of a prayer before the faces of the Great Ones in their onyx castle. It seemed likely that this merchant had caused his former capture by the slaves of the moon-things in Dylath-Leen, and that he now meant to do what the rescuing cats had baffled; taking the victim to some dread rendezvous with monstrous Nyarlathotep and telling with what boldness the seeking of unknown Kadath had been tried. Leng and the cold waste north of Inquanok must be close to the Other Gods, and there the passes to Kadath are well guarded.

The slant-eyed man was small, but the great hippocephalic bird was there to see he was obeyed; so Carter followed where he led, and passed within the circle of standing rocks and into the low arched doorway of that windowless stone monastery. There were no lights inside, but the evil merchant lit a small clay lamp bearing morbid bas-reliefs and prodded his prisoner on through mazes of narrow winding corridors. On the walls of the corridors were printed frightful scenes older than history, and in a style unknown to the archaeologists of earth. After countless aeons their pigments were brilliant still, for the cold and dryness of hideous Leng keep alive many primal things. Carter saw them fleetingly in the rays of that dim and moving lamp, and shuddered at the tale they told.

Through those archaic frescoes Leng's annals stalked; and the horned, hooved, and wide-mouthed almost-humans danced evilly amidst forgotten cities. There were scenes of old wars, wherein Leng's almost-humans fought with the bloated purple spiders of the neighbouring vales; and there were scenes also of the coming of the black galleys from the moon, and of the submission of Leng's people to the polypous and amorphous blasphemies that hopped and floundered and wriggled out of them. Those slippery greyish-white blasphemies they worshipped as gods, nor ever complained when scores of their best and fatted males were taken away in the black galleys. The monstrous moon-beasts made their camp on a jagged isle in the sea, and Carter could tell from the frescoes that this was none other than the lone nameless rock he had seen when sailing to Inquanok; that grey accursed rock which Inquanok's seamen shun, and from which vile howlings reverberate all through the night.

And in those frescoes was shewn the great seaport and capital of the almost-humans; proud and pillared betwixt the cliffs and the basalt wharves, and wondrous with high fanes and carven places. Great gardens and columned streets led from the cliffs and from each of the six sphinx-crowned gates to a vast central plaza, and in that plaza was a pair of winged colossal lions guarding the top of a subterrene staircase. Again and again were those huge winged lions shewn, their mighty flanks of diarite glistening in the grey twilight of the day and the cloudy phosphorescence of the night. And as Carter stumbled past their frequent and repeated pictures it came to him at last what indeed they were, and what city it was that the almost-humans had ruled so anciently before the coming of the black galleys. There could be no mistake, for the legends of dreamland are generous and profuse. Indubitably that primal city was no less a place than storied Sarkomand, whose ruins had bleached for a million years before the first true human saw the light, and whose twin titan lions guard eternally the steps that lead down from dreamland to the Great Abyss.

Other views shewed the gaunt grey peaks dividing Leng from Inquanok, and the monstrous Shantak-birds that build nests on the ledges half way up. And they shewed likewise the curious caves near the very topmost pinnacles, and how even the boldest of the Shantaks fly screaming away from them. Carter had seen those caves when he passed over them, and had noticed their likeness to the caves on Ngranek. Now he knew that the likeness was more than a chance one, for in these pictures were shewn their fearsome denizens; and those bat-wings, curving horns, barbed tails, prehensile paws and rubbery bodies were not strange to him. He had met those silent, flitting and clutching creatures before;

those mindless guardians of the Great Abyss whom even the Great Ones fear, and who own not Nyarlatho-tep but hoary Nodens as their lord. For they were the dreaded night-gaunts, who never laugh or smile because they have no faces, and who flop unendingly in the dark betwixt the Vale of Pnath and the passes to the outer world.

The slant-eyed merchant had now prodded Carter into a great domed space whose walls were carved in shocking bas-reliefs, and whose centre held a gaping circular pit surrounded by six malignly stained stone altars in a ring. There was no light in this vast evil-smelling crypt, and the small lamp of the sinister mer-chant shone so feebly that one could grasp details only little by little. At the farther end was a high stone dais reached by five steps; and there on a golden throne sat a lumpish figure robed in yellow silk figured with red and having a yellow silken mask over its face. To this being the slant-eyed man made certain signs with his hands, and the lurker in the dark replied by raising a disgust-ingly carven flute of ivory in silk-covered paws and blowing certain loathsome sounds from beneath its flowing yellow mask. This colloquy went on for some time, and to Carter there was something sickeningly familiar in the sound of that flute and the stench of the malodorous place. It made him think of a frightful red-litten city and of the revolting procession that once filed through it; of that, and of an awful climb through lunar countryside beyond, before the rescuing rush of earth's friendly cats. He knew that the creature on the dais was without doubt the high-priest not to be de-scribed, of which legend whispers such fiendish and abnormal possibilities, but he feared to think just what that abhorred high-priest might be.

Then the figured silk slipped a trifle from one of the greyish-white paws, and Carter knew what the noisome high-priest was. And in that hideous second stark fear drove him to something his reason would never have dared to attempt, for in all his shaken consciousness there was room only for one frantic will to escape from what squatted on that golden throne. He knew that hopeless labyrinths of stone lay betwixt him and the cold table-land outside, and that even on that table-land the noxious Shantek still waited; yet in spite of all this there was in his mind only the instant need to get away from that wriggling, silk-robed monstrosity.

The slant-eyed man had set the curious lamp upon one of the high and wickedly stained altar-stones by the pit, and had moved forward somewhat to talk to the high-priest with his hands. Carter, hitherto wholly passive, now gave that man a terrific push with all the wild strength of fear, so that the victim toppled at once into that gaping well which rumour holds to reach down to the hellish Vaults of Zin where gugs hunt shasts in the dark. In almost the same second he seized the lamp from the altar and darted out into the frescoed labyrinths, racing this way and that as chance determined and trying not to think of the stealthy padding of shapeless paws on the stones behind him, or of the silent wrigglings and crawlings which must be going on back there in lightless corridors.

After a few moments he regretted his thoughtless haste, and wished he had tried to follow backward the frescoes he had passed on the way in. True, they were so confused and duplicated that they could not have done him much good, but he wished none the less he had made the attempt. Those he now saw were even more horrible than those he had seen then, and he knew he was not in the corridors leading outside. In time he became quite sure he was not followed, and slackened his pace somewhat; but scarce had he breathed in half relief when a new peril beset him. His lamp was waning, and he would soon be in pitch blackness with no means of sight or guidance.

When the light was all gone he groped slowly in the dark, and prayed to the Great Ones for such help as they might afford. At times he felt the stone floor sloping up or down, and once he stumbled over a step for which no reason seemed to exist. The farther he went the damper it seemed to be, and when he was able to feel a junction or the mouth of a side passage he always chose the way which sloped downward the least. He believed, though, that his general course was down; and the vault-like smell and incrustations on the greasy walls and floor alike warned him he was burrowing deep in Leng's unwholesome table-land. But there was not any warning of the thing which came at last; only the thing itself with its terror and shock and breath-taking chaos. One moment he was groping slowly over the slippery floor of an almost level place, and the next he was shooting dizzily downward in the dark through a burrow which must have been well-nigh vertical.

Of the length of that hideous sliding he could never be sure, but it seemed to take hours of delirious nausea and ecstatic frenzy. Then he realized he was still, with the phosphorescent clouds of a northern night shining sickly above him. All around were crumbling walls and broken columns, and the pavement on which he lay was pierced by straggling grass and wrenched asunder by frequent shrubs and roots. Behind him a basalt cliff rose topless and perpendicular; its dark side sculptured into repellent scenes, and pierced by an arched and carven entrance to the inner blacknesses out of which he had come. Ahead stretched double rows of pillars, and the fragments and pedestals of pillars, that spoke of a broad and bygone street; and from the urns and basins along the way he knew it had been a great street of gardens. Far off at its end the pillars spread to mark a vast round plaza, and in that open circle there loomed gigantic under the lurid night clouds a pair of monstrous things. Huge winged lions of diarite they were, with blackness and shadow between them. Full twenty feet they reared their grotesque and unbroken heads, and snarled derisive on the ruins around them. And Carter knew right well what they must be, for legend tells of only one such twain. They were the changeless guardians of the Great Abyss, and these dark ruins were in truth primordial Sarkomand.

Carter's first act was to close and barricade the archway in the cliff with fallen blocks and odd debris that lay around. He wished no follower from Leng's hateful monastery, for along the way ahead would lurk enough of other dangers. Of how to get from Sarkomand to the peopled parts of dreamland he knew nothing at all; nor could he gain much by descending to the grottoes of the ghouls, since he knew they were no better informed than he. The three ghouls which had helped him through the city of Gugs to the outer world had not known how to reach Sarkomand in their journey back, but had planned to ask old traders in Dylath-Leen. He did not like to think of going again to the subterrene world of Gugs and risking once more that hellish tower of Koth with its Cyclopean steps leading to the enchanted wood, yet he felt he might have to try this course if all else failed. Over Leng's plateau past the lone monastery he dared not go unaided; for the high-priest's emissaries must be many, while at the journey's end there would no doubt be the Shantaks and perhaps other things to deal with. If he could get a boat he might sail back to Inquanok past the jagged and hideous rock in the sea, for the primal frescoes in the monastery labyrinth had shewn that this frightful place lies not far from Sarkomand's basalt quays. But to find a boat in this aeon-deserted city was no probable thing, and it did not appear likely that he could ever make one.

Such were the thoughts of Randolph Carter when a new impression began beating upon his mind. All this while there had stretched before him the great corpse-like width of fabled Sarkomand with its black broken pillars and crumbling sphinx-crowned gates and titan stones and monstrous winged lions against the sickly glow of those luminous night clouds. Now he saw far ahead and on the right a glow that no clouds could account for, and knew he was not alone in the silence of that dead city. The glow rose and fell fitfully, flickering with a greenish tinge which did not reassure the watcher. And when he crept closer, down the littered street and through some narrow gaps between tumbled walls, he perceived that it was a campfire near the wharves with many vague forms clustered darkly around it; and a lethal odour hanging heavily over all. Beyond was the oily lapping of the harbour water with a great ship riding at anchor, and Carter paused in stark terror when he saw that the ship was indeed one of the dreaded black galleys from the moon.

Then, just as he was about to creep back from that detestable flame, he saw a stirring among the vague dark forms and heard a peculiar and unmistakable sound. It was the frightened meeping of a ghoul, and in a moment it had swelled to a vertible chorus of anguish. Secure as he was in the shadow of monstrous ruins, Carter allowed his curiosity to conquer his fear, and crept forward again instead of retreating. Once in crossing an open street he wriggled worm-like on his stomach, and in another place he had to rise to his feet to avoid making a noise among heaps of fallen marble. But always he succeeded in avoiding discovery, so that in a short time he had found a spot behind a titan pillar where he could watch the whole green-litten scene of action. There around a hideous fire fed by the obnoxious stems of lunar fungi, there squatted a stinking circle of the toadlike moonbeasts and their almost human slaves. Some of these slaves were heating curious iron spears in the leaping flames, and at intervals applying their white-hot points to three tightly trussed prisoners that lay writhing before the leaders of the party. From the motions of their tenacles Carter could see that the blunt-snouted moonbeasts were enjoying the spectacle hugely, and vast was his horror when he suddenly recognised the frantic meeping and knew that the tortured ghouls were none other than the faithful trio which had guided him safely from the abyss, and had thereafter set out from the enchanted wood to find Sarkomand and the gate to their native deeps.

The number of malodorous moonbeasts about that greenish fire was very great, and Carter saw that he could do nothing now to save his former allies. Of how the ghouls had been captured he could not guess; but fancied that the grey toadlike blasphemies had heard them inquire in Dylath-Leen concerning the way to Sarkomand and had not wished them to approach so closely the hateful plateau of Leng and the high-priest not to be described. For a moment he pondered on what he ought to do, and recalled how near he was to the gate of the ghouls' black kingdom. Clearly it was wisest to creep east to the plaza of twin lions and descend at once to the gulf, where assuredly he would meet no horrors worse than those above, and where he might soon find ghouls eager to rescue their brethren and perhaps to wipe out the moonbeasts from the black galley. It occurred to him that the portal, like other gates to the abyss, might be guarded by flocks of night-gaunts; but he did not fear these faceless creatures now. He had learned that they are bound by solemn treaties with the ghouls, and the ghoul which was Pickman had taught him how to glibber a password they understood.

So Carter began another silent crawl through the ruins, edging slowly toward the great central plaza and the winged lions. It was ticklish work, but the moon-beasts were pleasantly busy and did not hear the slight noises which he twice made by accident among the scattered stones. At last he reached the open space and picked his way among the stunted trees and vines that had grown up therein. The gigantic lions loomed terrible above him in the sickly glow of the phosphorescent night clouds, but he manfully persisted toward them and presently crept round to their faces, knowing it was on that side he would find the mighty darkness which they guard. Ten feet apart crouched the mocking-faced beasts of diarite, brooding on Cyclopean pedestals whose sides were chiselled in fearsome bas-reliefs. Betwixt them was a tiled court with a central space which had once been railed with balusters of onyx. Midway in this space a black well opened, and Carter soon saw that he had indeed reached the yawning gulf whose crusted and mouldy stone steps lead down to the crypts of nightmare.

Terrible is the memory of that dark descent in which hours wore themselves away whilst Carter wound sightlessly round and round down a fathomless spiral of steep and slippery stairs. So worn and narrow were the steps, and so greasy with the ooze of inner earth, that the climber never quite knew when to expect a breathless fall and hurtling down to the ultimate pits; and he was likewise uncertain just when or how the guardian night-gaunts would suddenly pounce upon him, if indeed there were any stationed in this primeval passage. All about him was a stifling odour of nether gulfs, and he felt that the air of these choking depths was not made for mankind. In time he became very numb and somnolent, moving more from automatic impulse than from reasoned will; nor did he realize any change when he stopped moving altogether as something quietly seized him from behind. He was flying very rapidly through the air before a malevolent tickling told him that the rubbery night-gaunts had performed their duty.

Awaked to the fact that he was in the cold, damp clutch of the faceless flutterers, Carter remembered the password of the ghouls and glibbered it as loudly as he could amidst the wind and chaos of flight. Mindless though night-gaunts are said to be, the effect was instantaneous; for all tickling stopped at once, and the creatures hastened to shift their captive to a more comfortable position. Thus encouraged Carter ventured some explanations; telling of the seizure and torture of three ghouls by the moonbeasts, and of the need of assembling a party to rescue them. The night-gaunts, though inarticulate, seemed to understand what was said; and shewed greater haste and purpose in their flight. Suddenly the dense blackness gave place to the grey twilight of inner earth, and there opened up ahead one of those flat sterile plains on which ghouls love to squat and gnaw. Scattered tombstones and osseous fragments told of the denizens of that place; and as Carter gave a loud meep of urgent summons, a score of burrows emptied forth their leathery, dog-like tenants. The night-gaunts now flew low and set their passenger upon his feet, afterward withdrawing a little and forming a hunched semicircle on the ground while the ghouls greeted the newcomer.

Carter glibbered his message rapidly and explicitly to the grotesque company, and four of them at once departed through different burrows to spread the news to others and gather such troops as might be available for a rescue. After a long wait a ghoul of some importance appeared, and made significant signs to the night-gaunts, causing two of the latter to fly off into the dark. Thereafter there were constant accessions to the hunched flock of night-gaunts on the plain, till at length the slimy soil was fairly black with them. Meanwhile fresh ghouls crawled out of the burrows one by one, all glibbering excitedly and forming in crude battle array not far from the huddled night-gaunts. In time there appeared that proud and influential ghoul which was once the artist Richard Pickman of Boston, and to

him Carter glibbered a very full account of what had
occurred. The erstwhile Pickman, pleased to greet his
ancient friend again, seemed very much impressed, and
held a conference with other chiefs a little apart from
the growing throng.

Finally, after scanning the ranks with care, the assembled chiefs all meeped in unison and began glibbering orders to the crowds of ghouls and night-gaunts. A
large detachment of the horned flyers vanished at once,
while the rest grouped themselves two by two on their
knees with extended forelegs, awaiting the approach of
the ghouls one by one. As each ghoul reached the pair
of night-gaunts to which he was assigned, he was taken
up and borne away into the blackness; till at last the
whole throng had vanished save for Carter, Pickman,
and the other chiefs, and a few pairs of night-gaunts.
Pickman explained that night-gaunts are the advance
guard and battle steeds of the ghouls, and that the army
was issuing forth to Sarkomand to deal with the moonbeasts. Then Carter and the ghoulish chiefs approached
the waiting bearers and were taken up by the damp,
slippery paws. Another moment and all were whirling
in wind and darkness; endlessly up, up, up to the gate
of the winged lions and the spectral ruins of primal
Sarkomand.

When, after a great interval, Carter saw again the
sickly light of Sarkomand's nocturnal sky, it was to
behold the great central plaza swarming with militant
ghouls and night-gaunts. Day, he felt sure, must be
almost due; but so strong was the army that no surprise
of the enemy would be needed. The greenish flare near
the wharves still glimmered faintly, though the absence
of ghoulish meeping shewed that the torture of the

prisoners was over for the nonce. Softly glibbering directions to their steeds and to the flock of riderless night-gaunts ahead, the ghouls presently rose in wide whirring columns and swept on over the bleak ruins toward the evil flame. Carter was now beside Pickman in the front rank of ghouls, and saw as they approached the noisome camp that the moonbeasts were totally unprepared. The three prisoners lay bound and inert beside the fire, while their toadlike captors slumped drowsily about in no certain order. The almost-human slaves were asleep, even the sentinels shirking a duty which in this realm must have seemed to them merely perfunctory.

The final swoop of the night-gaunts and mounted ghouls was very sudden, each of the greyish toadlike blasphemies and their almost-human slaves being seized by a group of night-gaunts before a sound was made. The moonbeasts, of course, were voiceless; and even the slaves had little chance to scream before rubbery paws choked them into silence. Horrible were the writhings of those great jellyish abnormalities as the sardonic night-gaunts clutched them, but nothing availed against the strength of those black prehensile talons. When a moonbeast writhed too violently, a night-gaunt would seize and pull its quivering pink tentacles; which seemed to hurt so much that the victim would cease its struggles. Carter expected to see much slaughter, but found that the ghouls were far subtler in their plans. They glibbered certain simple orders to the night-gaunts which held the captives trusting the rest to instinct; and soon the hapless creatures were born silently away into the Great Abyss, to be distributed impartially amongst the Dholes, Gugs, ghasts and other dwellers in darkness whose modes of nourishment are not painless to their chosen victims. Meanwhile the three bound ghouls had been released and consoled by their conquering kins-folk, whilst various parties searched the neighborhood for possible remaining moonbeasts, and boarded the evil-smelling black galley at the wharf to make sure that nothing had escaped the general defeat. Surely enough, the capture had been thorough, for not a sign of further life could the victors detect. Carter, anxious to preserve a means of access to the rest of dreamland, urged them not to sink the anchored galley; and this request was freely granted out of gratitude for his act in reporting the plight of the captured trio. On the ship were found some very curious objects and decorations, some of which Carter cast at once into the sea.

Ghouls and night-gaunts now formed themselves in separate groups, the former questioning their rescued fellows anent past happenings. It appeared that the three had followed Carter's directions and proceeded from the enchanted wood to Dylath-Leen by way of Nir and the Skai, stealing human clothes at a lonely farmhouse and loping as closely as possible in the fash-ion of a man's walk. In Dylath-Leen's taverns their grotesque ways and faces had aroused much comment; but they had persisted in asking the way to Sarkomand until at last an old traveller was able to tell them. Then they knew that only a ship for Lelag-Leng would serve their purpose, and prepared to wait patiently for such a vessel.

But evil spies had doubtless reported much; for short-ly a black galley put into port, and the wide-mouthed ruby merchants invited the ghouls to drink with them in a tavern. Wine was produced from one of those sinister bottles grotesquely carven from a single ruby, and after that the ghouls found themselves prisoners on the black galley as Carter had found himself. This time, however, the unseen rowers steered not for the moon but for antique Sarkomand; bent evidently on taking their captives before the high-priest not to be described. They had touched at the jagged rock in the northern sea which Inquanok's mariners shun, and the ghouls had there seen for the first time the red masters of the ship; being sickened despite their own callousness by such extremes of malign shapelessness and fearsome odour. There, too, were witnessed the nameless pastimes of the toadlike resident garrison—such pastimes as give rise to the night-howlings which men fear. After that had come the landing at ruined Sarkomand and the beginning of the tortures, whose continuance the present rescue had prevented.

Future plans were next discussed, the three rescued ghouls suggesting a raid on the jagged rock and the extermination of the toadlike garrison there. To this, however, the night-gaunts objected; since the prospect of flying over water did not please them. Most of the ghouls favoured the design, but were at a loss how to follow it without the help of the winged night-gaunts. Thereupon Carter, seeing that they could not navigate the anchored galley, offered to teach them the use of the great banks of oars; to which proposal they eagerly assented. Grey day had now come, and under that leaden northern sky a picked detachment of ghouls filed into the noisome ship and took their seats on the rowers' benches. Carter found them fairly apt at learning, and before night had risked several experimental trips around the harbour. Not till three days later, however, did he deem it safe to attempt the voyage of conquest. Then, the rowers trained and the night-gaunts safely stowed in the forecastle, the party set sail at last; Pickman and the other chiefs gathering on deck and discussing modes of approach and procedure.

On the very first night the howlings from the rock were heard. Such was their timbre that all the galley's crew shook visibly; but most of all trembled the three rescued ghouls who knew precisely what those howlings meant. It was not thought best to attempt an attack by night, so the ship lay to under the phosphorescent clouds to wait for the dawn of a greyish day. When the light was ample and the howlings still the rowers resumed their strokes, and the galley drew closer and closer to that jagged rock whose granite pinnacles clawed fantastically at the dull sky. The sides of the rock were very steep; but on ledges here and there could be seen the bulging walls of queer windowless dwellings, and the low railings guarding travelled highroads. No ship of men had ever come so near the place, or at least, had never come so near and departed again; but Carter and the ghouls were void of fear and kept inflexibly on, rounding the eastern face of the rock and seeking the wharves which the rescued trio described as being on the southern side within a harbour formed of steep headlands.

The headlands were prolongations of the island proper, and came so closely together that only one ship at a time might pass between them. There seemed to be no watchers on the outside, so the galley was steered boldly through the flume-like strait and into the stagnant putrid harbour beyond. Here, however, all was bustle and activity; with several ships lying at anchor along a forbidding stone quay, and scores of almost-human slaves and moonbeasts by the waterfront handling crates and boxes or driving nameless and fabulous horrors hitched to lumbering lorries. There was a small stone town hewn out of the vertical cliff above the wharves, with the start of a winding road that spiralled out of sight toward higher ledges of the rock. Of what lay inside that prodigious peak of granite none might say, but the things one saw on the outside were far from encouraging.

At sight of the incoming galley the crowds on the wharves displayed much eagerness; those with eyes staring intently, and those without eyes wriggling their pink tentacles expectantly. They did not, of course, realize that the black ship had changed hands; for ghouls look much like the horned and hooved almost-humans, and the night-gaunts were all out of sight below. By this time the leaders had fully formed a plan; which was to loose the night-gaunts as soon as the wharf was touched, and then to sail directly away, leaving matters wholly to the instincts of those almost-mindless creatures. Marooned on the rock, the horned flyers would first of all seize whatever living things they found there, and afterward, quite helpless to think except in terms of the homing instinct, would forget their fears of water and fly swiftly back to the abyss; bearing their noisome prey to appropriate destinations in the dark, from which not much would emerge alive.

The ghoul that was Pickman now went below and gave the night-gaunts their simple instructions, while the ship drew very near to the ominous and malodorous wharves. Presently a fresh stir rose along the waterfront, and Carter saw that the motions of the galley had begun to excite suspicion. Evidently the steersman was not making for the right dock, and probably the watchers had noticed the difference between the hideous ghouls and the almost-human slaves whose places they were taking. Some silent alarm must have been given, for almost at once a horde of the mephitic moonbeasts began to pour from the little black doorways of the windowless houses and down the winding road at the right. A rain of curious javelins struck the galley as the prow hit the wharf, felling two ghouls and slightly wounding another; but at this point all the hatches were thrown open to emit a black cloud of whirring night-gaunts which swarmed over the town like a flock of horned and Cyclopean bats.

The jellyish moonbeasts had procured a great pole and were trying to push off the invading ship, but when the night-gaunts struck them they thought of such things no more. It was a very terrible spectacle to see those faceless and rubbery ticklers at their pastime, and tremendously impressive to watch the dense cloud of them spreading through the town and up the winding roadway to the reaches above. Sometimes a group of the black flutterers would drop a toadlike prisoner from aloft by mistake, and the manner in which the victim would burst was highly offensive to the sight and smell. When the last of the night-gaunts had left the galley the ghoulish leaders glibbered an order of withdrawal, and the rowers pulled quietly out of the harbour between the grey headlands while still the town was a chaos of battle and conquest.

The Pickman ghoul allowed several hours for the night-gaunts to make up their rudimentary minds and overcome their fear of flying over the sea, and kept the galley standing about a mile off the jagged rock while he waited, and dressed the wounds of the injured men. Night fell, and the grey twilight gave place to the sickly phosphorescence of low clouds, and all the while the leaders watched the high peaks of that accursed rock for signs of the night-gaunts' flight. Toward morning a black speck was seen hovering timidly over the topmost pinnacle, and shortly afterward the speck had become a swarm. Just before daybreak the swarm seemed to scatter, and within a quarter of an hour it had vanished wholly in the distance toward the northeast. Once or twice something seemed to fall from the thinning swarm into the sea; but Carter did not worry, since he knew from observation that the toadlike moonbeasts cannot swim. At length, when the ghouls were satisfied that all the night-gaunts had left for Sarkomand and the Great Abyss with their doomed burdens, the galley put back into the harbour betwixt the grey headlands; and all the hideous company landed and roamed curiously over the denuded rock with its towers and eyries and fortresses chiselled from the solid stone.

Frightful were the secrets uncovered in those evil and windowless crypts; for the remnants of unfinished pastimes were many, and in various stages of departure from their primal state. Carter put out of the way certain things which were after a fashion alive, and fled precipitately from a few other things about which he could not be very positive. The stench-filled houses were furnished mostly with grotesque stools and benches carven from moon-trees, and were painted inside with nameless and frantic designs. Countless weapons, implements, and ornaments lay about, including some large idols of solid ruby depicting singular beings not found on the earth. These latter did not, despite their material, invite either appropriation or long inspection; and Carter took the trouble to hammer five of them into very small pieces. The scattered spears and javelins he collected, and with Pickman's approval distributed among the ghouls. Such devices were new to the doglike lopers, but their relative simplicity made them easy to master after a few concise hints.

The upper parts of the rock held more temples than private homes, and in numerous hewn chambers were found terrible carven altars and doubtfully stained fonts and shrines for the worship of things more monstrous than the wild gods atop Kadath. From the rear of one great temple stretched a low black passage which Carter followed far into the rock with a torch till he came to a lightless domed hall of vast proportions, whose vaultings were covered with demoniac carvings and in whose centre yawned a foul and bottomless well like that in the hideous monastery of Leng where broods alone the high-priest not to be described. On the distant shadowy side, beyond the noisome well, he thought he discerned a small door of strangely wrought bronze; but for some reason he felt an unaccountable dread of opening it or even approaching it, and hastened back through the cavern to his unlovely allies as they shambled about with an ease and abandon he could scarcely feel. The ghouls had observed the unfinished pastimes of the moonbeasts, and had profited in their fashion. They had also found a hogshead of potent moon-wine, and were rolling it down to the wharves for removal and later use in diplomatic dealings, though the rescued trio, remembering its effect on them in Dylath-Leen, had warned their company to taste none of it. Of rubies from lunar mines there was a great store, both rough and polished, in one of the vaults near the water; but when the ghouls found they were not good to eat they lost all interest in them. Carter did not try to carry any away, since he knew too much about those which had mined them.

Suddenly there came an excited meeping from the sentries on the wharves, and all the loathsome foragers turned from their tasks to stare seaward and cluster round the waterfront. Betwixt the grey headlands a fresh black galley was rapidly advancing, and it would be but a moment before the almost-humans on deck would perceive the invasion of the town and give the alarm to the monstrous things below. Fortunately the ghouls still bore the spears and javelins which Carter had distributed amongst them; and at his command, sustained by the being that was Pickman, they now formed a line of battle and prepared to prevent the landing of the ship. Presently a burst of excitement on the galley told of the crew's discovery of the changed state of things, and the instant stoppage of the vessel proved that the superior numbers of the ghouls had been noted and taken into account. After a moment of hesitation the newcomers silently turned and passed out between the headlands again, but not for an instant did the ghouls imagine that the conflict was averted. Either the dark ship would seek reinforcements or the crew would try to land elsewhere on the island; hence a party of scouts was at once sent up toward the pinnacle to see what the enemy's course would be.

In a very few minutes the ghoul returned breathless to say that the moonbeasts and almost-humans were landing on the outside of the more easterly of the rugged grey headlands, and ascending by hidden paths and ledges which a goat could scarcely tread in safety. Almost immediately afterward the galley was sighted again through the flume-like strait, but only for a second. Then a few moments later, a second messenger panted down from aloft to say that another party was landing on the other headland; both being much more numerous than the size of the galley would seem to allow for. The ship itself, moving slowly with only one sparsely manned tier of oars, soon hove in sight betwixt the cliffs, and lay to in the foetid harbour as if to watch the coming fray and stand by for any possible use.

By this time Carter and Pickman had divided the ghouls into three parties, one to meet each of the two invading columns and one to remain in the town. The first two at once scrambled up the rocks in their respective directions, while the third was subdivided into a land party and a sea party. The sea party, commanded by Carter, boarded the anchored galley and rowed out to meet the undermanned galley of the newcomers; whereat the latter retreated through the strait to the open sea. Carter did not at once pursue it, for he knew he might be needed more acutely near the town.

Meanwhile the frightful detachments of the moon-beasts and almost-humans had lumbered up to the top of the headlands and were shockingly silhouetted on either side against the grey twilight sky. The thin hellish flutes of the invaders had now begun to whine, and the general effect of those hybrid, half-amorphous processions was as nauseating as the actual odour given off by the toadlike lunar blasphemies. Then the two parties of the ghouls swarmed into sight and joined the silhouetted panorama. Javelins began to fly from both sides, and the swelling meeps of the ghouls and the bestial howls of the almost-humans gradually joined the hellish whine of the flutes to form a frantick and indescribable chaos of daemon cacophony. Now and then bodies fell from the narrow ridges of the headlands into the sea outside or the harbour inside, in the latter case being sucked quickly under by certain submarine lurkers whose presence was indicated only by prodigious bubbles.

For half an hour this dual battle raged in the sky, till upon the west cliff the invaders were completely annihilated. On the east cliff, however, where the leader of the moonbeast party appeared to be present, the ghouls had not fared so well; and were slowly retreating to the slopes of the pinnacle proper. Pickman had quickly ordered reinforcements for this front from the party in the town, and these had helped greatly in the earlier stages of the combat. Then, when the western battle was over, the victorious survivors hastened across to the aid of their hard-pressed fellows; turning the tide and forcing the invaders back again along the narrow ridge of the headland. The almost-humans were by this time all slain, but the last of the toadlike horrors fought desperately with the great spears clutched in their powerful and disgusting paws. The time for javelins was now nearly past, and the fight became a hand-to-hand contest of what few spearmen could meet upon that narrow ridge.

As fury and recklessness increased, the number falling into the sea became very great. Those striking the harbour met nameless extinction from the unseen bubblers, but of those striking the open sea some were able to swim to the foot of the cliffs and land on tidal rocks, while the hovering galley of the enemy rescued several moonbeasts. The cliffs were unscalable except where the monsters had debarked, so that none of the ghouls on the rocks could rejoin their battle-line. Some were killed by javelins from the hostile galley or from the moonbeasts above, but a few survived to be rescued. When the security of the land parties seemed assured, Carter's galley sallied forth between the headlands and drove the hostile ship far out to sea; pausing to rescue such ghouls as were on the rocks or still swimming in the ocean. Several moonbeasts washed on rocks or reefs were speedily put out of the way.

Finally, the moonbeast galley being safely in the distance and the invading land army concentrated in one place, Carter landed a considerable force on the eastern headland in the enemy's rear; after which the fight was short-lived indeed. Attacked from both sides, the noisome flounderers were rapidly cut to pieces or pushed into the sea, till by evening the ghoulish chiefs agreed that the island was again clear of them. The hostile galley, meanwhile, had disappeared; and it was decided that the evil jagged rock had better be evacuated before any overwhelming horde of lunar horrors might be assembled and brought against the victors.

So by night Pickman and Carter assembled all the ghouls and counted them with care, finding that over a fourth had been lost in the day's battles. The wounded were placed on bunks in the galley, for Pickman always discouraged the old ghoulish custom of killing and eating one's own wounded, and the able-bodied troops were assigned to the oars or to such other places as they might most usefully fill. Under the low phosphorescent clouds of night the galley sailed, and Carter was not sorry to be departing from the island of unwholesome secrets, whose lightless domed hall with its bottomless well and repellent bronze door lingered restlessly in his fancy. Dawn found the ship in sight of Sarkomand's ruined quays of basalt, where a few night-gaunt sentries still waited, squatting like black horned gargoyles on the broken columns and crumbling sphinxes of that fearful city which lived and died before the years of man.

The ghouls made camp amongst the fallen stones of Sarkomand, despatching a messenger for enough night-gaunts to serve them as steeds. Pickman and the other chiefs were effusive in their gratitude for the aid Carter had lent them. Carter now began to feel that his plans were indeed maturing well, and that he would be able to command the help of these fearsome allies not only in quitting this part of dreamland, but in pursuing his ultimate quest for the gods atop unknown Kadath, and the marvellous sunset city they so strangely withheld from his slumbers. Accordingly he spoke of these things to the ghoulish leaders; telling what he knew of the cold waste wherein Kadath stands and of the monstrous Shantaks and the mountains carven into double-headed images which guard it. He spoke of the fear of Shantaks for night-gaunts, and of how the vast hippocephalic birds fly screaming from the black burrows high up on the gaunt grey peaks that divide Inquanok from hateful Leng. He spoke, too, of the things he had learned concerning night-gaunts from the frescoes in the windowless monastery of the high-priest not to be described; how even the Great Ones fear them, and how their ruler is not the crawling chaos Nyarlathotep at all, but hoary and immemorial Nodens, Lord of the Great Abyss.

All these things Carter glibbered to the assembled ghouls, and presently outlined that request which he had in mind and which he did not think extravagant considering the services he had so lately rendered the rubbery doglike lopers. He wished very much, he said, for the services of enough night-gaunts to bear him safely through the air past the realm of Shantaks and carven mountains, and up into the cold waste beyond the returning tracks of any other mortal. He desired to fly to the onyx castle atop unknown Kadath in the cold waste to plead with the Great Ones for the sunset city they denied him, and felt sure that the night-gaunts could take him thither without trouble; high above the perils of the plain, and over the hideous double heads of those carven sentinel mountains that squat eternally in the grey dusk. For the horned and faceless creatures there could be no danger from aught of earth since the Great Ones themselves dread them. And even were unexpected things to come from the Other Gods, who are prone to oversee the affairs of earth's milder gods, the night-gaunts need not fear; for the outer hells are indifferent matters to such silent and slippery flyers as own not Nyarlathotep for their master, but bow only to potent and archaic Nodens.

A flock of ten or fifteen night-gaunts, Carter glibbered, would surely be enough to keep any combination of Shantaks at a distance, though perhaps it might be well to have some ghouls in the party to manage the creatures, their ways being better known to their ghoulish allies than to men. The party could land him at some convenient point within whatever walls that fabulous onyx citadel might have, waiting in the shadows for his return or his signal whilst he ventured inside the castle to give prayer to the gods of earth. If any ghouls chose to escort him into the throne-room of the Great Ones, he would be thankful, for their presence would add weight and importance to his plea. He would not, however, insist upon this but merely wished transportation to and from the castle atop unknown Kadath; the final journey being either to the marvellous sunset city itself, in case the gods proved favourable, or back to the earthward Gate of Deeper Slumber in the Enchanted Wood in case his prayers were fruitless.

Whilst Carter was speaking all the ghouls listened with great attention, and as the moments advanced the sky became black with clouds of those night-gaunts for which messengers had been sent. The winged horrors settled in a semicircle around the ghoulish army, waiting respectfully as the doglike chieftains considered the wish of the earthly traveller. The ghoul that was Pickman glibbered gravely with his fellows and in the end Carter was offered far more than he had at most expected. As he had aided the ghouls in their conquest of the moonbeasts, so would they aid him in his daring voyage to realms whence none had ever returned; lending him not merely a few of their allied night-gaunts, but their entire army as then encamped, veteran fighting ghouls and newly assembled night-gaunts alike, save only a small garrison for the captured black galley and such spoils as had come from the jagged rock in the sea. They would set out through the air whenever he might wish, and once arrived on Kadath a suitable train of ghouls would attend him in state as he placed his petition before earth's gods in their onyx castle.

Moved by a gratitude and satisfaction beyond words, Carter made plans with the ghoulish leaders for his audacious voyage. The army would fly high, they decided, over hideous Leng with its nameless monastery and wicked stone villages; stopping only at the vast grey peaks to confer with the Shantak-frightening night-gaunts whose burrows honeycombed their summits. They would then, according to what advice they might receive from those denizens, choose their final course; approaching unknown Kadath either through the desert of carven mountains north of Inquanok, or through the more northerly reaches of repulsive Leng itself. Doglike and soulless as they are, the ghouls and night-gaunts had no dread of what those untrodden deserts might reveal; nor did they feel any deterring awe at the thought of Kadath towering lone with its onyx castle of mystery.

About midday the ghouls and night-gaunts prepared for flight, each ghoul selecting a suitable pair of horned steeds to bear him. Carter was placed well up toward the head of the column beside Pickman, and in front of the whole a double line of riderless night-gaunts was provided as a vanguard. At a brisk meep from Pickman the whole shocking army rose in a nightmare cloud above the broken columns and crumbling sphinxes of primordial Sarkomand; higher and higher, till even the great basalt cliff behind the town was cleared, and the cold, sterile table-land of Leng's outskirts laid open to sight. Still higher flew the black host, till even this table-land grew small beneath them; and as they worked northward over the wind-swept plateau of horror Carter saw once again with a shudder the circle of crude monoliths and the squat windowless building which he knew held that frightful silken-masked blasphemy from whose clutches he had so narrowly escaped. This time no descent was made as the army swept batlike over the sterile landscape, passing the feeble fires of the unwholesome stone villages at a great altitude, and pausing not at all to mark the morbid twistings of the hooved, horned almost-humans that dance and pipe eternally therein. Once they saw a Shantak-bird flying low over the plain, but when it saw them it screamed noxiously and flapped off to the north in grotesque panic.

At dusk they reached the jagged grey peaks that form the barrier of Inquanok, and hovered about these strange caves near the summits which Carter recalled as so frightful to the Shantaks. At the insistent meeping of the ghoulish leaders there issued forth from each lofty burrow a stream of horned black flyers with which the ghouls and night-gaunts of the party conferred at length by means of ugly gestures. It soon became clear that the best course would be that over the cold waste north of Inquanok, for Leng's northward reaches are full of unseen pitfalls that even the night-gaunts dislike; abysmal influences centering in certain white hemispherical buildings on curious knolls, which common folklore associates unpleasantly with the Other Gods and their crawling chaos Nyarlathotep.

Of Kadath the flutterers of the peaks knew almost nothing, save that there must be some mighty marvel toward the north, over which the Shantaks and the carven mountains stand guard. They hinted at rumoured abnormalities of proportion in those trackless leagues beyond, and recalled vague whispers of a realm where night broods eternally; but of definite data they had nothing to give. So Carter and his party thanked them kindly; and, crossing the topmost granite pinnacles to the skies of Inquanok, dropped below the level of the phosphorescent night clouds and beheld in the distance those terrible squatting gargoyles that were mountains till some titan hand carved fright into their virgin rock.

There they squatted in a hellish half-circle, their legs on the desert sand and their mitres piercing the luminous clouds; sinister, wolflike, and double-headed, with faces of fury and right hands raised, dully and malignly watching the rim of man's world and guarding with horror the reaches of a cold northern world that is not man's. From their hideous laps rose evil Shantaks of elephantine bulk, but these all fled with insane titters as the vanguard of night-gaunts was sighted in the misty sky. Northward above those gargoyle mountains the army flew, and over leagues of dim desert where never a landmark rose. Less and less luminous grew the clouds, till at length Carter could see only blackness around him; but never did the winged steeds falter, bred as they were in earth's blackest crypts, and seeing not with any eyes, but with the whole dank surface of their slippery forms. On and on they flew, past winds of dubious scent and sounds of dubious import; ever in thickest darkness, and covering such prodigious spaces that Carter wondered whether or not they could still be within earth's dreamland.

Then suddenly the clouds thinned and the stars shone spectrally above. All below was still black, but those pallid beacons in the sky seemed alive with a meaning and directiveness they had never possessed elsewhere. It was not that the figures of the constellations were different, but that the same familiar shapes now revealed a significance they had formerly failed to make plain. Everything focussed toward the north; every curve and asterism of the glittering sky became part of a vast design whose function was to hurry first the eye and then the whole observer onward to some secret and terrible goal of convergence beyond the frozen waste that stretched endlessly ahead. Carter looked toward the east where the great ridge of barrier peaks had towered along all the length of Inquanok and saw against the stars a jagged silhouette which told of its continued presence. It was more broken now, with yawning clefts and fantastically erratic pinnacles; and Carter studied closely the suggestive turnings and inclinations of that grotesque outline, which seemed to share with the stars some subtle northward urge.

They were flying past at a tremendous speed, so that the watcher had to strain hard to catch details; when all at once he beheld just above the line of the topmost peaks a dark and moving object against the stars, whose course exactly paralleled that of his own bizarre party. The ghouls had likewise glimpsed it, for he heard their low glibbering all about him, and for a moment he fancied the object was a gigantic Shantak, of a size vastly greater than that of the average specimen. Soon, however, he saw that this theory would not hold; for the shape of the thing above the mountains was not that of any hippocephalic bird. Its outline against the stars, necessarily vague as it was, resembled rather some huge mitred head, or pair of heads infinitely magnified; and its rapid bobbing flight through the sky seemed most peculiarly a wingless one. Carter could not tell which side of the mountains it was on, but soon perceived that it had parts below the parts he had first seen, since it blotted out all the stars in places where the ridge was deeply cleft.

Then came a wide gap in the range, where the hideous reaches of transmontane Leng were joined to the cold waste on this side by a low pass through which the stars shone wanly. Carter watched this gap with intense care, knowing that he might see outlined against the sky beyond it the lower parts of the vast thing that flew undulantly above the pinnacles. The object had now floated ahead a trifle, and every eye of the party was fixed on the rift where it would presently appear in full-length silhouette. Gradually the huge thing above the peaks neared the gap, slightly slackening its speed as if conscious of having outdistanced the ghoulish army. For another minute suspense was keen, and then the brief instant of full silhouette and revelation came; bringing to the lips of the ghouls an awed and half-choked meep of cosmic fear, and to the soul of the traveller a chill that has never wholly left it. For the mammoth bobbing shape that overtopped the ridge was only a head—a mitred double head—and below it in terrible vastness loped the frightful swollen body that bore it; the mountain-high monstrosity that walked in stealth and silence; the hyaena-like distortion of a giant anthropoid shape that trotted blackly against the sky, its repulsive pair of cone-capped heads reaching half way to the zenith.

Carter did not lose consciousness or even scream aloud, for he was an old dreamer; but he looked behind him in horror and shuddered when he saw that there were other monstrous heads silhouetted above the level of the peaks, bobbing along stealthily after the first one. And straight in the rear were three of the mighty mountain shapes seen full against the southern stars, tiptoeing wolflike and lumberingly, their tall mitres nodding thousands of feet in the air. The carven mountains, then, had not stayed squatting in that rigid semicircle north of Inquanok, with right hands uplifted. They had duties to perform, and were not remiss. But it was horrible, that they never spoke, and never even made a sound in walking.

Meanwhile the ghoul that was Pickman had glibbered an order to the night-gaunts, and the whole army soared higher into the air. Up toward the stars the grotesque column shot, till nothing stood out any longer against the sky; neither the grey granite ridge that was still nor the carven mitred mountains that walked. All was blackness beneath as the fluttering legion surged northward amidst rushing winds and invisible laughter in the aether, and never a Shantak or less mentionable entity rose from the haunted wastes to pursue them. The farther they went, the faster they flew, till soon their dizzying speed seemed to pass that of a rifle ball and approach that of a planet in its orbit. Carter wondered how with such speed the earth could still stretch beneath them, but knew that in the land of dream dimensions have strange properties. That they were in a realm of eternal night he felt certain, and he fancied that the constellations overhead had subtly emphasized their northward focus; gathering themselves up as it were to cast the flying army into the void of the boreal pole, as the folds of a bag are gathered up to cast out the last bits of substance therein.

Then he noticed with terror that the wings of the night-gaunts were not flapping any more. The horned and faceless steeds had folded their membranous appendages, and were resting quite passive in the chaos of wind that whirled and chuckled as it bore them on. A force not of earth had seized on the army, and ghouls and night-gaunts alike were powerless before a current which pulled madly and relentlessly into the north whence no mortal had ever returned. At length a lone pallid light was seen on the skyline ahead, thereafter rising steadily as they approached, and having beneath it a black mass that blotted out the stars. Carter saw that it must be some beacon on a mountain, for only a mountain could rise so vast as seen from so prodigious a height in the air.

Higher and higher rose the light and the blackness beneath it, till half the northern sky was obscured by the rugged conical mass. Lofty as the army was, that pale and sinister beacon rose above it, towering monstrous over all peaks and concernments of earth, and tasting the atomless aether where the cryptical moon and the mad planets reel. No mountain known of man was that which loomed before them. The high clouds far below were but a fringe for its foothills. The groping dizziness of topmost air was but a girdle for its loins. Scornful and spectral climbed that bridge betwixt earth and heaven, black in eternal night, and crowned with a pshent of unknown stars whose awful and significant outline grew every moment clearer. Ghouls meeped in wonder as they saw it, and Carter shivered in fear lest all the hurtling army be dashed to pieces on the unyielding onyx of that cyclopean cliff.

Higher and higher rose the light, till it mingled with the loftiest orbs of the zenith and winked down at the flyers with lurid mockery. All the north beneath it was blackness now; dread, stony blackness from infinite depths to infinite heights, with only that pale winking beacon perched unreachably at the top of all vision. Carter studied the light more closely, and saw at last what lines its inky background made against the stars. There were towers on that titan mountaintop; horrible domed towers in noxious and incalculable tiers and clusters beyond any dreamable workmanship of man; battlements and terraces of wonder and menace, all limned tiny and black and distant against the starry pshent that glowed malevolently at the uppermost rim of sight. Capping that most measureless of mountains was a castle beyond all mortal thought, and in it glowed the daemon-light. Then Randolph Carter knew that his quest was done, and that he saw above him the goal of all forbidden steps and audacious visions; the fabulous, the incredible home of the Great Ones atop unknown Kadath.

Even as he realised this thing, Carter noticed a change in the course of the helplessly wind-sucked party. They were rising abruptly now, and it was plain that the focus of their flight was the onyx castle where the pale light shone. So close was the great black mountain that its sides sped by them dizzily as they shot upward, and in the darkness they could discern nothing upon it. Vaster and vaster loomed the tenebrous towers of the nighted castle above, and Carter could see that it was well-nigh blasphemous in its immensity. Well might its stones have been quarried by nameless workmen in that horrible gulf rent out of the rock in the hill pass north of Inquanok, for such was its size that a man on its threshold stood even as air out on the steps of earth's loftiest fortress. The pshent of unknown stars above the myriad domed turrets glowed with a sallow, sickly flare, so that a kind of twilight hung about the murky walls of slippery onyx. The pallid beacon was now seen to be a single shining window high up in one of the loftiest towers, and as the helpless army neared the top of the mountain Carter thought he detected unpleasant shadows flitting across the feebly luminous expanse. It was a strangely arched window, of a design wholly alien to earth.

The solid rock now gave place to the giant foundations of the monstrous castle, and it seemed that the speed of the party was somewhat abated. Vast walls shot up, and there was a glimpse of a great gate through which the voyagers were swept. All was night in the titan courtyard, and then came the deeper blackness of inmost things as a huge arched portal engulfed the column. Vortices of cold wind surged dankly through sightless labyrinths of onyx, and Carter could never tell what cyclopean stairs and corridors lay silent along the route of his endless aerial twisting. Always upward led the terrible plunge in darkness, and never a sound, touch or glimpse broke the dense pall of mystery. Large as the army of ghouls and night-gaunts was, it was lost in the prodigious voids of that more than earthly castle. And when at last there suddenly dawned around him the lurid light of that single tower room whose lofty window had served as a beacon, it took Carter long to discern the far walls and high, distant ceiling, and to realize that he was indeed not again in the boundless air outside.

Randolph Carter had hoped to come into the throne-room of the Great ones with poise and dignity, flanked and followed by impressive lines of ghouls in ceremonial order, and offering his prayer as a free and potent master among dreamers. He had known that the Great Ones themselves are not beyond a mortal's power to cope with, and had trusted to luck that the Other Gods and their crawling chaos Nyarlathotep would not happen to come to their aid at the crucial moment, as they had so often done before when men sought out earth's gods in their home or on their mountains. And with his hideous escort he had half hoped to defy even the Other Gods if need were, knowing as he did that ghouls have no masters, and that night-gaunts own not Nyarlathotep but only archaic Nodens for their lord. But now he saw that supernal Kadath in its cold waste is indeed girt with dark wonders and nameless sentinels, and that the Other Gods are of a surety vigilant in guarding the mild, feeble gods of earth. Void as they are of lordship over ghouls and night-gaunts, the mindless, shapeless blasphemies of outer space can yet control them when they must; so that it was not in state as a free and potent master of dreamers that Randolph Carter came into the Great Ones' throne-room with his ghouls. Swept and herded by nightmare tempests from the stars, and dogged by unseen horrors of the northern waste, all that army floated captive and helpless in the lurid light, dropping numbly to the onyx floor when by some voiceless order the winds of fright dissolved.

Before no golden dais had Randolph Carter come, nor was there any august circle of crowned and haloed beings with narrow eyes, long-lobed ears, thin nose, and pointed chin whose kinship to the carven face on Ngranek might stamp them as those to whom a dreamer might pray. Save for the one tower room the onyx castle atop Kadath was dark, and the masters were not there. Carter had come to unknown Kadath in the cold waste, but he had not found the gods. Yet still the lurid light glowed in that one tower room whose size was so little less than that of all outdoors, and whose distant walls and roof were so nearly lost to sight in thin, curling mists. Earth's gods were not there, it was true, but of subtler and less visible presences there could be no lack. Where the mild gods are absent, the Other Gods are not unrepresented; and certainly, the onyx castle of castles was far from tenantless. In what outrageous form or forms terror would next reveal itself, Carter could by no means imagine. He felt that his visit had been expected, and wondered how close a watch had all along been kept upon him by the crawling chaos Nyarlathotep. It is Nyarlathotep, horror of infinite shapes and dread soul and messenger of the Other Gods, that the fungous moonbeasts serve; and Carter thought of the black galley that had vanished when the tide of battle turned against the toadlike abnormalities on the jagged rock in the sea.

Reflecting upon these things, he was staggering to his feet in the midst of his nightmare company when there rang without warning through that pale-litten and limitless chamber the hideous blast of a daemon trumpet. Three times pealed that frightful brazen scream, and when the echoes of the third blast had died chucklingly away Randolph Carter saw that he was alone. Whither, why and how the ghouls and night-gaunts had been snatched from sight was not for him to divine. He knew only that he was suddenly alone, and that whatever unseen powers lurked mockingly around him were no powers of earth's friendly dreamland. Presently from the chamber's uttermost reaches a new sound came. This, too, was a rhythmic trumpeting; but of a kind far removed from the three raucous blasts which had dissolved his goodly cohorts. In this low fanfare echoed all the wonder and melody of ethereal dream; exotic vistas of unimagined loveliness floating from each strange chord and subtly alien cadence. Odours of incense came to match the golden notes; and overhead a great light dawned, its colours changing in cycles unknown to earth's spectrum, and following the song of the trumpets in weird symphonic harmonies. Torches flared in the distance, and the beat of drums throbbed nearer amidst waves of tense expectancy.

Out of the thinning mists and the cloud of strange incenses filed twin columns of giant black slaves with loin-cloths of iridescent silk. Upon their heads were strapped vast helmet-like torches of glittering metal, from which the fragrance of obscure balsams spread in fumous spirals. In their right hands were crystal wands whose tips were carven into leering chimaeras, while their left hands grasped long thin silver trumpets which they blew in turn. Armlets and anklets of gold they had, and between each pair of anklets stretched a golden chain that held its wearer to a sober gait. That they were true black men of earth's dreamland was at once apparent, but it seemed less likely that their rites and costumes were wholly things of our earth. Ten feet from Carter the columns stopped, and as they did so each trumpet flew abruptly to its bearer's thick lips. Wild and ecstatic was the blast that followed, and wilder still the cry that chorused just after from dark throats somehow made shrill by strange artifice.

Then down the wide lane betwixt the two columns a lone figure strode; a tall, slim figure with the young face of an antique Pharaoh, gay with prismatic robes and crowned with a golden pshent that glowed with inherent light. Close up to Carter strode that regal figure; whose proud carriage and smart features had in them the fascination of a dark god or fallen archangel, and around whose eyes there lurked the languid sparkle of capricious humour. It spoke, and in its mellow tones there rippled the wild music of Lethean streams.

"Randolph Carter," said the voice, "you have come to see the Great Ones whom it is unlawful for men to see. Watchers have spoken of this thing, and the Other Gods have grunted as they rolled and tumbled mindlessly to the sound of thin flutes in the black ultimate void where broods the daemon-sultan whose name no lips dare speak aloud.

"When Barzai the Wise climbed Hatheg-Kla to see the Great Ones dance and howl above the clouds in the moonlight he never returned. The Other Gods were there, and they did what was expected. Zenig of Aphorat sought to reach unknown Kadath in the cold waste, and his skull is now set in a ring on the little finger of one whom I need not name.

"But you, Randolph Carter, have braved all things of earth's dreamland, and burn still with the flame of quest. You came not as one curious, but as one seeking his due, nor have you failed ever in reverence toward the mild gods of earth. Yet have these gods kept you from the marvellous sunset city of your dreams, and wholly through their own small covetousness; for verily, they craved the weird loveliness of that which your fancy had fashioned, and vowed that henceforward no other spot should be their abode.

"They are gone from their castle on unknown Kadath to dwell in your marvellous city. All through its palaces of veined marble they revel by day, and when the sun sets they go out in the perfumed gardens and watch the golden glory on temples and colonnades, arched bridges and silver-basined fountains, and wide streets with blossom-laden urns and ivory statues in gleaming rows. And when night comes they climb tall terraces in the dew, and sit on carved benches of porphyry scanning the stars, or lean over pale balustrades to gaze at the town's steep northward slopes, where one by one the little windows in old peaked gables shine softly out with the calm yellow light of homely candles.

"The gods love your marvellous city, and walk no more in the ways of the gods. They have forgotten the high places of earth, and the mountains that knew their youth. The earth has no longer any gods that are gods, and only the Other Ones from outer space hold sway on unremembered Kadath. Far away in a valley of your own childhood, Randolph Carter, play the heedless Great Ones. You have dreamed too well, O wise archdreamer, for you have drawn dream's gods away from the world of all men's visions to that which is wholly yours; having builded out of your boyhood's small fancies a city more lovely than all the phantoms that have gone before.

"It is not well that earth's gods leave their thrones for the spider to spin on, and their realm for the Others to sway in the dark manner of Others. Fain would the powers from outside bring chaos and horror to you, Randolph Carter, who are the cause of their upsetting, but that they know it is by you alone that the gods may be sent back to their world. In that half-waking dreamland which is yours, no power of uttermost night may pursue; and only you can send the selfish Great

Ones gently out of your marvellous sunset city, back through the northern twilight to their wonted place atop unknown Kadath in the cold waste.

"So, Randolph Carter, in the name of the Other Gods I spare you and charge you to seek that sunset city which is yours, and to send thence the drowsy truant gods for whom the dream world waits. Not hard to find is that roseal fever of the gods, that fanfare of supernal trumpets and clash of immortal cymbals, that mystery whose place and meaning have haunted you through the halls of waking and the gulfs of dreaming, and tormented you with hints of vanished memory and the pain of lost things awesome and momentous. Not hard to find is that symbol and relic of your days of wonder, for truly, it is but the stable and eternal gem wherein all that wonder sparkles crystallised to light your evening path. Behold! It is not over unknown seas but back over well-known years that your quest must go; back to the bright strange things of infancy and the quick sun-drenched glimpses of magic that old scenes brought to wide young eyes.

"For know you, that your gold and marble city of wonder is only the sum of what you have seen and loved in youth. It is the glory of Boston's hillside roofs and western windows aflame with sunset; of the flower-fragrant Common and the great dome on the hill and the tangle of gables and chimneys in the violet valley where the many-bridged Charles flows drowsily. These things you saw, Randolph Carter, when your nurse first wheeled you out in the springtime, and they will be the last things you will ever see with eyes of memory and of love. And there is antique Salem with its brooding years, and spectral Marblehead scaling its rocky precipices into past centuries, and the glory of Salem's towers and spires seen afar from Marblehead's pastures across the harbour against the setting sun.

"There is Providence quaint and lordly on its seven hills over the blue harbour, with terraces of green leading up to steeples and citadels of living antiquity, and Newport climbing wraithlike from its dreaming breakwater. Arkham is there, with its moss-grown gambrel roofs and the rocky rolling meadows behind it; and antediluvian Kingsport hoary with stacked chimneys and deserted quays and overhanging gables, and the marvel of high cliffs and the milky-misted ocean with tolling buoys beyond.

"Cool vales in Concord, cobbled lanes in Portsmouth, twilight bends of rustic New Hampshire roads where giant elms half hide white farmhouse walls and creaking well-sweeps. Glouscester's salt wharves and Truro's windy willows. Vistas of distant steepled towns and hills beyond hills along the North Shore, hushed stony slopes and low ivied cottages in the lee of huge boulders in Rhode Island's back country. Scent of the sea and fragrance of the fields; spell of the dark woods and joy of the orchards and gardens at dawn. These, Randolph Carter, are your city; for they are yourself. New England bore you, and into your soul she poured a liquid loveliness which cannot die. This loveliness, moulded, crystallised, and polished by years of memory and dreaming, is your terraced wonder of elusive sunsets; and to find that marble parapet with curious urns and carven rail, and descend at last these endless balustraded steps to the city of broad squares and prismatic fountains, you need only to turn back to the thoughts and visions of your wistful boyhood.

"Look! through that window shine the stars of eternal night. Even now they are shining above the scenes you have known and cherished, drinking of their charm that they may shine more lovely over the gardens of dream. There is Antares—he is winking at this moment over the roofs of Tremont Street, and you could see him from your window on Beacon Hill. Out beyond those stars yawn the gulfs from whence my mindless masters have sent me. Some day you too may traverse them, but if you are wise you will beware such folly; for of those mortals who have been and returned, only one preserves a mind unshattered by the pounding, clawing horrors of the void. Terrors and blasphemies gnaw at one another for space, and there is more evil in the lesser ones then in the greater; even as you know from the deeds of those who sought to deliver you into my hands, whilst I myself harboured no wish to shatter you, and would indeed have helped you hither long ago had I not been elsewhere busy, and certain that you would yourself find the way. Shun then, the outer hells, and stick to the calm, lovely things of your youth. Seek out your marvellous city and drive thence the recreant Great Ones, sending them back gently to those scenes which are of their own youth, and which wait uneasy for their return.

"Easier even then the way of dim memory is the way I will prepare for you. See! There comes hither a monstrous Shantak, led by a slave who for your peace of mind had best keep invisible. Mount and be ready—there! Yogash the black will help you on the scaly horror. Steer for that brightest star just south of the zenith—it is Vega, and in two hours will be just above the terrace of your sunset city. Steer for it only till you hear a far-off singing in the high aether. Higher than that lurks madness, so rein your Shantak when the first note lures. Look then back to earth, and you will see shining the deathless altar-flame of Ired-Naa from the sacred roof of a temple. That temple is in your desiderate sunset city, so steer for it before you heed the singing and are lost.

"When you draw nigh the city steer for the same high parapet whence of old you scanned the outspread glory, prodding the Shantak till he cry aloud. That cry the Great Ones will hear and know as they sit on their perfumed terraces, and there will come upon them such a homesickness that all of your city's wonders will not console them for the absence of Kadath's grim castle and the pshent of eternal stars that crowns it.

"Then must you land amongst them with the Shantak, and let them see and touch that noisome and hippocephalic bird; meanwhile discoursing to them of unknown Kadath, which you will so lately have left, and telling them how its boundless halls are lovely and unlighted, where of old they used to leap and revel in supernal radiance. And the Shantak will talk to them in the manner of Shantaks, but it will have no powers of persuasion beyond the recalling of elder days.

"Over and over must you speak to the wandering Great Ones of their home and youth, till at last they will weep and ask to be shewn the returning path they have forgotten. Thereat can you loose the waiting Shantak, sending him skyward with the homing cry of his kind; hearing which the Great Ones will prance and jump with antique mirth, and forthwith stride after the loathly bird in the fashion of gods, through the deep gulfs of heaven to Kadath's familiar towers and domes.

"Then will the marvellous sunset city be yours to cherish and inhabit for ever, and once more will earth's gods rule the dreams of men from their accustomed seat. Go now—the casement is open and the stars await outside. Already your Shantak wheezes and titters with impatience. Steer for Vega through the night, but turn when the singing sounds. Forget not this warning, lest horrors unthinkable suck you into the gulf of shrieking and ululant madness. Remember the Other Gods; they are great and mindless and terrible, and lurk in the outer voids. They are good gods to shun.

"*Hei! Aa-shanta 'nygh!* You are off! Send back earth's gods to their haunts on unknown Kadath, and pray to all space that you may never meet me in my thousand other forms. Farewell, Randolph Carter, and beware; *for I am Nyarlathotep, the Crawling Chaos.*"

And Randolph Carter, gasping and dizzy on his hideous Shantak, shot screamingly into space toward the cold blue glare of boreal Vega; looking but once behind him at the clustered and chaotic turrets of the onyx nightmare wherein still glowed the lone lurid light of that window above the air and the clouds of earth's dreamland. Great polypous horrors slid darkly past, and unseen bat wings beat multitudinous around him, but still he clung to the unwholesome mane of that loathly and hippocephalic scaled bird. The stars danced mockingly, almost shifting now and then to form pale signs of doom that one might wonder one had not seen and feared before; and ever the winds of nether howled of vague blackness and loneliness beyond the cosmos.

Then through the glittering vault ahead there fell a hush of portent, and all the winds and horrors slunk away as night things slink away before the dawn.

Trembling in waves that golden wisps of nebula made weirdly visible, there rose a timid hint of far-off melody, droning in faint chords that our own universe of stars knows not. And as that music grew, the Shantak raised its ears and plunged ahead, and Carter likewise bent to catch each lovely strain. It was a song, but not the song of any voice. Night and the spheres sang it, and it was old when space and Nyarlathotep and the Other Gods were born.

Faster flew the Shantak, and lower bent the rider, drunk with the marvel of strange gulfs, and whirling in the crystal coils of outer magic. Then came too late the warning of the evil one, the sardonic caution of the daemon legate who had bidden the seeker beware the madness of that song. Only to taunt had Nyarlathotep marked out the way to safety and the marvellous sunset city; only to mock had that black messenger revealed the secret of these truant gods whose steps he could so easily lead back at will. For madness and the void's wild vengeance are Nyarlathotep's only gifts to the presumptuous; and frantick though the rider strove to turn his disgusting steed, that leering, tittering Shantak coursed on impetuous and relentless, flapping its great slippery wings in malignant joy, and headed for those unhallowed pits whither no dreams reach; that last amorphous blight of nether-most confusion where bubbles and blasphemes at infinity's centre the mindless daemon-sultan Azathoth, whose name no lips dare speak aloud.

Unswerving and obedient to the foul legate's orders, that hellish bird plunged onward through shoals of shapeless lurkers and caperers in darkness, and vacuous herds of drifting entities that pawed and groped and groped and pawed; the nameless larvae of the Other Gods, that are like them blind and without mind, and possessed of singular hungers and thirsts.

Onward unswerving and relentless, and tittering hilariously to watch the chuckling and hysterics into which the risen song of night and the spheres had turned, that eldritch scaly monster bore its helpless rider; hurtling and shooting, cleaving the uttermost rim and spanning the outermost abysses; leaving behind the stars and the realms of matter, and darting meteor-like through stark formlessness toward those inconceivable, unlighted chambers beyond time wherein Azathoth gnaws shapeless and ravenous amidst the muffled, maddening beat of vile drums and the thin, monotonous whine of accursed flutes.

Onward—onward—through the screaming, cackling, and blackly populous gulfs—and then from some dim blessed distance there came an image and a thought to Randolph Carter the doomed. Too well had Nyarlathotep planned his mocking and his tantalising, for he had brought up that which no gusts of icy terror could quite efface. Home—New England—Beacon Hill—the waking world.

"For know you, that your gold and marble city of wonder is only the sum of what you have seen and loved in youth . . . the glory of Boston's hillside roofs and western windows aflame with sunset; of the flower-fragrant Common and the great dome on the hill and the tangle of gables and chimneys in the violet valley where the many-bridged Charles flows drowsily . . . this loveliness, moulded, crystallised, and polished by years of memory and reaming, is your terraced wonder of elusive sunsets; and to find that marble parapet with curious urns and carven rail, and descend at last those endless balustraded steps to the city of broad squares and prismatic fountains, you need only to turn back to the thoughts and visions of your wistful boyhood."

Onward—onward—dizzily onward to ultimate doom through the blackness where sightless feelers pawed and slimy snouts jostled and nameless things tittered and tittered and tittered. But the image and the thought had come, and Randolph Carter knew clearly that he was dreaming and only dreaming, and that somewhere in the background the world of waking and the city of his infancy still lay. Words came again—"You need only turn back to the thoughts and visions of your wistful boyhood." Turn—turn—blackness on every side, but Randolph Carter could turn.

Thick though the rushing nightmare that clutched his senses, Randolph Carter could turn and move. He could move, and if he chose he could leap off the evil Shantak that bore him hurtlingly doomward at the orders of Nyarlathotep. He could leap off and dare those depths of night that yawned interminably down, those depths of fear whose terrors yet could not exceed the nameless doom that lurked waiting at chaos' core. He could turn and move and leap—he could—he would—he would—he would.

Off that vast hippocephalic abomination leaped the doomed and desperate dreamer, and down through endless voids of sentient blackness he fell. Aeons reeled, universes died and were born again, stars became nebulae and nebulae became stars, and still Randolph Carter fell through those endless voids of sentient blackness.

Then in the slow creeping course of eternity the utmost cycle of the cosmos churned itself into another futile completion, and all things became again as they were unreckoned kalpas before. Matter and light were born anew as space once had known them; and comets, suns and worlds sprang flaming into life, though nothing survived to tell that they had been and gone, been and gone, always and always, back to no first beginning.

And there was a firmament again, and a wind, and a glare of purple light in the eyes of the falling dreamer. There were gods and presences and wills; beauty and evil, and the shrieking of noxious night robbed of its prey. For through the unknown ultimate cycle had lived a thought and a vision of a dreamer's boyhood, and now there were re-made a waking world and an old cherished city to body and to justify these things. Out of the void S'ngac the violet gas had pointed the way, and archaic Nodens was bellowing his guidance from unhinted deeps.

Stars swelled to dawns, and dawns burst into fountains of gold, carmine, and purple, and still the dreamer fell. Cries rent the aether as ribbons of light beat back the fiends from outside. And hoary Nodens raised a howl of triumph when Nyarlathotep, close on his quarry, stopped baffled by a glare that seared his formless hunting-horrors to grey dust. Randolph Carter had indeed descended at last the wide marmoreal flights to his marvellous city, for he was come again to the fair New England world that had wrought him.

So to the organ chords of morning's myriad whistles, and dawn's blaze thrown dazzling through purple panes by the great gold dome of the State House on the hill, Randolph Carter leaped shoutingly awake within his Boston room. Birds sang in hidden gardens and the perfume of trellised vines came wistful from arbours his grandfather had reared. Beauty and light glowed from classic mantel and carven cornice and walls grotesquely figured, while a sleek black cat rose yawning from hearthside sleep that his master's start and shriek had disturbed. And vast infinities away, past the Gate of Deeper Slumber and the enchanted wood and the garden lands and the Cerenarian Sea and the twilight reaches of Inquanok, the crawling chaos Nyarlathotep strode brooding into the onyx castle atop unknown Kadath in the cold waste, and taunted insolently the mild gods of earth whom he had snatched abruptly from their scented revels in the marvellous sunset city.

Celephais

IN A dream Kuranes saw the city in the valley, and the seacoast beyond, and the snowy peak overlooking the sea, and the gaily painted galleys that sail out of the harbour toward distant regions where the sea meets the sky. In a dream it was also that he came by his name of Kuranes, for when awake he was called by another name. Perhaps it was natural for him to dream a new name; for he was the last of his family, and alone among the indifferent millions of London, so there were not many to speak to him and to remind him who he had been. His money and lands were gone, and he did not care for the ways of the people about him, but preferred to dream and write of his dreams. What he wrote was laughed at by those to whom he showed it, so that after a time he kept his writings to himself, and finally ceased to write. The more he withdrew from the world about him, the more wonderful became his dreams; and it would have been quite futile to try to describe them on paper. Kuranes was not modern, and did not think like others who wrote. Whilst they strove to strip from life its embroidered robes of myth and to show in naked ugliness the foul thing that is reality, Kuranes sought for beauty alone. When truth and experience failed to reveal it, he sought it in fancy and illusion, and found it on his very doorstep, amid the nebulous memories of childhood tales and dreams.

There are not many persons who know what wonders are opened to them in the stories and visions of their youth; for when as children we listen and dream, we think but half-formed thoughts, and when as men we try to remember, we are dulled and prosaic with the poison of life. But some of us awake in the night with strange phantasms of enchanted hills and gardens, of fountains that sing in the sun, of golden cliffs overhanging murmuring seas, of plains that stretch down to sleeping cities of bronze and stone, and of shadowy companies of heroes that ride caparisoned white horses along the edges of thick forests; and then we know that we have looked back through the ivory gates into that world of wonder which was ours before we were wise and unhappy.

Kuranes came very suddenly upon his old world of childhood. He had been dreaming of the house where he had been born; the great stone house covered with ivy, where thirteen generations of his ancestors had lived, and where he had hoped to die. It was moonlight, and he had stolen out into the fragrant summer night, through the gardens, down the terraces, past the great oaks of the park, and along the long white road to the village. The village seemed very old, eaten away at the edge like the moon which had commenced to wane, and Kuranes wondered whether the peaked roofs of the small houses hid sleep or death. In the streets were spears of long grass, and the window-panes on either side broken or filmily staring. Kuranes had not lingered, but had plodded on as though summoned toward some goal. He dared not disobey the summons for fear it might prove an illusion like the urges and aspirations of waking life, which do not lead to any goal. Then he had been drawn down a lane that led off from the village street toward the channel cliffs, and had come to the end of things—to the precipice and the abyss where all the village and all the world fell abruptly into the unechoing emptiness of infinity, and where even the sky ahead was empty and unlit by the crumbling moon and the peering stars. Faith had urged him on, over the precipice and into the gulf, where he had floated down, down, down; past dark, shapeless, undreamed dreams, faintly glowing spheres that may have been partly dreamed dreams, and laughing winged things that seemed to mock the dreamers of all the worlds. Then a rift seemed to open in the darkness before him, and he saw the city of the valley, glistening radiantly far, far below, with a background of sea and sky, and a snow-capped mountain near the shore.

Kuranes had awaked the very moment he beheld the city, yet he knew from his brief glance that it was none other than Celephais, in the Valley of Ooth-Nargai beyond the Tanarian Hills where his spirit had dwelt all the eternity of an hour one summer afternoon very long ago, when he had slipt away from his nurse and let the warm sea-breeze lull him to sleep as he watched the clouds from the cliff near the village. He had protested then, when they had found him, waked him, and carried him home, for just as he was aroused he had been about to sail in a golden galley for those alluring regions where the sea meets the sky. And now he was equally resentful of awaking, for he had found his fabulous city after forty weary years.

But three nights afterward Kuranes came again to Celephais. As before, he dreamed first of the village that was asleep or dead, and of the abyss down which one must float silently; then the rift appeared again, and he beheld the glittering minarets of the city, and saw the graceful galleys riding at anchor in the blue harbour, and watched the gingko trees of Mount Aran swaying in the sea-breeze. But this time he was not snatched away, and like a winged being settled gradually over a grassy hillside till finally his feet rested gently on the turf. He had indeed come back to the valley of Ooth-Nargai and the splendid city of Celephais.

Down the hill amid scented grasses and brilliant flowers walked Kuranes, over the bubbling Naraxa on the small wooden bridge where he had carved his name so many years ago, and through the whispering grove to the great stone bridge by the city gate. All was as of old, nor were the marble walls discoloured, nor the polished bronze statues upon them tarnished. And Kuranes saw that he need not tremble lest the things he knew be vanished; for even the sentries on the ramparts were the same, and still as young as he remembered them. When he entered the city, past the bronze gates and over the onyx pavements, the merchants and camel-drivers greeted him as if he had never been away; and it was the same at the turquoise temple of Nath-Horthath, where the orchid-wreathed priests told him that there is no time in Ooth-Nargai, but only perpetual youth. Then Kuranes walked through the Street of Pillars to the seaward wall, where gathered the traders and sailors, and strange men from the regions where the sea meets the sky. There he stayed long, gazing out over the bright harbour where the ripples sparkled beneath an unknown sun, and where rode lightly the galleys from far places over the water. And he gazed also upon Mount Aran rising regally from the shore, its lower slopes green with swaying trees and its white summit touching the sky.

More than ever Kuranes wished to sail in a galley to the far places of which he had heard so many strange tales, and he sought again the captain who had agreed to carry him so long ago. He found the man, Athib, sitting on the same chest of spice he had sat upon before, and Athib seemed not to realize that any time had passed. Then the two rowed to a galley in the harbour, and giving orders to the oarmen, commenced to sail out into the billowy Cerenarian Sea that leads to the sky. For several days they glided undulatingly over the water, till finally they came to the horizon, where the sea meets the sky. Here the galley paused not at all, but floated easily in the blue of the sky among fleecy clouds tinted with rose. And far beneath the keel Kuranes could see strange lands and rivers and cities of surpassing beauty, spread indolently in the sunshine which seemed never to lessen or disappear. At length Athib told him that their journey was near its end, and that they would soon enter the harbour of Serannian, the pink marble city of the clouds, which is built on that ethereal coast where the west wind flows into the sky; but as the highest of the city's carven towers came into sight there was a sound somewhere in space, and Kuranes awaked in his London garret.

For many months after that Kuranes sought the marvellous city of Celephaïs and its sky-bound galleys in vain; and though his dreams carried him to many gorgeous and unheard-of-places, no one whom he met could tell him how to find Ooth-Nargai beyond the Tanarian Hills. One night he went flying over dark mountains where there were faint, lone campfires at great distances apart, and strange, shaggy herds with tinkling bells on the leaders, and in the wildest part of this hilly country, so remote that few men could ever have seen it, he found a hideously ancient wall or causeway of stone zigzagging along the ridges and valleys; too gigantic ever to have risen by human hands, and of such a length that neither end of it could be seen. Beyond that wall in the grey dawn he came to a land of quaint gardens and cherry trees, and when the sun rose he beheld such beauty of red and white flowers, green foliage and lawns, white paths, diamond brooks, blue lakelets, carven bridges, and red-roofed pagodas, that he for a moment forgot Celephais in sheer delight. But he remembered it again when he walked down a white path toward a red-roofed pagoda, and would have questioned the people of this land about it, had he not found that there were no people there, but only birds and bees and butterflies. On another night Kuranes walked up a damp stone spiral stairway endlessly, and came to a tower window overlooking a mighty plain and river lit by the full moon; and in the silent city that spread away from the river bank he thought he beheld some feature or arrangement which he had known before. He would have descended and asked the way to Ooth-Nargai had not a fearsome aurora sputtered up from some remote place beyond the horizon, showing the ruin and antiquity of the city, and the stagnation of the reedy river, and the death ly-

ing upon that land, as it had lain since King Kynara-
tholis came home from his conquests to find the vengeance of the gods.

So Kuranes sought fruitlessly for the marvellous city
of Celephais and its galleys that sail to Serannian in the
sky, meanwhile seeing many wonders and once barely
escaping from the high-priest not to be described, which
wears a yellow silken mask over its face and dwells all
alone in a prehistoric stone monastery in the cold desert
plateau of Leng. In time he grew so impatient of the
bleak intervals of day that he began buying drugs in
order to increase his periods of sleep. Hasheesh helped a
great deal, and once sent him to a part of space where
form does not exist, but where glowing gases study the
secrets of existence. And a violet-coloured gas told him
that this part of space was outside what he had called
infinity. The gas had not heard of planets and organisms
before, but identified Kuranes merely as one from the
infinity where matter, energy, and gravitation exist.
Kuranes was now very anxious to return to minaret-
studded Celephais, and increased his doses of drugs; but
eventually he had no more money left, and could buy
no drugs. Then one summer day he was turned out of
his garret, and wandered aimlessly through the streets,
drifting over a bridge to a place where the houses grew
thinner and thinner. And it was there that fulfillment
came, and he met the cortege of knights come from
Celephais to bear him thither forever.

Handsome knights they were, astride roan horses and
clad in shining armour with tabards of cloth-of-gold
curiously emblazoned. So numerous were they, that
Kuranes almost mistook them for an army, but they
were sent in his honour; since it was he who had

created Ooth-Nargai in his dreams, on which account he was now to be appointed its chief god for evermore. Then they gave Kuranes a horse and placed him at the head of the cavalcade, and all rode majestically through the downs of Surrey and onward toward the region where Kuranes and his ancestors were born. It was very strange, but as the riders went on they seemed to gallop back through Time; for whenever they passed through a village in the twilight they saw only such houses and villagers as Chaucer or men before him might have seen, and sometimes they saw knights on horseback with small companies of retainers. When it grew dark they travelled more swiftly, till soon they were flying uncannily as if in the air. In the dim dawn they came upon the village which Kuranes had seen alive in his childhood, and asleep or dead in his dreams. It was alive now, and early villagers curtsied as the horsemen clattered down the street and turned off into the lane that ends in the abyss of dreams. Kuranes had previously entered that abyss only at night, and wondered what it would look like by day; so he watched anxiously as the column approached its brink. Just as they galloped up the rising ground to the precipice a golden glare came somewhere out of the west and hid all the landscape in effulgent draperies. The abyss was a seething chaos of roseate and cerulean splendour, and invisible voices sang exultantly as the knightly entourage plunged over the edge and floated gracefully down past glittering clouds and silvery coruscations. Endlessly down the horsemen floated, their chargers pawing the aether as if galloping over golden sands; and then the luminous vapours spread apart to reveal a greater brightness, the brightness of the city Celephais, and the sea coast beyond, and the snowy peak overlooking the sea, and the gaily painted galleys that sail out of the harbour toward distant regions where the sea meets the sky.

And Kuranes reigned thereafter over Ooth-Nargai and all the neighboring regions of dream, and held his court alternately in Celephaïs and in the cloud-fashioned Serannian. He reigns there still, and will reign happily for ever, though below the cliffs at Innsmouth the channel tides played mockingly with the body of a tramp who had stumbled through the half-deserted village at dawn; played mockingly, and cast it upon the rocks by ivy-covered Trevor Towers, where a notably fat and especially offensive millionaire brewer enjoys the purchased atmosphere of extinct nobility.

The Silver Key

WHEN RANDOLPH CARTER was thirty he lost the key of the gate of dreams. Prior to that time he had made up for the prosiness of life by nightly excursions to strange and ancient cities beyond space, and lovely, unbelievable garden lands across ethereal seas; but as middle age hardened upon him he felt those liberties slipping away little by little, until at last he was cut off altogether. No more could his galleys sail up the river Oukranos past the gilded spires of Thran, or his elephant caravans tramp through perfumed jungles in Kled, where forgotten palaces with veined ivory columns sleep lovely and unbroken under the moon.

He had read much of things as they are, and talked with too many people. Well-meaning philosphers had taught him to look into the logical relations of things, and analyse the processes which shaped his thoughts and fancies. Wonder had gone away, and he had forgotten that all life is only a set of pictures in the brain, among which there is no difference betwixt those born of real things and those born of inward dreamings, and no cause to value the one above the other. Custom had dinned into his ears a superstitious reverence for that which tangibly and physically exists, and had made him secretly ashamed to dwell in visions. Wise men told him his simple fancies were inane and childish, and even more absurd because their actors persist in fancying them full of meaning and purpose as the blind cosmos grinds aimlessly on from nothing to something and from something back to nothing again, neither heeding nor knowing the wishes or existence of the minds that flicker for a second now and then in the darkness.

They had chained him down to things that are, and had then explained the workings of those things till mystery had gone out of the world. When he complained, and longed to escape into twilight realms where magic moulded all the little vivid fragments and prized associations of his mind into vistas of breathless expectancy and unquenchable delight, they turned him instead toward the newfound prodigies of science, bidding him find wonder in the atom's vortex and mystery in the sky's dimensions. And when he had failed to find these boons in things whose laws are known and measurable, they told him he lacked imagination, and was immature because he preferred dream-illusions to the illusions of our physical creation.

So Carter had tried to do as others did, and pretended that the common events and emotions of earthly minds were more important than the fantasies of rare and delicate souls. He did not dissent when they told him that the animal pain of a stuck pig or dyspeptic ploughman in real life is a greater thing than the peerless beauty of Narath with its hundred carven gates and domes of chalcedony, which he dimly remembered from his dreams; and under their guidance he cultivated a painstaking sense of pity and tragedy.

Once in a while, though, he could not help seeing how shallow, fickle, and meaningless all human aspirations are, and how emptily our real impulses contrast with those pompous ideals we profess to hold. Then he would have recourse to the polite laughter they had taught him to use against the extravagance and artificiality of dreams; for he saw that the daily life of our world is every inch as extravagant and artificial, and far less worthy of respect because of its poverty in beauty and its silly reluctance to admit its own lack of reason and purpose. In this way he became a kind of humorist, for he did not see that even humour is empty in a mindless universe devoid of any true standard of consistency or inconsistency.

In the first days of his bondage he had turned to the gentle churchly faith endeared to him by the naive trust of his fathers, for thence stretched mystic avenues which seemed to promise escape from life. Only on closer view did he mark the starved fancy and beauty, the stale and prosy triteness, and the owlish gravity and grotesque claims of solid truth which reigned boresomely and overwhelmingly among most of its professors; or feel to the full the awkwardness with which it sought to keep alive as literal fact the outgrown fears and guesses of a primal race confronting the unknown. It wearied Carter to see how solemnly people tried to make earthly reality out of old myths which every step of their boasted science confuted, and this misplaced seriousness killed the attachment he might have kept for the ancient creeds had they been content to offer the sonorous rites and emotional outlets in their true guise of ethereal fantasy.

But when he came to study those who had thrown off the old myths, he found them even more ugly than those who had not. They did not know that beauty lies in harmony, and that loveliness of life has no standard amidst an aimless cosmos save only its harmony with the dreams and the feelings which have gone before and blindly moulded our little spheres out of the rest of chaos. They did not see that good and evil and beauty and ugliness are only ornamental fruits of perspective, whose sole value lies in their linkage to what chance made our fathers think and feel, and whose finer details are different for every race and culture. Instead, they either denied these things altogether or transferred them to the crude, vague instincts which they shared with the beasts and peasants; so that their lives were dragged malodorously out in pain, ugliness, and disproportion, yet filled with a ludicrous pride at having escaped from something no more unsound than that which still held them. They had traded the false gods of fear and blind piety for those of license and anarchy.

Carter did not taste deeply of these modern freedoms; for their cheapness and squalor sickened a spirit loving beauty alone while his reason rebelled at the flimsy logic with which their champions tried to gild brute impulse with a sacredness stripped from the idols they had discarded. He saw that most of them, in common with their cast-off priest-craft, could not escape from the delusion that life has a meaning apart from that which men dream into it; and could not lay aside the crude notion of ethics and obligations beyond those of beauty, even when all Nature shrieked of its unconsciousness and impersonal unmorality in the light of their scientific discoveries. Warped and bigoted with preconceived illusions of justice, freedom, and consistency, they cast off the old lore and the old way with the old beliefs; nor ever stopped to think that that lore and those ways were the sole makers of their present thoughts and judgments, and the sole guides and standards in a meaningless universe without fixed aims or stable points of reference. Having lost these artificial settings, their lives grew void of direction and dramatic interest; till at length they strove to drown their ennui in bustle and pretended usefulness, noise and excitement, barbaric display and animal sensation. When these things palled, disappointed, or grew nauseous through revulsion, they cultivated irony and bitterness, and found fault with the social order. Never could they realize that their brute foundations were as shifting and contradictory as the gods of their elders, and that the satisfaction of one moment is the bane of the next. Calm, lasting beauty comes only in dream, and this solace the world had thrown away when in its worship of the real it threw away the secrets of childhood and innocence.

Amidst this chaos of hollowness and unrest Carter tried to live as befitted a man of keen thought and good heritage. With his dreams fading under the ridicule of the age he could not believe in anything, but the love of harmony kept him close to the ways of his race and station. He walked impassive through the cities of men, and sighed because no vista seemed fully real; because every flash of yellow sunlight on tall roofs and every glimpse of balustraded plazas in the first lamps of evening served only to remind him of dreams he had once known, and to make him homesick for ethereal lands he no longer knew how to find. Travel was only a mockery; and even the Great War stirred him but little, though he served from the first in the Foreign Legion of France. For a while he sought friends, but soon grew weary of the crudeness of their emotions, and the sameness and earthiness of their visions. He felt vaguely glad that all his relatives were distant and out of touch with him, for they would not have understood his mental life. That is, none but his grandfather and great-uncle Christopher could, and they were long dead.

Then he began once more the writing of books, which he had left off when dreams first failed him. But here, too, was there no satisfaction or fulfillment; for the touch of earth was upon his mind, and he could not think of lovely things as he had done of yore. Ironic humour dragged down all the twilight minarets he reared, and the earthy fear of improbability blasted all the delicate and amazing flowers in his faery gardens. The convention of assumed pity spilt mawkishness on his characters, while the myth of an important reality and significant human events and emotions debased all his high fantasy into thin-veiled allegory and cheap social satire. His new novels were successful as his old ones had never been; and because he knew how empty they must be to please an empty herd, he burned them and ceased his writing. They were very graceful novels, in which he urbanely laughed at the dreams he lightly sketched; but he saw that their sophistication had sapped all their life away.

It was after this that he cultivated deliberate illusion, and dabbled in the notions of the bizarre and the eccentric as an antidote for the commonplace. Most of these, however, soon showed their poverty and barrenness;

and he saw that the popular doctrines of occultism are as dry and inflexible as those of science, yet without even the slender palliative of truth to redeem them. Gross stupidity, falsehood, and muddled thinking are not dream; and form no escape from life to a mind trained above their own level. So Carter bought stranger books and sought out deeper and more terrible men of fantastic erudition; delving into arcana of consciousness that few have trod, and learning things about the secret pits of life, legend, and immemorial antiquity which disturbed him ever afterward. He decided to live on a rarer plane, and furnished his Boston home to suit his changing moods; one room for each, hung in appropriate colours, furnished with befitting books and objects, and provided with sources of the proper sensations of light, heat, sound, taste, and odour.

Once he heard of a man in the south who was shunned and feared for the blasphemous things he read in prehistoric books and clay tablets smuggled from India and Arabia. Him he visited, living with him and sharing his studies for seven years, till horror overtook them one midnight in an unknown and archaic graveyard, and only one emerged where two had entered. Then he went back to Arkham, the terrible witch-haunted old town of his forefathers in New England, and had experiences in the dark, amidst the hoary willows and tottering gambrel roofs, which made him seal forever certain pages in the diary of a wild-minded ancestor. But these horrors took him only to the edge of reality, and were not of the true dream country he had known in youth; so that at fifty he despaired of any rest or contentment in a world grown too busy for beauty and too shrewd for dreams.

Having perceived at last the hollowness and futility of real things, Carter spent his days in retirement, and in wistful disjointed memories of his dream-filled youth. He thought it rather silly that he bothered to keep on living at all, and got from a South American acquaintance a very curious liquid to take him to oblivion without suffering. Inertia and force of habit, however, caused him to defer action; and he lingered indecisively among thoughts of old times, taking down the strange hangings from his walls and refitting the house as it was in his early boyhood—purple panes, Victorian furniture, and all.

With the passage of time he became almost glad he had lingered, for his relics of youth and his cleavage from the world made life and sophistication seem very distant and unreal; so much so that a touch of magic and expectancy stole back into his nightly slumbers. For years those slumbers had known only such twisted reflections of every-day things as the commonest slumbers know, but now there returned a flicker of something stranger and wilder; something of vaguely awesome imminence which took the form of tensely clear pictures from his childhood days, and made him think of little inconsequential things he had long forgotten. He would often awake calling for his mother and grandfather, both in their graves a quarter of a century.

Then one night his grandfather reminded him of the key. The grey old scholar, as vivid as in life, spoke long and earnestly of their ancient line, and of the strange visions of the delicate and sensitive men who composed it. He spoke of the flame-eyed Crusader who learnt wild secrets of the Saracens that held him captive; and of the first Sir Randolph Carter who studied magic when Elizabeth was queen. He spoke, too, of that Edmund Carter who had just escaped hanging in the Salem witchcraft, and who had placed in an antique box a great silver key handed down from his ancestors. Before Carter awaked, the gentle visitant had told him where to find that box; that carved oak box of archaic wonder whose grotesque lid no hand had rised for two centuries.

In the dust and shadows of the great attic he found it, remote and forgotten at the back of a drawer in a tall chest. It was about a foot square, and its Gothic carvings were so fearful that he did not marvel no person since Edmund Carter had dared to open it. It gave forth no noise when shaken, but was mystic with the scent of unremembered spices. That it held a key was indeed only a dim legend, and Randolph Carter's father had never known such a box existed. It was bound in rusty iron, and no means was provided for working the formidable lock. Carter vaguely understood that he would find within it some key to the lost gate of dreams, but of where and how to use it his grandfather had told him nothing.

An old servant forced the carven lid, shaking as he did so at the hideous faces leering from the blackened wood, and at some unplaced familarity. Inside, wrapped in a discoloured parchment, was a huge key of tarnished silver covered with cryptical arabesques; but of any legible explanation there was none. The parchment was voluminous, and held only the strange hieroglyphs of an unknown tongue written with an antique reed. Carter recognized the characters as those he had seen on a certain papyrus scroll belonging to that terrible scholar of the South who had vanished one midnight in a nameless cemetery. The man had always shivered when he read this scroll, and Carter shivered now.

But he cleaned the key, and kept it by him nightly in its aromatic box of ancient oak. His dreams were meanwhile increasing in vividness, and though showing him none of the strange cities and incredible gardens of the old days, were assuming a definite cast whose purpose could not be mistaken. They were calling him back along the years, and with the mingled wills of all his fathers were pulling him toward some hidden and ancestral source. Then he knew he must go into the past and merge himself with old things, and day after day he thought of the hills to the north where haunted Arkham and the rushing Miskatonic and the lonely rustic homestead of his people lay.

In the brooding fire of autumn Carter took the old remembered way past graceful lines of rolling hill and stone-walled meadow, distant vale and hanging woodland, curving road and nestling farmstead, and the crystal windings of the Miskatonic, crossed here and there by rustic bridges of wood or stone. At one bend he saw the group of giant elms among which an ancestor had oddly vanished a century and a half before, and shuddered as the wind blew meaningly through them. Then there was the crumbling farmhouse of old Goody Fowler the witch, with its little evil windows and great roof sloping nearly to the ground on the north side. He speeded up his car as he passed it, and did not slacken till he had mounted the hill where his mother and her fathers before her were born, and where the old white house still looked proudly across the road at the breathlessly lovely panorama of rocky slope and verdant valley, with the distant spires of Kingsport on the horizon, and hints of the archaic, dream-laden sea in the farthest background.

Then came the steeper slope that held the old Carter place he had not seen in over forty years. Afternoon was far gone when he reached the foot, and at the bend half way up he paused to scan the outspread countryside golden and glorified in the slanting floods of magic poured out by a western sun. All the strangeness and expectancy of his recent dreams seemed present in this hushed and unearthly landscape, and he thought of the unknown solitudes of other planets as his eyes traced out the velvet and deserted lawns shining undulant between their tumbled walls, and clumps of faery forest setting off far lines of purple hills beyond hills, and the spectral wooded valley dipping down in shadow to dank hollows where trickling waters crooned and gurgled among swollen and distorted roots.

Something made him feel that motors did not belong in the realm he was seeking, so he left his car at the edge of the forest, and putting the great key in his coat pocket walked on up the hill. Woods now engulfed him utterly, though he knew the house was on a high knoll that cleared the trees except to the north. He wondered how it would look, for it had been left vacant and untended through his neglect since the death of his strange great-uncle Christopher thirty years before. In his boyhood he had revelled through long visits there, and had found weird marvels in the woods beyond the orchard.

Shadows thickened around him, for the night was near. Once a gap in the trees opened up to the right, so that he saw off across leagues of twilight meadow and spied the old Congregational steeple on Central Hill in

Kingsport; pink with the last flush of day, the panes of the little round windows blazing with reflected fire. Then, when he was in deep shadow again, he recalled with a start that the glimpse must have come from childish memory alone, since the old white church had long been torn down to make room for the Congregational Hospital. He had read of it with interest, for the paper had told about some strange burrows or passages found in the rocky hill beneath.

Through his puzzlement a voice piped, and he started again at its familiarity after long years. Old Benijah Corey had been his Uncle Christopher's hired man, and was aged even in those far-off times of his boyhood visits. Now he must be well over a hundred, but that piping voice could come from no one else. He could distinguish no words, yet the tone was haunting and unmistakable. To think that "old Benijy" should still be alive!

"Mister Randy! Mister Randy! Wharbe ye? D'ye want to skeer yer Aunt Marthy plumb to death? Hain't she tuld ye to keep nigh the place in the arternoon an' git back afur dark? Randy! Ran ... dee! ... He's the beatin'est boy fer runnin' off in the woods I ever see; haff the time a-settin' moonin' raound that snake-den in the upper timberlot! ... Hey yew, Ran ... dee!"

Randolph Carter stopped in the pitch darkness and rubbed his hand across his eyes. Something was queer. He had been somewhere he ought not to be; had strayed very far away to places where he had not belonged, and was now inexcusably late. He had not noticed the time on the Kingsport steeple, though he could easily have made it out with his pocket telescope; but he knew his lateness was something very strange and unprecedented.

He was not sure he had his little telescope with him, and put his hand in his blouse pocket to see. No, it was not there, but there was the big silver key he had found in a box somewhere. Uncle Chris had told him something odd once about an old unopened box with a key in it, but Aunt Martha had stopped the story abruptly, saying it was no kind of thing to tell a child whose head was already too full of queer fancies. He tried to recall just where he had found the key, but something seemed very confused. He guessed it was in the attic at home in Boston, and dimly remembered bribing Parks with half his week's allowance to help him open the box and keep quiet about it; but when he remembered this, the face of Parks came up very strangely, as if the wrinkles of long years had fallen upon the brisk little Cockney.

"Ran ... dee! Ran ... dee! Hi! Hi! Randy!"

A swaying lantern came around the black bend, and old Benijah pounced on the silent and bewildered form of the pilgrim.

"Durn ye, boy, so thar ye be! Ain't ye got a tongue in yer head, that ye can't answer a body? I ben callin' this haff hour, an' ye must a heerd me long ago! Dun't ye know yer Aunt Marthy's all a-fidget over yer bein' off arter dark? Wait till I tell yer Uncle Chris when he gits hum! Ye'd orta know these here woods ain't no fitten place to be traipsin' this hour! They's things abroad what dun't do nobody no good, as my gran'-sir' knowed afur me. Come, Mister Randy, or Hannah wunt keep supper no longer!"

So Randolph Carter was marched up the road where wondering stars glimmered through high autumn boughs. And dogs barked as the yellow light of small-paned windows shone out at the farther turn, and the

Pleiades twinkled across the open knoll where a great gambrel roof stood black against the dim west. Aunt Martha was in the doorway, and did not scold too hard when Benijah shoved the truant in. She knew Uncle Chris well enough to expect such things of the Carter blood. Randolph did not show his key, but ate his supper in silence and protested only when bedtime came. He sometimes dreamed better when awake, and he wanted to use that key.

In the morning Randolph was up early, and would have run off to the upper timber lot if Uncle Chris had not caught him and forced him into his chair by the breakfast table. He looked impatiently around the low-pitched room with the rag carpet and exposed beams and corner-posts, and smiled only when the orchard boughs scratched at the leaded panes of the rear window. The trees and the hills were close to him, and formed the gates of that timeless realm which was his true country.

Then, when he was free, he felt in his blouse pocket for the key; and being reassured, skipped off across the orchard to the rise beyond, where the wooded hill climbed again to heights above even the treeless knoll. The floor of the forest was mossy and mysterious, and great lichened rocks rose vaguely here and there in the dim light like Druid monoliths among the swollen and twisted trunks of a sacred grove. Once in his ascent Randolph crossed a rushing stream whose falls a little way off sang runic incantations to the lurking fauns and aegipans and dryads.

Then he came to the strange cave in the forest slope, the dreaded "snake-den" which country folk shunned, and away from which Benijah had warned him again and again. It was deep; far deeper than anyone but Randolph suspected, for the boy had found a fissure in the farthermost black corner that led to a loftier grotto beyond—a haunting sepulchral place whose granite walls held a curious illusion of conscious artifice. On this occasion he crawled in as usual, lighting his way with matches filched from the sitting-room match-safe, and edging through the final crevice with an eagerness hard to explain even to himself. He could not tell why he approached the farther wall so confidently, or why he instinctively drew forth the great silver key as he did so. But on he went, and when he danced back to the house that night he offered no excuses for his lateness, nor heeded in the least the reproofs he gained for ignoring the noontide dinner-horn altogether.

Now it is agreed by all the distant relatives of Randolph Carter that something occurred to heighten his imagination in his tenth year. His cousin, Ernest B. Aspinwall, Esq., of Chicago, is fully ten years his senior; and distinctly recalls a change in the boy after the autumn of 1883. Randolph had looked on scenes of fantasy that few others can ever have beheld, and stranger still were some of the qualities which he showed in relation to very mundane things. He seemed, in fine, to have picked up an odd gift of prophecy; and reacted unusually to things which, though at the time without meaning, were later found to justify the singular impressions. In subsequent decades as new inventions, new names, and new events appeared one by one in the book of history, people would now and then recall wonderingly how Carter had years before let fall some careless word of undoubted connection with what was then far in the future. He did not himself understand these words, or know why certain things made him feel certain emotions; but fancied that some unremembered dream must be responsible. It was as early as 1897 that he turned pale when some traveller mentioned the French town of Belloy-en-Santerre, and friends remembered it when he was almost mortally wounded there in 1916, while serving with the Foreign Legion in the Great War.

Carter's relatives talk much of these things because he has lately disappeared. His little old servant Parks, who for years bore patiently with his vagaries, last saw him on the morning he drove off alone in his car with a key he had recently found. Parks had helped him get the key from the old box containing it, and had felt strangely affected by the grotesque carvings on the box, and by some other odd quality he could not name. When Carter left, he had said he was going to visit his old ancestral country around Arkham.

Half way up Elm Mountain, on the way to the ruins of the old Carter place, they found his motor set carefully by the roadside; and in it was a box of fragrant wood with carvings that frightened the countrymen who stumbled on it. The box held only a queer parchment whose characters no linguist or palaeographer has been able to decipher or identify. Rain had long effaced any possible footprints, though Boston investigators had something to say about evidences of disturbances among the fallen timbers of the Carter place. It was, they averred, as though someone had groped about the ruins at no distant period. A common white handkerchief found among forest rocks on the hillside beyond cannot be identified as belonging to the missing man.

There is talk of apportioning Randolph Carter's estate among his heirs, but I shall stand firmly against this course because I do not believe he is dead. There are twists of time and space, of vision and reality, which only a dreamer can divine; and from what I know of Carter I think he had merely found a way to traverse these mazes. Whether or not he will ever come back, I cannot say. He wanted the lands of dream he had lost, and yearned for the days of his childhood. Then he found a key, and I somehow believe he was able to use it to strange advantage.

I shall ask him when I see him, for I expect to meet him shortly in a certain dream-city we both used to haunt. It is rumoured in Ulthar, beyond the River Skai, that a new king reigns on the opal throne of Ilek-Vad, that fabulous town of turrets atop the hollow cliffs of glass overlooking the twilight sea wherein the bearded and finny Gnorri build their singular labyrinths, and I believe I know how to interpret this rumour. Certainly, I look forward impatiently to the sight of that great silver key, for in its cryptical arabesques there may stand symbolised all the aims and mysteries of a blindly impersonal cosmos.

Through the Gates
of The Silver Key*

1

IN A vast room hung with strangely figured arras and carpeted with Boukhara rugs of impressive age and workmanship, four men were sitting around a document-strewn table. From the far corners, where odd tripods of wrought iron were now and then replenished by an incredibly aged Negro in somber livery, came the hypnotic fumes of olibanum; while in a deep niche on one side there ticked a curious, coffin-shaped clock whose dial bore baffling hieroglyphs and whose four hands did not move in consonance with any time system known on this planet. It was a singular and disturbing room, but well fitted to the business then at hand. For there, in the New Orleans home of this continent's greatest mystic, mathematician and orientalist, there was being settled at last the estate of a scarcely less great mystic, scholar, author and dreamer who had vanished from the face of the earth four years before.

Randolph Carter, who had all his life sought to escape from the tedium and limitations of waking reali-

* Written in collaboration with E. Hoffman Price.

ty in the beckoning vistas of dreams and fabled avenues of other dimensions, disappeared from the sight of man on the seventh of October, 1928, at the age of fifty-four. His career had been a strange and lonely one, and there were those who inferred from his curious novels many episodes more bizarre than any in his recorded history. His association with Harley Warren, the South Carolina mystic whose studies in the primal Naacal language of the Himalayan priests had led to such outrageous conclusions, had been close. Indeed, it was he who—one mist-mad, terrible night in an ancient graveyard—had seen Warren descend into a dank and nitrous vault, never to emerge. Carter lived in Boston, but it was from the wild, haunted hills behind hoary and witch-accursed Arkham that all his forebears had come. And it was amid these ancient, cryptically brooding hills that he had ultimately vanished.

His old servant, Parks—who died early in 1930— had spoken of the strangely aromatic and hideously carven box he had found in the attic, and of the undecipherable parchments and queerly figured silver key which that box had contained: matters of which Carter had also written to others. Carter, he said, had told him that this key had come down from his ancestors, and that it would help him to unlock the gates to his lost boyhood, and to strange dimensions and fantastic realms which he had hiterto visited only in vague, brief, and elusive dreams. Then one day Carter took the box and its contents and rode away in his car, never to return.

Later on, people found the car at the side of an old, grass-grown road in the hills behind crumbling Arkham—the hills where Carter's forebears had once dwelt, and where the ruined cellar of the great Carter homestead still gaped to the sky. It was in a grove of tall elms near by that another of the Carters had mysteriously vanished in 1781, and not far away was the half-rotted cottage where Goody Fowler, the witch, had brewed her ominous potions still earlier. The region had been settled in 1692 by fugitives from the witchcraft trials in Salem, and even now it bore a name for vaguely ominous things scarcely to be envisaged. Edmund Carter had fled from the shadow of Gallows Hill just in time, and the tales of his sorceries were many. Now, it seemed, his lone descendant had gone somewhere to join him!

In the car they found the hideously carved box of fragrant wood, and the parchment which no man could read. The silver key was gone—presumably with Carter. Further than that there was no certain clue. Detectives from Boston said that the fallen timbers of the old Carter place seemed oddly disturbed, and somebody found a handkerchief on the rock-ridged, sinisterly wooded slope behind the ruins near the dreaded cave called the Snake Den.

It was then that the country legends about the Snake Den gained a new vitality. Farmers whispered of the blasphemous uses to which old Edmund Carter the wizard had put that horrible grotto, and added later tales about the fondness which Randolph Carter himself had had for it when a boy. In Carter's boyhood the venerable gambrel-roofed homestead was still standing and tenanted by his great-uncle Christopher. He had visited there often, and had talked singularly about the Snake Den. People remembered what he had said about a deep fissure and an unknown inner cave beyond, and speculated on the change he had shown after spending one whole memorable day in the cavern when he was nine. That was in October, too—and ever after that he had seemed to have a uncanny knack at prophesying future events.

It had rained late in the night that Carter vanished, and no one was quite able to trace his footprints from the car. Inside the Snake Den all was amorphous liquid mud, owing to the copious seepage. Only the ignorant rustics whispered about the prints they thought they spied where the great elms overhang the road, and on the sinister hillside near the Snake Den, where the handkerchief was found. Who could pay attention to whispers that spoke of stubby little tracks like those which Randolph Carter's square-toed boots made when he was a small boy? It was as crazy a notion as that other whisper—that the tracks of old Benijah Corey's peculiar heelless boots had met the stubby little tracks in the road. Old Benijah had been the Carters' hired man when Randolph was young; but he had died thirty years ago.

It must have been these whispers—plus Carter's own statement to Parks and others that the queerly arabesqued silver key would help him unlock the gates of his lost boyhood—which caused a number of mystical students to declare that the missing man had actually doubled back on the trail of time and returned through forty-five years to that other October day in 1883 when he had stayed in the Snake Den as a small boy. When he came out that night, they argued, he had somehow made the whole trip to 1928 and back; for did he not thereafter know of things which were to happen later?

And yet he had never spoken of anything to happen after 1928.

One student—an elderly eccentric of Providence, Rhode Island, who had enjoyed a long and close correspondence with Carter—had a still more elaborate theory, and believed that Carter had not only returned to boyhood, but achieved a further liberation, roving at will through the prismatic vistas of boyhood dream. After a strange vision this man published a tale of Carter's vanishing in which he hinted that the lost one now reigned as king on the opal throne of Ilek-Vad, that fabulous town of turrets atop the hollow cliffs of glass overlooking the twilight sea wherein the bearded and finny Gnorri build their singular labyrinths.

It was this old man, Ward Phillips, who pleaded most loudly against the apportionment of Carter's estate to his heirs—all distant cousins—on the ground that he was still alive in another time-dimension and might well return some day. Against him was arrayed the legal talent of one of the cousins, Ernest K. Aspinwall of Chicago, a man ten years Carter's senior, but keen as a youth in forensic battles. For four years the contest had raged, but now the time for apportionment had come, and this vast, strange room in New Orleans was to be the scene of the arrangements.

It was the home of Carter's literary and financial executor—the distinguished Creole student of mysteries and Eastern antiquities, Etienne-Laurent de Marigny. Carter had met de Marigny during the war, when they both served in the French Foreign Legion, and had at once cleaved to him because of their similar tastes and outlook. When, on a memorable joint furlough, the learned young Creole had taken the wistful Boston dreamer to Bayonne, in the south of France, and had shown him certain terrible secrets in the nighted and immemorial crypts that burrow beneath that brooding, eon-weighted city, the friendship was forever sealed. Carter's will had named de Marigny as executor, and now that avid scholar was reluctantly presiding over the settlement of the estate. It was sad work for him, for like the old Rhode Islander he did not believe that Carter was dead. But what weight had the dreams of mystics against the harsh wisdom of the world?

Around the table in that strange room in the old French Quarter sat the men who claimed an interest in the proceedings. There had been the usual legal advertisements of the conference in papers wherever Carter's heirs were thought to live; yet only four now sat listening to the abnormal ticking of that coffin-shaped clock which told no earthly time, and to the bubbling of the courtyard fountain beyond half-curtained, fan-lighted windows. As the hours wore on, the faces of the four were half shrouded in the curling fumes from the tripods, which, piled recklessly with fuel, seemed to need less and less attention from the silently gliding and increasingly nervous old Negro.

There was Etienne de Marigny himself—slim, dark, handsome, mustached, and still young. Aspinwall, representing the heirs, was white-haired, apoplectic-faced, side-whiskered, and portly. Phillips, the Providence mystic, was lean, grey, long-nosed, clean-shaven, and stoop-shouldered. The fourth man was non-committal in age—lean, with a dark, bearded, singularly immobile face of very regular contour, bound with the turban of a high-caste Brahman and having night-black, burning, almost irisless eyes which seemed to gaze out from a vast distance behind the features. He had announced himself as the Swami Chandraputra, an adept from Benares, with important information to give; and both de Marigny and Phillips—who had corresponded with him—had been quick to recognize the genuineness of his mystical pretensions. His speech had an oddly forced, hollow, metallic quality, as if the use of English taxed his vocal apparatus; yet his language was as easy, correct and idomatic as any native Anglo-Saxon's. In general attire he was the normal European civilian, but his loose clothes sat peculiarly badly on him, while his bushy black beard, Eastern turban, and large, white mittens gave him an air of exotic eccentricity.

De Marigny, fingering the parchment found in Carter's car, was speaking.

"No, I have not been able to make anything of the parchment. Mr. Phillips, here, also gives it up. Colonel Churchward declares it is not Naacal, and it looks nothing at all like the hieroglyphics on that Easter Island war-club. The carvings on that box, though, do strangely suggest Easter Island images. The nearest thing I can recall to these parchment characters—notice how all the letters seem to hang down from horizontal word-bars—is the writing in a book poor Harley Warren once had. It came from India while Carter and I were visiting him in 1919, and he never would tell us anything about it—said it would be better if we didn't know, and hinted that it might have come originally from some place other than the Earth. He took it with him in December, when he went down into the vault in that old graveyard—but neither he nor the book ever came to the surface again. Some time ago I sent our friend here—the Swami Chandraputra—a memory-sketch of some of those letters, and also a photostatic copy of the Carter parchment. He believes he may be able to shed light on them after certain references and consultations.

"But the key—Carter sent me a photograph of that. Its curious arabesques were not letters, but seem to have belonged to the same culture-tradition as the parchment. Carter always spoke of being on the point of solving the mystery, though he never gave details. Once he grew almost poetic about the whole business. That antique silver key, he said, would unlock the successive doors that bar our free march down the mighty corridors of space and time to the very Border which no man has crossed since Shaddad with his terrific genius built and concealed in the sands of Arabia Petræa the prodigious domes and uncounted minarets of thousand-pillared Irem. Half-starved dervishes—wrote Carter—and thirst-crazed nomads have returned to tell of that monumental portal, and of the hand that is sculptured above the keystone of the arch, but no man has passed and retraced his steps to say that his footprints on the garnet-strewn sands within bear witness to his visit. The key, he surmised, was that for which the cyclopean sculptured hand vainly grasps.

"Why Carter didn't take the parchment as well as the key, we can not say. Perhaps he forgot it—or perhaps he forbore to take it through recollection of one who had taken a book of like characters into a vault and never returned. Or perhaps it was really immaterial to what he wished to do."

As de Marigny paused, old Mr. Phillips spoke a harsh, shrill voice.

"We can know of Randolph Carter's wandering only what we dream. I have been to many strange places in dreams, and have heard many strange and significant things in Ulthar, beyond the River Skai. It does not appear that the parchment was needed, for certainly Carter reentered the world of his boyhood dreams, and is now a king in Ilek-Vad."

Mr. Aspinwall grew doubly apoplectic-looking as he sputtered: "Can't somebody shut the old fool up? We've had enough of these moonings. The problem is to divide the property, and it's about time we got to it."

For the first time Swami Chandraputra spoke in his queerly alien voice.

"Gentlemen, there is more to this matter than you think. Mr. Aspinwall does not do well to laugh at the evidence of dreams. Mr. Phillips has taken an incomplete view—perhaps because he has not dreamed enough. I, myself, have done much dreaming. We in India have always done that, just as all the Carters seem to have done it. You, Mr. Aspinwall, as a maternal cousin, are naturally not a Carter. My own dreams, and certain other sources of information, have told me a great deal which you still find obscure. For example, Randolph Carter forgot that parchment which he couldn't decipher—yet it would have been well for him had he remembered to take it. You see, I have really learned pretty much what happened to Carter after he left his car with the silver key at sunset on that seventh of October, four years ago."

Aspinwall audibly sneered, but the others sat up with heightened interest. The smoke from the tripods increased, and the crazy ticking of that coffin-shaped clock seemed to fall into bizarre patterns like the dots and dashes of some alien and insoluble telegraph message from outer space. The Hindoo leaned back, half closed his eyes, and continued in that oddly laboured yet idiomatic speech, while before his audience there began to float a picture of what had happened to Randolph Carter.

2

The hills beyond Arkham are full of a strange magic—something, perhaps, which the old wizard Edmund Carter called down from the stars and up from the crypts of nether earth when he fled there from Salem in 1692. As soon as Randolph Carter was back among them he knew that he was close to one of the gates which a few audacious, abhorred and alien-souled men have blasted through titan walls betwixt the world and the outside absolute. Here, he felt, and on this day of the year, he could carry out with success the message he had deciphered months before from the arabesques of that tarnished and incredibly ancient silver key. He knew now how it must be rotated, and how it must be held up to the setting sun, and what syllables of ceremony must be intoned into the void at the ninth and last turning. In a spot as close to a dark polarity and induced gate as this, it could not fail in its primary functions. Certainly, he would rest that night in the lost boyhood for which he had never ceased to mourn.

He got out of the car with the key in his pocket, walking up-hill deeper and deeper into the shadowy core of that brooding, haunted countryside of winding road, vine-grown stone wall, black woodland, gnarled, neglected orchard, gaping-windowed, deserted farmhouse, and nameless ruin. At the sunset hour, when the distant spires of Kingsport gleamed in the ruddy blaze, he took out the key and made the needed turnings and intonations. Only later did he realise how soon the ritual had taken effect.

Then in the deepening twilight he had heard a voice out of the past: Old Benijah Corey, his great-uncle's hired man. Had not old Benijah been dead for thirty years? Thirty years before *when*. What was time? Where had he been? Why was it strange that Benijah should be calling him on this seventh of October 1883? Was he not out later than Aunt Martha had told him to stay? What was this key in his blouse pocket, where his little telescope—given him by his father on his ninth birthday, two months before—ought to be? Had he found it in the attic at home? Would it unlock the mystic pylon which his sharp eye had traced amidst the jagged rocks at the back of that inner cave behind the Snake Den on the hill? That was the place they always coupled with old Edmund Carter the wizard. People wouldn't go there, and nobody but him had ever noticed or squirmed through the root-choked fissure to that great black inner chamber with the pylon. Whose hands had carved that hint of a pylon out of the living rock? Old Wizard Edmund's—or *others* that he had conjured up and commanded?

That evening little Randolph ate supper with Uncle Chris and Aunt Martha in the old gambrel-roofed farmhouse.

Next morning he was up early and out through the twisted-boughed apple orchard to the upper timber lot where the mouth of the Snake Den lurked black and forbidding amongst grotesque, overnourished oaks. A nameless expectancy was upon him, and he did not even notice the loss of his handkerchief as he fumbled in his blouse pocket to see if the queer silver key was safe. He crawled through the dark orifice with tense, adventurous assurance, lighting his way with matches taken from the sitting-room. In another moment he had wriggled through the root-choked fissure at the farther end, and was in the vast, unknown inner grotto whose ultimate rock wall seemed half like a monstrous and consciously shapen pylon. Before that dank, dripping wall he stood silent and awestruck, lighting one match after another as he gazed. Was that stony bulge above the keystone of the imagined arch really a gigantic sculptured hand? Then he drew forth the silver key, and made motions and intonations whose source he could only dimly remember. Was anything forgotten? He knew only that he wished to cross the barrier to the untrammelled land of his dreams and the gulfs where all dimensions dissolved in the absolute.

3

What happened then is scarcely to be described in words. It is full of those paradoxes, contradictions and anomalies which have no place in waking life, but which fill our more fantastic dreams and are taken as matters of course till we return to our narrow, rigid, objective world of limited causation and tri-dimensional logic. As the Hindoo continued his tale, he had difficul-

ty in avoiding what seemed—even more than the notion of a man transferred through the years to boyhood—
an air of trivial, puerile extravagance. Mr. Aspinwall, in
disgust, gave an apoplectic snort and virtually stopped
listening.

For the rite of the silver key, as practised by Randolph
Carter in that black, haunted cave within a cave, did
not prove unavailing. From the first gesture and syllable
an aura of strange, awesome mutation was apparent—a
sense of incalculable disturbance and confusion in time
and space, yet one which held no hint of what we
recognize as motion and duration. Imperceptibly, such
things as age and location ceased to have any significance whatever. The day before, Randolph Carter had
miraculously leaped a gulf of years. Now there was no
distinction between boy and man. There was only the
entity Randolph Carter, with a certain store of images
which had lost all connection with terrestrial scenes and
circumstances of acquisition. A moment before, there
had been an inner cave with vague suggestions of a
monstrous arch and gigantic sculptured hand on the
farther wall. Now there was neither cave nor absence
of cave; neither wall nor absence of wall. There was
only a flux of impressions not so much visual as cere-
bral, amidst which the entity that was Randolph Carter
experienced perceptions or registrations of all that his
mind revolved on, yet without any clear consciousness
of the way in which he received them.

By the time the rite was over, Carter knew that he
was in no region whose place could be told by Earth's
geographers, and in no age whose date history could fix;
for the nature of what was happening was not wholly
unfamiliar to him. There were hints of it in the crypti-

cal Pnakotic fragments, and a whole chapter in the forbidden *Necronomicon* of the mad Arab, Abdul Alhazred, had taken on significance when he had deciphered the designs graven on the silver key. A gate had been unlocked—not, indeed, the Ultimate Gate, but one leading from Earth and time to that extension of Earth which is outside time, and from which in turn the Ultimate Gate leads fearsomely and perilously to the Last Void which is outside all earths, all universes, and all matter.

There would be a Guide—and a very terrible one; a Guide who had been an entity of Earth millions of years before, when man was undreamed of, and when forgotten shapes moved on a steaming planet building strange cities among whose last, crumbling ruins the first mammals were to play. Carter remembered what the monstrous *Necronomicon* had vaguely and disconcertingly adumbrated concerning that Guide:

"And while there are those," the mad Arab had written, *"who have dared to seek glimpses beyond the Veil, and to accept HIM as guide, they would have been more prudent had they avoided commerce with HIM; for it is written in the Book of Thoth how terrific is the price of a single glimpse. Nor may those who pass ever return, for in the vastnesses transcending our world are shapes of darkness that seize and bind. The Affair that shambleth about in the night, the evil that defieth the Elder Sign, the Herd that stand watch at the secret portal each tomb is known to have and that thrive on that which groweth out of the tenants thereof:—all these Blacknesses are lesser than HE WHO guardeth the Gateway: HE WHO will guide the rash one beyond all the worlds into the Abyss of unnamable*

devourers. For He is 'UMR AT-TAWIL, *the Most Ancient One, which the scribe rendereth as THE PROLONGED OF LIFE."*

Memory and imagination shaped dim half-pictures with uncertain outlines amidst the seething chaos, but Carter knew that they were of memory and imagination only. Yet he felt that it was not chance which built these things in his consciousness, but rather some vast reality, ineffable and undimensioned, which surrounded him and strove to translate itself into the only symbols he was capable of grasping. For no mind of Earth may grasp the extensions of shape which interweave in the oblique gulfs outside time and the dimensions we know.

There floated before Carter a cloudy pageantry of shapes and scenes which he somehow linked with Earth's primal, eon-forgotten past. Monstrous living things moved deliberately through vistas of fantastic handiwork that no sane dream ever held, and landscapes bore incredible vegetation and cliffs and mountains and masonry of no human pattern. There were cities under the sea, and denizens thereof; and towers in great deserts where globes and cylinders and nameless winged entities shot off into space, or hurtled down out of space. All this Carter grasped, though the images bore no fixed relation to one another or to him. He himself had no stable form or position, but only such shifting hints of form and position as his whirling fancy supplied.

He had wished to find the enchanted regions of his boyhood dreams, where galleys sail up the river Oukranos past the gilded spires of Thran, and elephant caravans tramp through perfumed jungles in Kled, beyond forgotten palaces with veined ivory columns that sleep lovely and unbroken under the moon. Now, intoxicated with wider visions, he scarcely knew what he sought. Thoughts of infinite and blasphemous daring rose in his mind, and he knew he would face the dreaded Guide without fear, asking monstrous and terrible things of him.

All at once the pageant of impressions seemed to achieve a vague kind of stabilization. There were great masses of towering stone, carven into alien and incomprehensible designs and disposed according to the laws of some unknown, inverse geometry. Light filtered down from a sky of no assignable colour in baffling, contradictory directions, and played almost sentiently over what seemed to be a curved line of gigantic hieroglyphed pedestals more hexagonal than otherwise, and surmounted by cloaked, ill-defined shapes.

There was another shape, too, which occupied no pedestal, but which seemed to glide or float over the cloudy, floor-like lower level. It was not exactly permanent in outline, but held transient suggestions of something remotely preceding or paralleling the human form, though half as large again as an ordinary man. It seemed to be heavily cloaked, like the shapes on the pedestals, with some neutral-coloured fabric; and Carter could not detect any eye-holes through which it might gaze. Probably it did not need to gaze, for it seemed to belong to an order of beings far outside the merely physical in organization and faculties.

A moment later Carter knew that this was so, for the Shape had spoken to his mind without sound or language. And though the name it uttered was a dreaded and terrible one, Randolph Carter did not flinch in fear.

Instead, he spoke back, equally without sound or language, and made those obeisances which the hideous *Necronomicon* had taught him to make. For this shape was nothing less than that which all the world has feared since Lomar rose out of the sea, and the Children of the Fire Mist came to Earth to teach the Elder Lore to man. It was indeed the frightful Guide and Guardian of the Gate—'UMR AT-TAWIL, the ancient one, which the scribe rendereth the PROLONGED OF LIFE.

The Guide knew, as he knew all things, of Carter's quest and coming, and that this seeker of dreams and secrets stood before him unafraid. There was no horror or malignity in what he radiated, and Carter wondered for a moment whether the mad Arab's terrific blasphemous hints came from envy and a baffled wish to do what was now about to be done. Or perhaps the Guide reserved his horror and malignity for those who feared. As the radiations continued, Carter eventually interpreted them in the form of words.

"I am indeed that Most Ancient One," said the Guide, "of whom you know. We have awaited you—the Ancient Ones and I. You are welcome, even though long delayed. You have the key, and have unlocked the First Gate. Now the Ultimate Gate is ready for your trial. If you fear, you need not advance. You may still go back unharmed, the way you came. But if you chose to advance——"

The pause was ominous, but the radiations continued to be friendly. Carter hesitated not a moment, for a burning curiosity drove him on.

"I will advance," he radiated back, "and I accept you as my Guide."

At this reply the Guide seemed to make a sign by

certain motions of his robe which may or may not have involved the lifting of an arm or some homologous member. A second sign followed, and from his well-learned lore Carter knew that he was at last very close to the Ultimate Gate. The light now changed to another inexplicable colour, and the shapes on the quasi-hexagonal pedestals became more clearly defined. As they sat more erect, their outlines became more like those of men, though Carter knew that they could not be men. Upon their cloaked heads there now seemed to rest tall, uncertainly coloured miters, strangely suggestive of those on certain nameless figures chiselled by a forgotten sculptor along the living cliffs of a high, forbidden mountain in Tartary; while grasped in certain folds of their swathings were long sceptres whose carven heads bodied forth a grotesque and archaic mystery.

Carter guessed what they were and whence they came, and Whom they served; and guessed, too, the price of their service. But he was still content, for at one mighty venture he was to learn all. Damnation, he reflected, is but a word bandied about by those whose blindness leads them to condemn all who can see, even with a single eye. He wondered at the vast conceit of those who had babbled of the *malignant* Ancient Ones, as if They could pause from their everlasting dreams to wreack a wrath on mankind. As well, he thought, might a mammoth pause to visit frantic vengeance on an angleworm. Now the whole assemblage on the vaguely hexagonal pillars was greeting him with a gesture of those oddly carven sceptres and radiating a message which he understood:

"We salute you, Most Ancient One, and you, Randolph Carter, whose daring has made you one of us."

Carter saw now that one of the pedestals was vacant, and a gesture of the Most Ancient One told him it was reserved for him. He saw also another pedestal, taller than the rest, and at the centre of the oddly curved line—neither semicircle nor ellipse, parabola nor hyperbola—which they formed. This, he guessed, was the Guide's own throne. Moving and rising in a manner hardly definable, Carter took his seat; and as he did so he saw that the Guide had seated himself.

Gradually and mistily it became apparent that the Most Ancient One was holding something—some object clutched in the outflung folds of his robe as if for the sight, or what answered for sight, of the cloaked Companions. It was a large sphere, or apparent sphere, of some obscurely iridescent metal, and as the Guide put it forward a low, pervasive half-impression of *sound* began to rise and fall in intervals which seemed to be rhythmic even though they followed no rhythm of Earth. There was a suggestion of chanting—or what human imagination might interpret as chanting. Presently the quasi-sphere began to grow luminous, and as it gleamed up into a cold, pulsating light of unassignable colour, Carter saw that its flickerings conformed to the alien rhythm of the chant. Then all the mitred, sceptre-bearing Shapes on the pedestals commenced a slight, curious swaying in the same inexplicable rhythm, while nimbuses of unclassifiable light—resembling that of the quasi-sphere—played around their shrouded heads.

The Hindoo paused in his tale and looked curiously at the tall, coffin-shaped clock with the four hands and hieroglyphed dial, whose crazy ticking followed no known rhythm of Earth.

"You, Mr. de Marigny," he suddenly said to his learned host, "do not need to be told the particularly alien rhythm to which those cowled Shapes on the hexagonal pillars chanted and nodded. You are the only one else—in America—who has had a taste of the Outer Extension. That clock—I suppose it was sent to you by the Yogi poor Harley Warren used to talk about—the seer who said that he alone of living men had been to Yian-Ho, the hidden legacy of eon-old Leng, and had borne certain things away from that dreadful and forbidden city. I wonder how many of its subtler properties you know? If my dreams and readings be correct, it was made by those who knew much of the First Gateway. But let me go on with my tale."

At last, continued the Swami, the swaying and the suggestion of chanting ceased, the lambent nimbuses around the now drooping and motionless heads faded, while the cloaked shapes slumped curiously on their pedestals. The quasi-sphere, however, continued to pulsate with inexplicable light. Carter felt that the Ancient Ones were sleeping as they had been when he first saw them, and he wondered out of what cosmic dreams his coming had aroused them. Slowly there filtered into his mind the truth that this strange chanting ritual had been one of instruction, and that the Companions had been chanted by the Most Ancient One into a new and peculiar kind of sleep in order that their dreams might open the Ultimate Gate to which the silver key was a passport. He knew that in the profundity of this deep sleep they were contemplating unplumbed vastnesses of utter and absolute outsideness, and that they were to accomplish that which his presence had demanded.

The Guide did not share this sleep, but seemed still to be giving instructions in some subtle, soundless way. Evidently he was implanting images of those things which he wished the Companions to dream: and Carter knew that as each of the Ancient Ones pictured the prescribed thought, there would be born the nucleus of a manifestation visible to his earthly eyes. When the dreams of all the Shapes had achieved a oneness, that manifestation would occur, and everything he required be materialized, through concentration. He had seen such things on Earth—in India, where the combined, projected will of a circle of adepts can make a thought take tangible substance, and in hoary Atlaanât, of which few even dare speak.

Just what the Ultimate Gate was, and how it was to be passed, Carter could not be certain; but a feeling of tense expectancy surged over him. He was conscious of having a kind of body, and of holding the fateful silver key in his hand. The masses of towering stone opposite him seemed to possess the evenness of a wall, toward the centre of which his eyes were irresistibly drawn. And then suddenly he felt the mental currents of the Most Ancient One cease to flow forth.

For the first time Carter realized how terrific utter silence, mental and physical, may be. The earlier moments had never failed to contain some perceptible rhythm, if only the faint, cryptical pulse of the Earth's dimensional extension, but now the hush of the abyss seemed to fall upon everything. Despite his intimations of body, he had no audible breath, and the glow of 'Umr at-Tawil's quasi-sphere had grown petrifiedly fixed and unpulsating. A potent nimbus, brighter than those which had played round the heads of the Shapes, blazed frozenly over the shrouded skull of the terrible Guide.

A dizziness assailed Carter, and his sense of lost orientation waxed a thousandfold. The strange lights seemed to hold the quality of the most impenetrable blacknesses heaped upon blacknesses while about the Ancient Ones, so close on their pseudo-hexagonal thrones, there hovered an air of the most stupefying remoteness. Then he felt himself wafted into immeasurable depths, with waves of perfumed warmth lapping against his face. It was as if he floated in a torrid, rose-tinctured sea; a sea of drugged wine whose waves broke foaming against shores of brazen fire. A great fear clutched him as he half saw that vast expanse of surging sea lapping against its far-off coast. But the moment of silence was broken—the surgings were speaking to him in a language that was not of physical sound or articulate words.

"The Man of Truth is beyond good and evil," intoned a voice that was not a voice. *"The Man of Truth has ridden to All-Is-One. The Man of Truth has learned that Illusion is the One Reality, and that Substance is the Great Impostor."*

And now, in that rise of masonry to which his eyes had been so irresistibly drawn, there appeared the outline of a titanic arch not unlike that which he thought he had glimpsed so long ago in that cave within a cave, on the far, unreal surface of the three-dimensioned Earth. He realized that he had been using the silver key— moving it in accord with an unlearned and instinctive ritual closely akin to that which had opened the Inner Gate. That rose-drunken sea which lapped his cheeks was, he realized, no more or less than the adamantine mass of the solid wall yielding before his spell, and the vortex of thought with which the Ancient Ones had aided his spell. Still guided by instinct and blind determination, he floated forward—and through the Ultimate Gate.

4

Randolph Carter's advance through the cyclopean bulk of masonry was like a dizzy precipitation through the measureless gulfs between the stars. From a great distance he felt triumphant, godlike surges of deadly sweetness, and after that the rustling of great wings, and impressions of sound like the chirpings and murmurings of objects unknown on Earth or in the solar system. Glancing backward, he saw not one gate alone but a multiplicity of gates, at some of which clamoured Forms he strove not to remember.

And then, suddenly, he felt a greater terror than that which any of the Forms could give—a terror from which he could not flee because it was connected with himself. Even the First Gateway had taken something of stability from him, leaving him uncertain about his bodily form and about his relationship to the mistily defined objects around him, but it had not disturbed his sense of unity. He had still been Randolph Carter, a fixed point in the dimensional seething. Now, beyond the Ultimate Gateway, he realized in a moment of consuming fright that he was not one person, but many persons.

He was in many places at the same time. On Earth,

on October 7, 1883, a little boy named Randolph Carter was leaving the Snake Den in the hushed evening light and running down the rocky slope, and through the twisted-boughed orchard toward his Uncle Christopher's house in the hills beyond Arkham; yet at that same moment, which was also somehow in the earthly year of 1928, a vague shadow not less Randolph Carter was sitting on a pedestal among the Ancient Ones in Earth's transdimensional extension. Here, too, was a third Randolph Carter, in the unknown and formless cosmic abyss beyond the Ultimate Gate. And elsewhere, in a chaos of scenes whose infinite multiplicity and monstrous diversity brought him close to the brink of madness, were a limitless confusion of beings which he knew were as much himself as the local manifestation now beyond the Ultimate Gate.

There were Carters in settings belonging to every known and suspected age of Earth's history, and to remoter ages of earthly entity transcending knowledge, suspicion, and credibility; Carters of forms both human and non-human, vertebrate and invertebrate, conscious and mindless, animal and vegetable. And more, there were Carters having nothing in common with earthly life, but moving outrageously amidst backgrounds of other planets and systems and galaxies and cosmic continua; spores of eternal life drifting from world to world, universe to universe, yet all equally himself. Some of the glimpses recalled dreams—both faint and vivid, single and persistent—which he had had through the long years since he first began to dream; and a few possessed a haunting, fascinating and almost horrible familiarity which no earthly logic could explain.

Faced with this realization, Randolph Carter reeled in

the clutch of supreme horror—horror such as had not been hinted even at the climax of that hideous night when two had ventured into an ancient and abhorred necropolis under a waning moon and only one had emerged. No death, no doom, no anguish can arouse the surpassing despair which flows from a loss of *identity*. Merging with nothingness is peaceful oblivion; but to be aware of existence and yet to know that one is no longer a definite being distinguished from other beings— that one no longer has a *self*—that is the nameless summit of agony and dread.

He knew that there had been a Randolph Carter of Boston, yet could not be sure whether he—the fragment or facet of an entity beyond the Ultimate Gate— had been that one or some other. His *self* had been annihilated; and yet he—if indeed there could, in view of that utter nullity of individual existence, be such a thing as *he*—was equally aware of being in some inconceivable way a legion of selves. It was as though his body had been suddenly transformed into one of those many-limbed and many-headed effigies sculptured in Indian temples, and he contemplated the aggregation in a bewildered attempt to discern which was the original and which the additions—if indeed (supremely monstrous thought!) there *were* any original as distinguished from other embodiments.

Then, in the midst of these devastating reflections, Carter's beyond-the-gate fragment was hurled from what had seemed the nadir of horror to black, clutching pits of a horror still more profound. This time it was largely external—a force of personality which at once confronted and surrounded and pervaded him, and which in addition to its local presence, seemed also to be a part of himself, and likewise to be co-existent with all time and conterminous with all space. There was no visual image, yet the sense of entity and the awful concept of combined localism and identity and infinity lent a paralysing terror beyond anything which any Carter-fragment had hitherto deemed capable of existing.

In the face of that awful wonder, the quasi-Carter forgot the horror of destroyed individuality. It was an All-in-One and One-in-All of limitless being and self—not merely a thing of one space-time continuum, but allied to the ultimate animating essence of existence's whole unbounded sweep—the last, utter sweep which has no confines and which outreaches fancy and mathematics alike. It was perhaps that which certain secret cults of Earth had whispered of as *Yog-Sothoth,* and which has been a deity under other names; that which the crustaceans of Yuggoth worship as the Beyond-One, and which the vaporous brains of the spiral nebulæ know by an untranslatable sign—yet in a flash the Carter-facet realized how slight and fractional all these conceptions are.

And now the Being was addressing the Carter-facet in prodigious waves that smote and burned and thundered—a concentration of energy that blasted its recipient with well-nigh unendurable violence, and that paralleled in an unearthly rhythm the curious swaying of the Ancient Ones, and the flickering of the monstrous lights, in that baffling region beyond the First Gate. It was as though suns and worlds and universes had converged upon one point whose very position in space they had conspired to annihilate with an impact of resistless fury. But amidst the greater terror one lesser terror was diminished; for the searing waves appeared somehow to isolate the Beyond-the-Gate Carter from his infinity of duplicates—to restore, as it were, a certain amount of the illusion of identity. After a time the hearer began to translate the waves into speech-forms known to him, and his sense of horror and oppression waned. Fright became pure awe, and what had seemed blasphemously abnormal seemed now only ineffably majestic.

"Randolph Carter," it seemed to say, "my manifestations on your planet's extension, the Ancient Ones, have sent you as one who would lately have returned to small lands of dream which he had lost, yet who with greater freedom has risen to greater and nobler desires and curiosities. You wished to sail up golden Oukranos, to search out forgotten ivory cities in orchid-heavy Kled, and to reign on the opal throne of Ilek-Vad, whose fabulous towers and numberless domes rise mighty toward a single red star in a firmament alien to your Earth and to all matter. Now, with the passing of two Gates, you wish loftier things. You would not flee like a child from a scene disliked to a dream beloved, but would plunge like a man into that last and inmost of secrets which lies behind all scenes and dreams.

"What you wish, I have found good; and I am ready to grant that which I have granted eleven times only to beings of your planet—five times only to those you call men, or those resembling them. I am ready to show you the Ultimate Mystery, to look on which is to blast a feeble spirit. Yet before you gaze full at that last and first of secrets you may still wield a free choice, and return if you will through the two Gates with the Veil still unrent before your eyes."

5

A sudden shutting-off of the waves left Carter in a chilling and awesome silence full of the spirit of desolation. On every hand pressed the illimitable vastness of the void; yet the seeker knew that the Being was still there. After a moment he thought of words whose mental substance he flung into the abyss: "I accept. I will not retreat."

The waves surged forth again, and Carter knew that the Being had heard. And now there poured from that limitless Mind a flood of knowledge and explanation which opened new vistas to the seeker, and prepared him for such a grasp of the cosmos as he had never hoped to possess. He was told how childish and limited is the notion of a tri-dimensional world, and what an infinity of directions there are besides the known directions of up-down, forward-backward, right-left. He was shown the smallness and tinsel emptiness of the little Earth gods, with their petty, human interests and connections—their hatreds, rages, loves and vanities; their craving for praise and sacrifice, and their demands for faiths contrary to reason and nature.

While most of the impressions translated themselves to Carter as words, there were others to which other senses gave interpretation. Perhaps with eyes and perhaps with imagination he perceived that he was in a region of dimensions beyond those conceivable to the eye and brain of man. He saw now, in the brooding shadows of that which had been first a vortex of power and then an illimitable void, a sweep of creation that dizzied his senses. From some inconceivable vantage-point he looked upon prodigious forms whose multiple extensions transcended any conception of being, size and boundaries which his mind had hitherto been able to hold, despite a lifetime of cryptical study. He began to understand dimly why there could exist at the same time the little boy Randolph Carter in the Arkham farm-house in 1883, the misty form on the vaguely hexagonal pillar beyond the First Gate, the fragment now facing the Presence in the limitless abyss, and all the other Carters his fancy or perception envisaged.

Then the waves increased in strength and sought to improve his understanding, reconciling him to the multiform entity of which his present fragment was an infinitesimal part. They told him that every figure of space is but the result of the intersection by a plane of some corresponding figure of one more dimension—as a square is cut from a cube, or a circle from a sphere. The cube and sphere, of three dimensions, are thus cut from corresponding forms of four dimensions, which men know only through guesses and dreams; and these in turn are cut from forms of five dimensions, and so on up to the dizzy and reachless heights of archetypal infinity. The world of men and of the gods of men is merely an infinitesimal phase of an infinitesimal thing—the three-dimensional phase of that small wholeness reached by the First Gate, where 'Umr at-Tawil dictates dreams to the Ancient Ones. Though men hail it as reality, and band thoughts of its many-dimensioned original as unreality, it is in truth the very opposite. That which we call substance and reality is shadow and illusion, and that which we call shadow and illusion is substance and reality.

Time, the waves went on, is motionless, and without beginning or end. That it has motion and is the cause of change is an illusion. Indeed, it is itself really an illusion, for except to the narrow sight of beings in limited dimensions there are no such things as past, present and future. Men think of time only because of what they call change, yet that too is illusion. All that was, and is, and is to be, exists simultaneously.

These revelations came with a godlike solemnity which left Carter unable to doubt. Even though they lay almost beyond his comprehension, he felt that they must be true in the light of that final cosmic reality which belies all local perspectives and narrow partial views; and he was familiar enough with profound speculations to be free from the bondage of local and partial conceptions. Had his whole quest not been based upon a faith in the unreality of the local and partial?

After an impressive pause the waves continued, saying that what the denizens of few-dimensioned zones call change is merely a function of their consciousness, which views the external world from various cosmic angles. As the Shapes produced by the cutting of a cone seem to vary with the angles of cutting—being circle, ellipse, parabola or hyperbola according to that angle, yet without any change in the cone itself—so do the local aspects of an unchanged and endless reality seem to change with the cosmic angle of regarding. To this variety of angles of consciousness the feeble beings of the inner worlds are slaves, since with rare exceptions they can not learn to control them. Only a few students of forbidden things have gained inklings of this control, and have thereby conquered time and change. But the entities outside the Gates command all angles, and view the myriad parts of the cosmos in terms of fragmentary change-involving perspective, or of the changeless totality beyond perspective, in accordance with their will.

As the waves paused again, Carter began to comprehend, vaguely and terrifiedly, the ultimate background of that riddle of lost individuality which had at first so horrified him. His intuition pieced together the fragments of revelation, and brought him closer and closer to a grasp of the secret. He understood that much of the frightful revelation would have come upon him— splitting up his ego amongst myriads of earthly counterparts—inside the First Gate, had not the magic of 'Umr at-Tawil kept it from him in order that he might use the silver key with precision for the Ultimate Gate's opening. Anxious for clearer knowledge, he sent out waves of thought, asking more of the exact relationship between his various facets—the fragment now beyond the Ultimate Gate, the fragment still on the quasi-hexogonal pedestal beyond the First Gate, the boy of 1883, the man of 1928, the various ancestral beings who had formed his heritage and the bulwark of his ego, and the nameless denizens of the other eons and other worlds which that first hideous flash of ultimate perception had identified with him. Slowly the waves of the Being surged out in reply, trying to make plain what was almost beyond the reach of an earthly mind.

All descended lines of beings of the finite dimensions, continued the waves, and all stages of growth in each one of these beings, are merely manifestations of one archetypal and eternal being in the space outside dimensions. Each local being—son, father, grandfather, and so on—and each stage of individual being—infant, child, boy, man—is merely one of the infinite phases of that same archetypal and eternal being, caused by a variation in the angle of the consciousness-plane which cuts it. Randolph Carter at all ages; Randolph Carter and all his ancestors, both human and pre-human, terrestrial and pre-terrestrial; all these were only phases of one ultimate, eternal "Carter" outside space and time—phantom projections differentiated only by the angle at which the plane of consciousness happened to cut the eternal archetype in each case.

A slight change of angle could turn the student of today into the child of yesterday; could turn Randolph Carter into that wizard, Edmund Carter who fled from Salem to the hills behind Arkham in 1692, or that Pickman Carter who in the year 2169 would use strange means in repelling the Mongol hordes from Australia; could turn a human Carter into one of those earlier entities which had dwelt in primal Hyperborea and worshipped black, plastic Tsathoggua after flying down from Kythamil, the double planet that once revolved around Arcturus; could turn a terrestrial Carter to a remotely ancestral and doubtfully shaped dweller on Kythamil itself, or a still remoter creature of trans-galactic Stronti, or a four-dimensional gaseous consciousness in an older space-time continuum, or a vegetable brain of the future on a dark, radio-active comet of inconceivable orbit—and so on, in endless cosmic cycle.

The archetypes, throbbed the waves, are the people of the Ultimate Abyss—formless, ineffable, and guessed at only by rare dreamers on the low-dimensioned worlds. Chief among such was this informing Being itself ... *which indeed was Carter's own archetype.* The glutless zeal of Carter and all his forebears for forbidden cosmic secrets was a natural result of derivation from the Supreme Archetype. On every world all great wizards, all great thinkers, all great artists, are facets of It.

Almost stunned with awe, and with a kind of terrifying delight, Randolph Carter's consciousness did homage to that transcendent Entity from which it was derived. As the waves paused again he pondered in the mighty silence, thinking of strange tributes, stranger questions, and still stranger requests. Curious concepts flowed conflictingly through a brain dazed with unaccustomed vistas and unforeseen disclosures. It occurred to him that, if these disclosures were literally true, he might bodily visit all those infinitely distant ages and parts of the universe which he had hitherto known only in dreams, could he but command the magic to change the angle of his consciouness-plane. And did not the silver key supply that magic? Had it not first changed him from a man in 1928 to a boy in 1883, and then to something quite outside time? Oddly, despite his present apparent absence of body; he knew that the key was still with him.

While the silence still lasted, Randolph Carter radiated forth the thoughts and questions which assailed him. He knew that in this ultimate abyss he was equidistant from every facet of his archetype—human or non-human, terrestrial or extra-terrestrial, galactic or trans-galactic; and his curiosity regarding the other phases of his being—especially those phases which were farthest from an earthly 1928 in time and space, or which had most persistently haunted his dreams throughout life—was at fever heat. He felt that his archetypal Entity could at will send him bodily to any of these phases of bygone and distant life by changing his consciousness-plane and despite the marvels he had undergone he burned for the further marvel of walking in the flesh through those grotesque and incredible scenes which visions of the night had fragmentarily brought him.

Without definite intention he was asking the Presence for access to a dim, fantastic world whose five multi-coloured suns, alien constellations, dizzily black crags, clawed, tapir-snouted denizens, bizarre metal towers, unexplained tunnels, and cryptical floating cylinders had intruded again and again upon his slumbers. That world, he felt vaguely, was in all the conceivable cosmos the one most freely in touch with others; and he longed to explore the vistas whose beginnings he had glimpsed, and to embark through space to those still remoter worlds with which the clawed, snouted denizens trafficked. There was no time for fear. As at all crises of his strange life, sheer cosmic curiosity triumphed over everything else.

When the waves resumed their awesome pulsing, Carter knew that his terrible request was granted. The Being was telling him of the nighted gulfs through which he would have to pass, of the unknown quintuple star in an unsuspected galaxy around which the alien world revolved, and of the burrowing inner horrors against which the clawed, snouted race of that world perpetually fought. It told him, too, of how the angle of his personal consciousness-plane, and the angle of his consciousness-plane regarding the space-time elements of the sought-for world, would have to be tilted simultaneously in order to restore to that world the Carter-facet which had dwelt there.

The Presence warned him to be sure of his symbols if he wished ever to return from the remote and alien world he had chosen, and he radiated back an impatient affirmation; confident that the silver key, which he felt was with him and which he knew had tilted both world and personal planes in throwing him back to 1883, contained those symbols which were meant. And now the Being, grasping his impatience, signified its readiness to accomplish the monstrous precipitation. The waves abruptly ceased, and there supervened a momentary stillness tense with nameless and dreadful expectancy.

Then, without warning, came a whirring and drumming that swelled to a terrific thundering. Once again Carter felt himself the focal point of an intense concentration of energy which smote and hammered and seared unbearably in the now-familiar rhythm of outer space, and which he could not classify as either the blasting heat of a blazing star, or the all-petrifying cold of the ultimate abyss. Bands and rays of colour utterly foreign to any spectrum of our universe played and wove and interlaced before him, and he was conscious of a frightful velocity of motion. He caught one fleeting glimpse of a figure sitting *alone* upon a cloudy throne more hexagonal than otherwise. . . .

6

As the Hindoo paused in his story he saw that de Marigny and Phillips were watching him absorbedly. Aspinwall pretended to ignore the narrative and kept his eyes ostentatiously on the papers before him. The alien-rhythmed ticking of the coffin-shaped clock took on a new and portentous meaning, while the fumes from the choked, neglected tripods wove themselves into fantastic and inexplicable shapes, and formed disturbing combinations with the grotesque figures of the draft-swayed tapestries. The old Negro who had tended them was gone—perhaps some growing tension had frightened him out of the house. An almost apologetic hesitancy hampered the speaker as he resumed in his oddly laboured yet idiomatic voice.

"You have found these things of the abyss hard to believe," he said, "but you will find the tangible and material things ahead still harder. That is the way of our minds. Marvels are doubly incredible when brought into three dimensions from the vague regions of possible dream. I shall not try to tell you much—that would be another and very different story. I will tell only what you absolutely have to know."

Carter, after that final vortex of alien and polychromatic rhythm, had found himself in what for a moment he thought was his old insistent dream. He was, as many a night before, walking amidst throngs of clawed, snouted beings through the streets of a labyrinth of inexplicably fashioned metal under a blaze of diverse solar colour; and as he looked down he saw that his body was like those of the others—rugose, partly squamous, and curiously articulated in a fashion mainly insect-like yet not without a caricaturish resemblence to the human outline. The silver key was still in his grasp, though held by a noxious-looking claw.

In another moment the dream-sense vanished, and he

felt rather as one just awakened from a dream. The ultimate abyss—the Being—the entity of absurd, outlandish race called Randolph Carter on a world of the future not yet born—some of these things were parts of the persistent recurrent dreams of the wizard Zkauba on the planet Yaddith. They were too persistent—they interfered with his duties in weaving spells to keep the frightful Dholes in their burrows, and became mixed up with his recollections of the myriad real worlds he had visited in light-beam envelopes. And now they had become quasi-real as never before. This heavy, material silver key in his right upper claw, exact image of one he had dreamt about, meant no good. He must rest and reflect, and consult the tablets of Nhing for advice on what to do. Climbing a metal wall in a lane off the main concourse, he entered his apartment and approached the rack of tablets.

Seven day-fractions later Zkauba squatted on his prism in awe and half despair, for the truth had opened up a new and conflicting set of memories. Nevermore could he know the peace of being one entity. For all time and space he was two: Zkauba the wizard of Yaddith, disgusted with the thought of the repellent earth-mammal Carter that he was to be and had been, and Randolph Carter, of Boston on the Earth, shivering with fright at the clawed, snouted thing which he had once been, and had become again.

The time units spent on Yaddith, croaked the Swami —whose laboured voice was beginning to show signs of fatigue—made a tale in themselves which could not be related in brief compass. There were trips to Stronti and Mthura and Kath, and other worlds in the twenty-eight galaxies accessible to the light-beam envelopes of the creatures of Yaddith, and trips back and forth through eons of time with the aid of the silver key and various other symbols known to Yaddith's wizards. There were hideous struggles with the bleached viscous Dholes in the primal tunnels that honeycombed the planet. There were awed sessions in libraries amongst the massed lore of ten thousand worlds living and dead. There were tense conferences with other minds of Yaddith, including that of the Arch-Ancient Buo. Zkauba told no one of what had befallen his personality, but when the Randolph Carter facet was uppermost he would study furiously every possible means of returning to the Earth and to human form, and would desperately practise human speech with the alien throat-organs so ill adapted to it.

The Carter-facet had soon learned with horror that the silver key was unable to effect his return to human form. It was, as he deduced too late from things he remembered, things he dreamed, and things he inferred from the lore of Yaddith, a product of Hyperborea on Earth; with power over the personal consciousness-angles of human beings alone. It could, however, change the planetary angle and send the user at will through time in an unchanged body. There had been an added spell which gave it limitless powers it otherwise lacked; but this, too, was a human discovery—peculiar to a spatially unreachable region, and not to be duplicated by the wizards of Yaddith. It had been written on the undecipherable parchment in the hideously carven box with the silver key, and Carter bitterly lamented that he had left it behind. The now inaccessible Being of the abyss had warned him to be sure of his symbols, and had doubtless thought he lacked nothing.

As time wore on he strove harder and harder to utilize the monstrous lore of Yaddith in finding a way back to the abyss and the omnipotent Entity. With his new knowledge he could have done much toward reading the cryptic parchment; but that power, under present conditions, was merely ironic. There were times, however, when the Zkauba-facet was uppermost and when he strove to erase the conflicting Carter-memories which troubled him.

Thus long spaces of time wore on—ages longer than the brain of man could grasp, since the beings of Yaddith die only after prolonged cycles. After many hundreds of revolutions the Carter-facet seemed to gain on the Zkauba-facet, and would spend vast periods calculating the distance of Yaddith in space and time from the human Earth that was to be. The figures were staggering—eons of light-years beyond counting—but the immemorial lore of Yaddith fitted Carter to grasp such things. He cultivated the power of dreaming himself momentarily Earthward, and learned many things about our planet that he had never known before. But he could not dream the needed formula on the missing parchment.

Then at last he conceived a wild plan of escape from Yaddith—which began when he found a drug that would keep his Zkauba-facet always dormant, yet without dissolution of the knowledge and memories of Zkauba. He thought that his calculations would let him perform a voyage with a light-wave envelope such as no being of Yaddith had ever performed—a *bodily* voyage through nameless eons and across incredible galactic reaches to the solar system and the Earth itself.

Once on Earth, though in the body of a clawed, snouted thing, he might be able somehow to find—and finish deciphering—the strangely hieroglyphed parchment he had left in the car at Arkham; and with its aid—and the key's—resume his normal terrestrial semblance.

He was not blind to the perils of the attempt. He knew that when he had brought the planet-angle to the right eon (a thing impossible to do while hurtling through space), Yaddith would be a dead world dominated by triumphant Dholes, and that his escape in the light-wave envelope would be a matter of grave doubt. Likewise was he aware of how he must achieve suspended animation, in the manner of an adept, to endure the eon-long flight through fathomless abysses. He knew, too, that—assuming his voyage succeeded—he must immunize himself to the bacterial and other earthly conditions hostile to a body from Yaddith. Furthermore, he must provide a way of feigning human shape on Earth until he might recover and decipher the parchment and resume that shape in truth. Otherwise he would probably be discovered and destroyed by the people in horror as a thing that should not be. And there must be some gold—luckily obtainable on Yaddith—to tide him over that period of quest.

Slowly Carter's plans went forward. He provided a light-wave envelope of abnormal toughness, able to stand both the prodigious time-transition and the unexampled flight through space. He tested all his calculations, and sent forth his Earthward dreams again and again, bringing them as close as possible to 1928. He practised suspended animation with marvellous success. He discovered just the bacterial agent he needed, and worked out the varying gravity-stress to which he must become used. He artfully fashioned a waxen mask and loose costume enabling him to pass among men as a human being of a sort, and devised a doubly potent spell with which to hold back the Dholes at the moment of his starting from the dead, black Yaddith of the inconceivable future. He took care, too, to assemble a large supply of the drugs—unobtainable on Earth—which would keep his Zkauba-facet in abeyance till he might shed the Yaddith body, nor did he neglect a small store of gold for earthly use.

The starting-day was a time of doubt and apprehension. Carter climbed up to his envelope-platform, on the pretext of sailing for the triple star Nython, and crawled into the sheath of shining metal. He had just room to perform the ritual of the silver key, and as he did so he slowly started the levitation of his envelope. There was an appalling seething and darkening of the day, and hideous racking of pain. The cosmos seemed to reel irresponsibly, and the other constellations danced in a black sky.

All at once Carter felt a new equilibrium. The cold of interstellar gulfs gnawed at the outside of his envelope, and he could see that he floated free in space—the metal building from which he had started having decayed years before. Below him the ground was festering with gigantic Dholes; and even as he looked, one reared up several hundred feet and levelled a bleached, viscous end at him. But his spells were effective, and in another moment he was falling away from Yaddith, unharmed.

7

In that bizarre room in New Orleans, from which the old black servant had instinctively fled, the odd voice of Swami Chandraputra grew hoarser still.

"Gentlemen," he continued, "I will not ask you to believe these things until I have shown you special proof. Accept it, then, as a myth, when I tell you of the *thousands of light-years—thousands of years of time, and uncounted billions of miles* that Randolph Carter hurtled through space as a nameless, alien entity in a thin envelope of electron-activated metal. He timed his period of suspended animation with utmost care, planning to have it end only a few years before the time of landing on the Earth in or near 1928.

"He will never forget that awakening. Remember, gentlemen, that before that eon-long sleep *he had lived consciously for thousands of terrestrial years amidst the alien and horrible wonders of Yaddith.* There was a hideous gnawing of cold, a cessation of menacing dreams, and a glance through the eye-plates of the envelope. Stars, clusters, nebulæ, on every hand—*and at last their outlines bore some kinship to the constellations of Earth that he knew.*

"Some day his descent into the solar system may be told. He saw Kynarth and Yuggoth on the rim, passed close to Neptune and glimpsed the hellish white fungi that spot it, learned an untellable secret from the close-glimpsed mists of Jupiter, and saw the horror on one of the satellites, and gazed at the cyclopean ruins that sprawl over Mars' ruddy disc. When the Earth drew near he saw it as a thin crescent which swelled alarmingly in size. He slackened speed, though his sensations of homecoming made him wish to lose not a moment. I will not try to tell you of these sensations as I learned them from Carter.

"Well, toward the last Carter hovered about in the Earth's upper air waiting till daylight came over the Western Hemisphere. He wanted to land where he had left—near the Snake Den in the hills behind Arkham. If any of you have been away from home long—and I know one of you has—I leave it to you how the sight of New England's rolling hills and great elms and gnarled orchards and ancient stone walls must have affected him.

"He came down at dawn in the lower meadow of the old Carter place, and was thankful for the silence and solitude. It was autumn, as when he had left, and the smell of the hills was balm to his soul. He managed to drag the metal envelope up the slope of the timber lot into the Snake Den, though it would not go through the weed-choked fissure to the inner cave. It was there also that he covered his alien body with the human clothing and waxen mask which would be necessary. He kept the envelope here for over a year, till certain circumstances made a new hiding-place necessary.

"He walked to Arkham—incidentally practising the management of his body in human posture and against terrestrial gravity—and got his gold changed to money at a bank. He also made some inquiries—posing as a foreigner ignorant of much English—and found that the year was 1930, only two years after the goal he had aimed at.

"Of course, his position was horrible. Unable to assert his identity, forced to live on guard every moment, with certain difficulties regarding food, and with a need to conserve the alien drug which kept his Zkauba-facet dormant, he felt that he must act as quickly as possible. Going to Boston and taking a room in the decaying West End, where he could live cheaply and inconspicuously, he at once established inquiries concerning Randolph Carter's estate and effects. It was then that he learned how anxious Mr. Aspinwall, here, was to have the estate divided, and how valiantly Mr. de Marigny and Mr. Phillips strove to keep it intact."

The Hindoo bowed, though no expression crossed his dark, tranquil, and thickly bearded face.

"Indirectly," he continued, "Carter secured a good copy of the missing parchment and began working on its deciphering. I am glad to say that I was able to help in all this—for he appealed to me quite early, and through me came in touch with other mystics throughout the world. I went to live with him in Boston—a wretched place in Chambers Street. As for the parchment—I am pleased to help Mr. de Marigny in his perplexity. To him let me say that the language of those hieroglyphics is not Naacal, but R'lyehian, which was brought to Earth by the spawn of Cthulhu countless ages ago. It is, of course, a translation—there was an Hyperborean original millions of years earlier in the primal tongue of Tsath-yo.

"There was more to decipher than Carter had looked for, but at no time did he give up hope. Early this year he made great strides through a book he imported from Nepal, and there is no question but that he will win before long. Unfortunately, however, one handicap has developed—the exhaustion of the alien drug which keeps the Zkauba-facet dormant. This is not, however, as great a calamity as was feared. Carter's personality is gaining in the body, and when Zkauba comes uppermost—for shorter and shorter periods, and now only when evoked by some unusual excitement—he is generally too dazed to undo any of Carter's work. He can not find the metal envelope that would take him back to Yaddith, for although he almost did, once, Carter hid it anew at a time when the Zkauba-facet was wholly latent. All the harm he has done is to frighten a few people and create certain nightmare rumours among the Poles and Lithuanians of Boston's West End. So far, he had never injured the careful disguise prepared by the Carter-facet, though he sometimes throws it off so that parts have to be replaced. I have seen what lies beneath—and it is not good to see.

"A month ago Carter saw the advertisement of this meeting, and knew that he must act quickly to save his estate. He could not wait to decipher the parchment and resume his human form. Consequently he deputed me to act for him.

"Gentlemen, I say to you that Randolph Carter is not dead; that he is temporarily in an anomalous condition, but that within two or three months at the outside he will be able to appear in proper form and demand the custody of his estate. I am prepared to offer proof if necessary. Therefore I beg that you will adjourn this meeting for an indefinite period."

8

De Marigny and Phillips stared at the Hindoo as if hypnotized, while Aspinwall emitted a series of snorts and bellows. The old attorney's disgust had by now surged into open rage, and he pounded the table with an apoplectically veined fist. When he spoke, it was in a kind of bark.

"How long is this foolery to be borne? I've listened an hour to this madman—this faker—and now he has the damned effrontery to say Randolph Carter is alive— to ask us to postpone the settlement for no good reason! Why don't you throw the scoundrel out, de Marigny? Do you mean to make us all the butts of a charlatan or idiot?"

De Marigny quietly raised his hand and spoke softly.

"Let us think slowly and clearly. This has been a very singular tale, and there are things in it which I, as a mystic not altogether ignorant, recognize as far from impossible. Furthermore—since 1930 I have received letters from the Swami which tally with his account."

As he paused, old Mr. Phillips ventured a word.

"Swami Chandraputra spoke of proofs. I, too, recognize much that is significant in this story, and I have myself had many oddly corroborative letters from the Swami during the last two years; but some of these statements are very extreme. Is there not something tangible which can be shown?"

At last the impassive-faced Swami replied, slowly and hoarsely, and drawing an object from the pocket of his loose coat as he spoke.

"While none of you here has ever *seen* the silver key itself, Messrs. de Marigny and Phillips have seen photographs of it. *Does this look familiar to you?*"

He fumblingly laid on the table, with his large, white-mittened hand, a heavy key of tarnished silver—nearly five inches long, of unknown and utterly exotic workmanship, and covered from end to end with hieroglyphs of the most bizarre description. De Marigny and Phillips gasped.

"That's it!" cried de Marigny. "The camera doesn't lie. I couldn't be mistaken!

But Aspinwall had already launched a reply.

"Fools! What does it prove? If that's really the key that belonged to my cousin, it's up to this foreigner—this damned nigger—to explain how he got it! Randolph Carter vanished with the key four years ago. How do we know he wasn't robbed and murdered? He was half crazy himself, and in touch with still crazier people.

"Look here, you nigger—where did you get that key? Did you kill Randolph Carter?"

The Swami's features, abnormally placid, did not change; but the remote, irisless black eyes behind them blazed dangerously. He spoke with great difficulty.

"Please control youself, Mr. Aspinwall. There is another form of proof that I *could* give, but its effect upon everybody would not be pleasant. Let us be reasonable. Here are some papers obviously written since 1930, and in the unmistakable style of Randolph Carter."

He clumsily drew a long envelope from inside his loose coat and handed it to the sputtering attorney as de Marigny and Phillips watched with chaotic thoughts and a dawning feeling of supernal wonder.

"Of course the handwriting is almost illegible—but remember that Randolph Carter now has no hands well adapted to forming human script."

Aspinwall looked through the papers hurriedly, and was visibly perplexed, but he did not change his demeanour. The room was tense with excitement and nameless dread, and the alien rhythm of the coffin-shaped clock had an utterly diabolic sound to de Marigny and Phillips, though the lawyer seemed affected not at all.

Aspinwall spoke again. "These look like clever forgeries. If they aren't, they may mean that Randolph Carter has been brought under the control of people with no good purpose. There's only one thing to do—have this faker arrested. De Marigny, will you telephone for the police?"

"Let us wait," answered their host. "I do not think this case calls for the police. I have a certain idea. Mr. Aspinwall, this gentleman is a mystic of real attainments. He says he is in the confidence of Randolph Carter. Will it satisfy you if he can answer certain questions which could be answered only by one in such confidence? I know Carter, and can ask such questions. Let me get a book which I think will make a good test."

He turned toward the door to the library, Phillips dazedly following in a kind of automatic way. Aspinwall remained where he was, studying closely the Hindoo who confronted him with abnormally impassive face. Suddenly, as Chandraputra clumsily restored the silver key to his pocket, the lawyer emitted a guttural shout.

"Hey, by Heaven I've got it! This rascal is in disguise. I don't believe he's an East Indian at all. That face—it isn't a face, but a *mask!* I guess his story put that into my head, but it's true. It never moves, and that turban and beard hide the edges. This fellow's a common crook! He isn't even a foreigner—I've been watching his language. He's a Yankee of some sort. And look at those mittens—he knows his fingerprints could be spotted. Damn you, I'll pull that thing off—"

"Stop!" The hoarse, oddly alien voice of the Swami held a tone beyond all mere-earthly fright. "I told you there was *another form of proof which I could give if necessary*, and I warned you not to provoke me to it. This red-faced old meddler is right—I'm not really an East Indian. *This face is a mask, and what it covers is not human.* You others have guessed—I felt that minutes ago. It wouldn't be pleasant if I took that mask off—let it alone, Ernest. I may as well tell you that *I am Randolph Carter.*"

No one moved. Aspinwall snorted and made vague motions. De Marigny and Phillips, across the room, watched the workings of the red face and studied the back of the turbaned figure that confronted him. The clock's abnormal ticking was hideous, and the tripod fumes and swaying arras danced a dance of death. The half-choking lawyer broke the silence.

"No you don't, you crook—you can't scare me! You've reasons of your own for not wanting that mask off. Maybe we'd know who you are. Off with it—"

As he reached forward, the Swami seized his hand with one of his own clumsily mittened members, evoking a curious cry of mixed pain and surprise. De Marigny started toward the two, but paused confused as the pseudo-Hindoo's shout of protest changed to a wholly inexplicable rattling and buzzing sound. Aspinwall's red face was furious, and with his free hand he made another lunge at his opponent's bushy beard. This time he succeeded in getting a hold, and at his frantic tug the whole waxen visage came loose from the turban and clung to the lawyer's apoplectic fist.

As it did so, Aspinwall uttered a frightful gurgling cry, and Phillips and de Marigny saw his face convulsed with a wilder, deeper and more hideous epilepsy of stark panic than ever they had seen on human countenance before. The pseudo-Swami had meanwhile released his other hand and was standing as if dazed, making buzzing noises of a most abnormal quality. Then the turbaned figure slumped oddly into a posture scarcely human, and began a curious, fascinated sort of shuffle toward the coffin-shaped clock that ticked out its cosmic and abnormal rhythm. His now uncovered face was turned away, and de Marigny and Phillips could not see what the lawyer's act had disclosed. Then their attention was turned to Aspinwall, who was sinking ponderously to the floor. The spell was broken—but when they reached the old man he was dead.

Turning quickly to the shuffling Swami's receding back, de Marigny saw one of the great white mittens drop listlessly off a dangling arm. The fumes of the olibanum were thick, and all that could be glimpsed of the revealed hand was something long and black. Before the Creole could reach the retreating figure, old Mr. Phillips laid a restraining hand on his shoulder.

"Don't!" he whispered. "We don't know what we're up against. That other facet, you know—Zkauba, the wizard of Yaddith. ..."

The turbaned figure had now reached the abnormal

clock, and the watchers saw through the dense fumes a blurred black claw fumbling with the tall, hieroglyphed door. The fumbling made a queer, clicking sound. Then the figure entered the coffin-shaped case and pulled the door shut after it.

De Marigny could no longer be restrained, but when he reached and opened the clock it was empty. The abnormal ticking went on, beating out the dark, cosmic rhythm which underlies all mystical gate-openings. On the floor the great white mitten, and the dead man with a bearded mask clutched in his hand, had nothing further to reveal.

* * * * *

A year passed, and nothing has been heard of Randolph Carter. His estate is still unsettled. The Boston address from which one "Swami Chandraputra" sent inquiries to various mystics in 1930-31-32 was indeed tenanted by a strange Hindoo, but he left shortly before the date of the New Orleans conference and has never been seen since. He was said to be dark, expressionless, and bearded, and his landlord thinks the swarthy mask—which was duly exhibited—looks very much like him. He was never, however, suspected of any connection with the nightmare apparitions whispered of by local Slavs. The hills behind Arkham were searched for the "metal envelope," but nothing of the sort was ever found. However, a clerk in Arkham's First National Bank does recall a queer turbaned man who cashed an odd bit of gold bullion in October, 1930.

De Marigny and Phillips scarcely know what to make of the business. After all, what was proved?

There was a story. There was a key which might have been forged from one of the pictures Carter had freely distributed in 1928. There were papers—all indecisive. There was a masked stranger, but who now living saw behind the mask? Amidst the strain and the olibanum fumes that act of vanishing in the clock might easily have been a dual hallucination. Hindoos know much of hypnotism. Reason proclaims the "Swami" a criminal with designs on Randolph Carter's estate. But the autopsy said that Aspinwall had died of shock. Was it rage *alone* which caused it? And some things in that story ...

In a vast room hung with strangely figured arras and filled with olibanum fumes, Etienne-Laurent de Marigny often sits listening with vague sensations to the abnormal rhythm of that hieroglyphed, coffin-shaped clock.

The White Ship

I AM Basil Elton, keeper of the North Point light that
my father and grandfather kept before me. Far from
the shore stands the grey light-house, above sunken
slimy rocks that are seen when the tide is low, but
unseen when the tide is high. Past that beacon for a
century have swept the majestic barques of the seven
seas. In the days of my grandfather there were many; in
the days of my father not so many; and now there are
so few that I sometimes feel strangely alone, as though
I were the last man on our planet.

From far shores came those white-sailed argosies of
old; from far Eastern shores where warm suns shine
and sweet odours linger about strange gardens and gay
temples. The old captains of the sea came often to my
grandfather and told him of these things which in turn
he told to my father, and my father told to me in the
long autumn evenings when the wind howled eerily
from the East. And I have read more of these things,
and of many things besides, in the books men gave me
when I was young and filled with wonder.

But more wonderful than the lore of old men and

the lore of books is the secret lore of ocean. Blue,
green, grey, white or black; smooth, ruffled, or moun-
tainous; that ocean is not silent. All my days have I
watched it and listened to it, and I know it well. At first
it told to me only the plain little tales of calm beaches
and near ports, but with the years it grew more friendly
and spoke of other things; of things more strange and
more distant in space and in time. Sometimes at twilight
the grey vapors of the horizon have parted to grant me
glimpses of the ways beyond; and some times at night
the deep waters of the sea have grown clear and phosphorescent, to grant me glimpses of the ways beneath.
And these glimpses have been as often of the ways that
were and the ways that might be, as of the ways that
are; for ocean is more ancient than the mountains, and
freighted with the memories and the dreams of Time.

Out of the South it was that the White Ship used to
come when the moon was full and high in the heavens.
Out of the South it would glide very smoothly and
silently over the sea. And whether the sea was rough or
calm, and whether the wind was friendly or adverse, it
would always glide smoothly and silently, its sail distant and its long strange tiers of oars moving rhythmi-
cally. One night I espied upon the deck a man, bearded
and robed, and he seemed to beckon me to embark for
far unknown shores. Many times afterward I saw him
under the full moon, and ever did he beckon me.

Very brightly did the moon shine on the night I
answered the call, and I walked out over the waters to
the White Ship on a bridge of moonbeams. The man
who had beckoned now spoke a welcome to me in a
soft language I seemed to know well, and the hours
were filled with soft songs of the oarsmen as we glided

away into a mysterious South, golden with the glow of that full, mellow moon.

And when the day dawned, rosy and effulgent, I beheld the green shore of far lands, bright and beautiful, and to me unknown. Up from the sea rose lordly terraces of vendure, tree-studded, and shewing here and there the gleaming white roofs and colonnades of strange temples. As we drew nearer the green shore the bearded man told me of that land, the land of Zar, where dwell all the dreams and thoughts of beauty that come to men once and then are forgotten. And when I looked upon the terraces again I saw that what he said was true, for among the sights before me were many things I had once seen through the mists beyond the horizon and in the phosphorescent depths of ocean. There too were forms and fantasies more splendid than any I had ever known; the visions of young poets who died in want before the world could learn of what they had seen and dreamed. But we did not set foot upon the sloping meadows of Zar, for it is told that he who treads them may nevermore return to his native shore.

As the White Ship sailed silently away from the templed terraces of Zar, we beheld on the distant horizon ahead the spires of a mighty city; and the bearded man said to me, "This is Thalarion, the City of a Thousand Wonders, wherein reside all those mysteries that man has striven in vain to fathom." And I looked again, at closer range, and saw that the city was greater than any city I had known or dreamed of before. Into the sky the spires of its temples reached, so that no man might behold their peaks; and far back beyond the horizon stretched the grim, grey walls, over which one might spy only a few roofs, weird and ominous, yet adorned with rich friezes and alluring sculptures. I yearned mightily to enter this fascinating yet repellent city, and besought the bearded man to land me at the shone pier by the huge carven gate Akariel; but he gently denied my wish, saying, "Into Thalarion, the City of a Thousand Wonders, many have passed but none returned. Therein walk only daemons and mad things that are no longer men, and the streets are white with the unburied bones of those who have looked upon the eidolon Lathi, that reigns over the city." So the White Ship sailed on past the walls of Thalarion, and followed for many days a southward-flying bird, whose glossy plumage matched the sky out of which it had appeared.

Then came we to a pleasant coast gay with blossoms of every hue, where as far inland as we could see basked lovely groves and radiant arbours beneath a meridian sun. From bowers beyond our view came bursts of song and snatches of lyric harmony, interspersed with faint laughter so delicious that I urged the rowers onward in my eagerness to reach the scene. And the bearded man spoke no word, but watched me as we approached the lily-lined shore. Suddenly a wind blowing from over the flowery meadows and leafy woods brought a scent at which I trembled. The wind grew stronger, and the air was filled with the lethal, charnel odour of plague-stricken towns and uncovered cemeteries. And as we sailed madly away from that damnable coast the bearded man spoke at last, saying, "This is Xura, the Land of Pleasures Unattained."

So once more the White Ship followed the bird of heaven, over warm blessed seas fanned by caressing, aromatic breezes. Day after day and night after night did we sail, and when the moon was full we would listen to soft songs of the oarsmen, sweet as on that distant night when we sailed away from my far native land. And it was by moonlight that we anchored at last in the harbour of Sona-Nyl, which is guarded by twin headlands of crystal that rise from the sea and meet in a resplendent arch. This is the Land of Fancy, and we walked to the verdant shore upon a golden bridge of moonbeams.

In the Land of Sona-Nyl there is neither time not space, neither suffering nor death; and there I dwelt for many aeons. Green are the groves and pastures, bright and fragrant the flowers, blue and musical the streams, clear and cool the fountains, and stately and gorgeous the temples, castles, and cities of Sona-Nyl. Of that land there is no bound, for beyond each vista of beauty rises another more beautiful. Over the countryside and amidst the splendour of cities can move at will the happy folk, of whom all are gifted with unmarred grace and unalloyed happiness. For the aeons that I dwelt there I wandered blissfully through gardens where quaint pagodas peep from pleasing clumps of bushes, and where the white walks are bordered with delicate blossoms. I climbed gentle hills from whose summits I could see entrancing panoramas of loveliness, with steepled towns nestling in verdant valleys, and with the golden domes of gigantic cities glittering on the infinitely distant horizon. And I viewed by moonlight the sparkling sea, the crystal headlands, and the placid harbour wherein lay anchored the White Ship.

It was against the full moon one night in the immemorial year of Tharp that I saw outlined the beckoning form of the celestial bird, and felt the first stirrings of unrest. Then I spoke with the bearded man, and told

him of my new yearnings to depart for remote
Cathuria, which no man hath seen, but which all believe to lie beyond the basalt pillars of the West. It is
the Land of Hope, and in it shine the perfect ideals of
all that we know elsewhere; or at least so men relate.
But the bearded man said to me. "Beware of those
perilous seas wherein men say Cathuria lies. In Sona-
Nyl there is no pain or death, but who can tell what lies
beyond the basalt pillars of the West?" Natheless at the
next full moon I boarded the White Ship, and with the
reluctant bearded man left the happy harbour for untravelled seas.

And the bird of heaven flew before, and led us
toward the basalt pillars of the West, but this time the
oarsman sang no soft songs under the full moon. In my
mind I would often picture the unknown Land of
Cathuria with its splendid groves and palaces, and
would wonder what new delights there awaited me.
"Cathuria," I would say to myself, "is the abode of gods
and the land of unnumbered cities of gold. Its forests
are of aloe and sandalwood, even as the fragrant groves
of Camorin, and among the trees flutter gay birds sweet
with song. On the green and flowery mountains of
Cathuria stand temples of pink marble, rich with carven
and painted glories, and having in their courtyards cool
fountains of silver, where purr with ravishing music the
scented waters that come from the grotto-born river
Narg. And the cities of Cathuria are cinctured with
golden walls, and their pavements also are of gold. In
the gardens of these cities are strange orchids, and perfumed lakes whose beds are of coral and amber. At
night the streets and the gardens are lit with gay lan-
thorns fashioned from the three-coloured shell of the

tortoise, and here resound the soft notes of the singer and the lutanist. And the houses of the cities of Cathuria are all palaces, each built over a fragrant canal bearing the waters of the sacred Narg. Of marble and porphyry are the houses, and roofed with glittering gold that reflects the rays of the sun and enhances the splendour of the cities as blissful gods view them from the distant peaks. Fairest of all is the palace of the great monarch Dorieb, whom some say to be a demi-god and others a god. High is the palace of Dorieb, and many are the turrets of marble upon its walls. In its wide halls many multitudes assemble, and here hang the trophies of the ages. And the roof is of pure gold, set upon tall pillars of ruby and azure, and having such carven figures of gods and heroes that he who looks up to those heights seems to gaze upon the living Olympus. And the floor of the palace is of glass, under which flow the cunningly lighted waters of the Narg, gay with gaudy fish not known beyond the bounds of lovely Cathuria."

Thus would I speak to myself of Cathuria, but ever would the bearded man warn me to turn back to the happy shores of Sona-Nyl; for Sona-Nyl is known of men, while none hath ever beheld Cathuria.

And on the thirty-first day that we followed the bird, we beheld the basalt pillars of the West. Shrouded in mist they were, so that no man might peer beyond them or see their summits—which indeed some say reach even to the heavens. And the bearded man again implored me to turn back, but I heeded him not; for from the mists beyond the basalt pillars I fancied there came the notes of singers and lutanists; sweeter than the sweetest songs of Sona-Nyl, and sounding mine own praises; the praises of me, who had voyaged far from the full moon and dwelt in the Land of Fancy. So to the sound of melody the White Ship sailed into the mist betwixt the basalt pillars of the West. And when the music ceased and the mist lifted, we beheld not the Land of Cathuria, but a swift-rushing resistless sea, over which our helpless barque was borne toward some unknown goal. Soon to our ears came the distant thunder of falling waters, and to our eyes appeared on the far horizon ahead the titanic spray of a monstrous cataract, wherein the oceans of the world drop down to abysmal nothingness. Then did the bearded man say to me, with tears on his cheek, "We have rejected the beautiful Land of Sona-Nyl, which we may never behold again. The gods are greater than men, and they have conquered." And I closed my eyes before the crash I knew would come, shutting out the sight of the celestial bird which flapped its mocking blue wings over the brink of the torrent.

Out of that crash came darkness, and I heard the shrieking of men and of things which were not men. From the East tempestuous winds arose, and chilled me as I crouched on the slab of damp stone which had risen beneath my feet. Then as I heard another crash I opened my eyes and beheld myself upon the platform of that lighthouse whence I had sailed so many aeons ago. In the darkness below there loomed the vast blurred outlines of a vessel breaking up on the cruel rocks, and as I glanced out over the waste I saw that the light had failed for the first time since my grandfather had assumed its care.

And in the later watches of the night, when I went within the tower, I saw on the wall a calendar which still remained as when I had left it at the hour I sailed away. With the dawn I descended the tower and looked for wreckage upon the rocks, but what I found was only this: a strange dead bird whose hue was as of the azure sky, and a single shattered spar, of a whiteness greater than that of the wave-tips or of the mountain snow.

And thereafter the ocean told me its secrets no more; and though many times since has the moon shone full and high in the heavens, the White Ship from the South came never again.

The Strange High House
In The Mist

IN THE morning mist comes up from the sea by the cliffs beyond Kingsport. White and feathery it comes from the deep to its brothers the clouds, full of dreams of dank pastures and caves of leviathan. And later, in still summer rains on the steep roofs of poets, the clouds scatter bits of those dreams, that men shall not live without rumour of old strange secrets, and wonders that planets tell planets alone in the night. When tales fly thick in the grottoes of tritons, and conches in seaweed cities blow wild tunes learned from the Elder Ones, then great eager mists flock to heaven laden with lore, and oceanward eyes on the rocks see only a mystic whiteness, as if the cliff's rim were the rim of all earth, and the solemn bells of buoys tolled free in the aether of faery.

Now north of archaic Kingsport the crags climb lofty and curious, terrace on terrace, till the northernmost hangs in the sky like a grey frozen wind-cloud. Alone it is, a bleakpoint jutting in limitless space, for there the coast turns sharp where the great Miskatonic pours out of the plains past Arkham, bringing woodland legends

229

and little quaint memories of New England's hills. The sea-folk in Kingsport look up at that cliff as other sea-folk look up at the pole-star, and time the night's watches by the way it hides or shows the Great Bear, Cassiopeia, and the Dragon. Among them it is one with the firmament, and truly, it is hidden from them when the mist hides the stars or the sun. Some of the cliffs they love, as that whose grotesque profile they call Father Neptune, or that whose pillared steps they term "The Causeway"; but this one they fear because it is so near the sky. The Portuguese sailors coming in from a voyage cross themselves when they first see it, and the old Yankees believe it would be much a graver matter than death to climb it, if indeed that were possible. Nevertheless there is an ancient house on that cliff, and at evening men see lights in the small-paned windows.

The ancient house has always been there, and people say One dwells within who talks with the morning mists that come up from the deep, and perhaps sees singular things oceanward at those times when the cliff's rim becomes the rim of all earth, and solemn buoys toll free in the white aether of faery. This they tell from hearsay, for that forbidding crag is always unvisited, and natives dislike to train telescopes on it. Summer boarders have indeed scanned it with jaunty binoculars, but have never seen more than the grey primeval roof, peaked and shingled, whose eaves come nearly to the grey foundations, and the dim yellow light of the little windows peeping out from under those eaves in the dusk. These summer people do not believe that the same One has lived in the ancient house for hundreds of years, but can not prove their heresy to any real Kingsporter. Even the Terrible Old Man who talks to leaden pendulums in bottles, buys groceries with centuried Spanish gold, and keeps stone idols in the yard of his antediluvian cottage in Water Street can only say these things were the same when his grandfather was a boy, and that must have been inconceivable ages ago, when Belcher or Shirley or Pownall or Bernard was Governor of His Majesty's Province of the Massachusetts-Bay.

Then one summer there came a philosopher into Kingsport. His name was Thomas Olney, and he taught ponderous things in a college by Narragansett Bay. With stout wife and romping children he came, and his eyes were weary with seeing the same things for many years, and thinking the same well-disciplined thoughts. He looked at the mists from the diadem of Father Neptune, and tried to walk into their white world of mystery along the titan steps of The Causeway. Morning after morning he would lie on the cliffs and look over the world's rim at the cryptical aether beyond, listening to spectral bells and the wild cries of what might have been gulls. Then, when the mist would lift and the sea stand out prosy with the smoke of steamers, he would sigh and descend to the town, where he loved to thread the narrow olden lanes up and down hill, and study the crazy tottering gables and odd-pillared doorways which had sheltered so many generations of sturdy sea-folk. And he even talked with the Terrible Old Man, who was not fond of strangers, and was invited into his fearsomely archaic cottage where low ceilings and wormy panelling hear the echoes of disquieting soliloquies in the dark small hours.

Of course it was inevitable that Olney should mark the grey unvisited cottage in the sky, on that sinister northward crag which is one with the mists and the firmament. Always over Kingsport it hung, and always its mystery sounded in whispers through Kingsport's crooked alleys. The Terrible Old Man wheezed a tale that his father had told him, of lightning that shot one night up from that peaked cottage to the clouds of higher heaven; and Granny Orne, whose tiny gambrel-roofed abode in Ship Street is all covered with moss and ivy, croaked over something her grandmother had heard at second-hand, about shapes that flapped out of the eastern mists straight into the narrow single door of that unreachable place—for the door is set close to the edge of the crag toward the ocean, and glimpsed only from ships at sea.

At length, being avid for new strange things and held back by neither the Kingsporter's fear nor the summer boarder's usual indolence, Olney made a very terrible resolve. Despite a conservative training—or because of it, for humdrum lives breed wistful longings of the unknown—he swore a great oath to scale that avoided northern cliff and visit the abnormally antique grey cottage in the sky. Very plausibly his saner self argued that the place must be tenanted by people who reached it from inland along the easier ridge beside the Miskatonic's estuary. Probably they traded in Arkham, knowing how little Kingsport liked their habitation, or perhaps being unable to climb down the cliff on the Kingsport side. Olney walked out along the lesser cliffs to where the great crag leaped insolently up to consort with celestial things, and became very sure that no human feet could mount it or descend it on that beetling southern slope. East and north it rose thousands of feet perpendicular from the water, so only the western side, inland and toward Arkham remained.

One early morning in August Olney set out to find a path to the inaccessible pinnacle. He worked northwest along pleasant back roads, past Hooper's Pond and the old brick powder-house to where the pastures slope up to the ridge above the Miskatonic and give a lovely vista of Arkham's white Georgian steeples across leagues of river and meadow. Here he found a shady road to Arkham, but no trail at all in the seaward direction he wished. Woods and fields crowded up to the high bank of the river's mouth, and bore not a sign of man's presence; not even a stone wall or a straying cow, but only the tall grass and giant trees and tangles of briars that the first Indian might have seen. As he climbed slowly east, higher and higher above the estuary on his left and nearer and nearer the sea, he found the way growing in difficulty till he wondered how ever the dwellers in that disliked place managed to reach the world outside, and whether they came often to market in Arkham.

Then the trees thinned, and far below him on his right he saw the hills and antique roofs and spires of Kingsport. Even Central Hill was a dwarf from this height, and he could just make out the ancient graveyard by the Congregational Hospital, beneath which rumour said some terrible caves or burrows lurked. Ahead lay sparse grass and scrub blueberry bushes, and beyond them the naked rock of the crag and the thin peak of the dreaded grey cottage. Now the ridge narrowed, and Olney grew dizzy at his loneness in the sky, south of him the frightful precipice above Kingsport north of him the vertical drop of nearly a mile to the river's mouth. Suddenly a great chasm opened before him, ten feet deep, so that he had to let himself down by his hands and drop to a slanting floor, and then crawl perilously up a natural defile in the opposite wall. So this was the way the folk of the uncanny house journeyed betwixt earth and sky!

When he climbed out of the chasm a morning mist was gathering, but he clearly saw the lofty and unhallowed cottage ahead; walls as grey as the rock, and high peak standing bold against the milky white of the seaward vapours. And he perceived that there was no door on this landward end, but only a couple of small lattice windows with dingy bull's-eye panes leaded in Seventeenth Century fashion. All around him was cloud and chaos, and he could see nothing below the whiteness of illimitable space. He was alone in the sky with this queer and very disturbing house; and when he sidled around to the front and saw that the wall stood flush with the cliff's edge, so that the single narrow door was not to be reached save from the empty aether, he felt a distinct terror that altitude could not wholly explain. And it was very odd that shingles so worm-eaten could survive, or bricks so crumbled still form a standing chimney.

As the mist thickened, Olney crept around to the windows on the north and west and south sides, trying them but finding them all locked. He was vaguely glad they were locked, because the more he saw of that house the less he wished to get in. Then a sound halted him. He heard a lock rattle and a bolt shoot, and a long creaking follow as if a heavy door were slowly and cautiously opened. This was on the oceanward side that he could not see, where the narrow portal opened on blank space thousands of feet in the misty sky above the waves.

Then there was heavy, deliberate tramping in the cottage, and Olney heard the windows opening, first on the north side opposite him, and then on the west side just around the corner. Next would come the south windows, under the great low eaves on the side where he stood; and it must be said that he was more than uncomfortable as he thought of the detestable house on one side and the vacancy of upper air on the other. When a fumbling came in the nearer casements he crept around to the west again, flattening himself against the wall beside the now opened windows. It was plain that the owner had come home; but he had not come from the land, nor from any ballon or airship that could be imagined. Steps sounded again, and Olney edged round to the north; but before he could find a haven a voice called softly, and he knew he must confront his host.

Stuck out of the west window was a great black-bearded face whose eyes were phosphorescent with the imprint of unheard-of sights. But the voice was gentle, and of a quaint olden kind, so that Olney did not shudder when a brown hand reached out to help him over the sill and into that low room of black oak wainscots and carved Tudor furnishings. The man was clad in very ancient garments, and had about him an unplacable nimbus of sea-lore and dreams of tall galleons. Olney does not recall many of the wonders he told, or even who he was; but says that he was strange and kindly, and filled with the magic of unfathomed voids of time and space. The small room seemed green with a dim aqueous light, and Olney saw that the far windows to the east were not open, but shut against the misty aether with dull thick panes like the bottoms of old bottles.

That bearded host seemed young, yet looked out of eyes steeped in the elder mysteries; and from the tales of marvellous ancient things he related, it must be guessed that the village folk were right in saying he had communed with the mists of the sea and the clouds of the sky ever since there was any village to watch his taciturn dwelling from the plain below. And the day wore on, and still Olney listened to rumours of old times and far places, and heard how the kings of Atlantis fought with the slippery blasphemies that wriggled out of rifts in ocean's floor, and how the pillared and weedy temple of Poseidonis is still glimpsed at midnight by lost ships, who know by its sight that they are lost. Years of the Titans were recalled, but the host grew timid when he spoke of the dim first age of chaos before the gods or even the Elder Ones were born, and when *the other gods* came to dance on the peak of Hatheg-Kla in the stony desert near Ulthar, beyond the River Skai.

It was at this point that there came a knocking on the door; that ancient door of nail-studded oak beyond which lay only the abyss of white cloud. Olney started in fright, but the bearded man motioned him to be still, and tiptoed to the door to look out through a very small peephole. What he saw he did not like, so pressed his fingers to his lips and tiptoed around to shut and lock all the windows before returning to the ancient settle beside his guest. Then Olney saw lingering against the translucent squares of each of the little dim windows in succession a queer black outline as the caller moved inquisitively about before leaving; and he was glad his host had not answered the knocking. For there are strange objects in the great abyss, and the seeker of dreams must take care not to stir up or meet the wrong ones.

Then the shadows began to gather; first little furtive ones under the table, and then bolder ones in the dark panelled corners. And the bearded man made enigmatical gestures of prayer, and lit tall candles in curiously wrought brass candle-sticks. Frequently he would glance at the door as if he expected some one, and at length his glance seemed answered by a singular rapping which must have followed some very ancient and secret code. This time he did not even glance through the peephole, but swung the great oak bar and shot the bolt, unlatching the heavy door and flinging it wide to the stars and the mist.

And then to the sound of obscure harmonies there floated into that room from the deep all the dreams and memories of earth's sunken Mighty Ones. And golden flames played about weedy locks, so that Olney was dazzled as he did them homage. Trident-bearing Neptune was there, and sportive tritons and fantastic nereids, and upon dolphins' backs was balanced a vast crenulate shell wherein rode the grey and awful form of primal Nodens, Lord of the Great Abyss. And the conches of the tritons gave weird blasts, and the nereids made strange sounds by striking on the grotesque resonant shells of unknown lurkers in black sea-caves. Then hoary Nodens reached forth a wizened hand and helped Olney and his host into the vast shell, whereat the conches and the gongs set up a wild and awesome clamour. And out into the limitless aether reeled that fabulous train, the noise of whose shouting was lost in the echoes of thunder.

All night in Kingsport they watched that lofty cliff when the storm and the mists gave them glimpses of it, and when toward the small hours the little dim windows went dark they whispered of dread and disaster. And Olney's children and stout wife prayed to the bland proper god of Baptists, and hoped that the traveller would borrow an umbrella and rubbers unless the rain stopped by morning. Then dawn swam dripping and mist-wreathed out of the sea, and the buoys tolled solemn in vortices of white aether. And at noon elfin horns rang over the ocean as Olney, dry and light-footed, climbed down from the cliffs to antique Kingsport with the look of far places in his eyes. He could not recall what he had dreamed in the sky-perched hut of that still nameless hermit, or say how he had crept down that crag untraversed by other feet. Nor could he talk of these matters at all save with the Terrible Old Man, who afterward mumbled queer things in his long white beard; vowing that the man who came down from that crag was not wholly the man who went up, and that somewhere under that grey peaked roof, or amidst inconceivable reaches of that sinister white mist, there lingered still the lost spirit of him who was Thomas Olney.

And ever since that hour, through dull dragging years of greyness and weariness, the philosopher has laboured and eaten and slept and done uncomplaining the suitable deeds of a citizen. Not any more does he long for the magic of farther hills, or sigh for secrets that peer like green reefs from a bottomless sea. The sameness of his days no longer gives him sorrow, and well-disciplined thoughts have grown enough for his imagination. His good wife waxes stouter and his children older and prosier and more useful, and he never fails to smile correctly with pride when the occasion calls for it. In his glance there is not any restless light, and if he ever listens for solemn bells or far elfin horns it is only at night when old dreams are wandering. He has never seen Kingsport again, for his family disliked the funny old houses and complained that the drains were impossibly bad. They have a trim bungalow now at Bristol Highlands, where no tall crags tower, and the neighbours are urban and modern.

But in Kingsport strange tales are abroad, and even the Terrible Old Man admits a thing untold by his grandfather. For now, when the wind sweeps boisterous out of the north past the high ancient house that is one with the firmament, there is broken at last that ominous, brooding silence ever before the bane of Kingsport's maritime cotters. And old folk tell of pleasing voices heard singing there, and of laughter that swells with joys beyond earth's joys; and say that at evening the little low windows are brighter than formerly. They say, too, that the fierce aurora comes oftener to that spot, shining blue in the north with visions of frozen worlds while the crag and the cottage hang black and fantastic against wild coruscations. And the mists of the dawn are thicker, and sailors are not quite so sure that all the muffled seaward ringing is that of the solemn buoys.

Worst of all, though, is the shrivelling of old fears in the hearts of Kingsport's young men, who grow prone to listen at night to the north wind's faint distant sounds. They swear no harm or pain can inhabit that high peaked cottage, for in the new voices gladness beats, and with them the tinkle of laughter and music.

What tales the sea-mists may bring to that haunted and northernmost pinnacle they do not know, but they long to extract some hint of the wonders that knock at the cliff-yawning door when clouds are thickest. And patriarchs dread lest some day one by one they seek out that inaccessible peak in the sky, and learn what centuried secrets hide beneath the steep shingled roof which is part of the rocks and the stars and the ancient fears of Kingsport. That those venturesome youths will come back they do not doubt, but they think a light may be gone from their eyes, and a will from their hearts. And they do not wish quaint Kingsport with its climbing lanes and archaic gables to drag listless down the years while voice by voice the laughing chorus grows stronger and wilder in that unknown and terrible eyrie where mists and the dreams of mists stop to rest on their way from the sea to the skies.

They do not wish the souls of their young men to leave the pleasant hearths and gambrel-roofed taverns of old Kingsport, nor do they wish the laughter and song in that high rocky place to grow louder. For as the voice which has come has brought fresh mists from the sea and from the north fresh lights, so do they say that still other voices will bring more mists and more lights, till perhaps the olden gods (whose existence they hint only in whispers for fear the Congregational parson shall hear) may come out of the deep and from unknown Kadath in the cold waste and make their dwelling on that evilly appropriate crag so close to the gentle hills and valleys of quiet, simple fisher folk. This they do not wish, for to plain people things not of earth are unwelcome; and besides, the Terrible Old Man often recalls what Olney said about a knock that the lone dweller feared, and a shape seen black and inquisitive against the mist through those queer translucent windows of leaded bull's-eyes.

All these things, however, the Elder Ones only may decide; and meanwhile the morning mist still comes up by that lonely vertiginous peak with the steep ancient house, that grey low-eaved house where none is seen but where evening brings furtive lights while the north wind tells of strange revels. White and feathery it comes from the deep to its brothers the clouds, full of dreams of dank pastures and caves of leviathan. And when tales fly thick in the grottoes of tritons, and conches in seaweed cities blow wild tunes learned from the Elder Ones, then great eager vapours flock to heaven laden with lore; and Kingsport, nestling uneasy on its lesser cliffs below that awesome hanging sentinel of rock, sees oceanward only a mystic whiteness, as if the cliff's rim were the rim of all earth, and the solemn bells of the buoys tolled free in the aether of faery.